Praise for *An A*

"[Hilma Wolitzer is an] American literary treasure. . . . Wolitzer uses her gift for her chosen medium, long-form fiction, to deliver a message far broader than this deceptively accessible novel first seems to address. *An Available Man* is not just a cautionary tale of geriatric loneliness and sex. It's a meditation—and then, a breathtaking roller-coaster ride, and then, a meditation again—on what we lose when we allow loss and longing to make us unavailable to ourselves."

—*The Boston Globe*

"Funny, wise and touching. . . . Wolitzer writes so well and knows so much that her books combine absurdity with poignancy in a deft and captivating way."

—*The Washington Post*

"Impressively readable . . . Wolitzer is such a capable storyteller. . . . [This novel] succeeds, precisely because the writer understands that it's not a childish insistence on finding everything delightful but the full complexity of experience that gives a romance, late-life or otherwise, its real beauty."

—*The Philadelphia Enquirer*

"Wolitzer is, by turns, funny, shocking, poignant and wise."

—*Star Tribune*

"I absolutely loved *An Available Man* (and not, I swear, because I'm partial to widowers). For a start, Edward Schuyler is someone I desperately wish I could invite to my next dinner party (and not, I swear, because there are half a dozen women I'd like him to meet). This is a book to savor page by page, filled with astute detail, both comic and mournful, about what it's like to be middle-aged and lonely yet not give up on the search for love."

—Julia Glass, author of *The Widower's Tale* and the National Book Award–winning *Three Junes*

"Heartbreaking, maddening, comical, and poignant . . . This sweet story of a man's diving back into the dating pool at an older age will especially appeal to readers in that demographic."

—*Library Journal*

"Comic, tender, and delicious, in *An Available Man*, the broken-hearted rise again to heal and find love anew. Hilma Wolitzer is a national treasure, and she's at her best here in the story of Edward Schuyler, a grieving widower who must put down his binoculars to see the world with new eyes. You will love it!"

—Adriana Trigiani, bestselling author of *Big Stone Gap* and *Very Valentine*

"Wolitzer [writes] of the pain of losing a partner and its aftermath . . . with remarkable insight, grace, and humor. A warm, keenly incisive view of life's vicissitudes by a writer too seldom heard from."

—*Booklist* (starred review)

"Wolitzer's rapturously charming look at love in late life plumbs the depths of grief and longing to reveal the heady shine of new possibilities. What can I say? With its cast of exuberantly alive characters and a wise and witty plot, this book is love at first sight."

—Caroline Leavitt, *New York Times* bestselling author of *Pictures of You*

"Families are Wolitzer's turf, and she's an observant and often humorous chronicler of domesticity and the stuff that comes with it: illness, loss, boredom, crankiness, and, on good days, love."

—*Publishers Weekly*

"Hilma Wolitzer is a master of the domestic world, and her writing is graceful, stylish, intelligent and so, so funny! This is a lovely novel, an elegant bouquet of family life, made up of tenderness and confusion, grief and solace, uncertainty and commitment, and the unexpectedness of love."

—Roxana Robinson, author of *Cost*

"I'm completely in love with this particular available man, and with the words that brought him to life for me. This book is very dear to my heart. What a gratifying read: wit! poignancy! authenticity! I asked myself constantly, How does Hilma Wolitzer do it?"

—Elinor Lipman, author of *Then She Found Me*

By Hilma Wolitzer

NOVELS

An Available Man

Summer Reading

The Doctor's Daughter

Tunnel of Love

Silver

In the Palomar Arms

Hearts

In the Flesh

Ending

NONFICTION

The Company of Writers

NOVELS FOR YOUNG READERS

Wish You Were Here

Toby Lived Here

Out of Love

Introducing Shirley Braverman

An Available Man

An Available Man

a novel

HILMA WOLITZER

BALLANTINE BOOKS TRADE PAPERBACKS
NEW YORK

2013 Ballantine Books Trade Paperback Edition

Published in the United States by Ballantine Books, an imprint of The Random House Publishing Group, a division of Random House, Inc., New York.

BALLANTINE and colophon are registered trademarks of Random House, Inc.

RANDOM HOUSE READER'S CIRCLE & Design is a registered trademark of Random House, Inc.

Originally published in hardcover in the United States by Ballantine Books, an imprint of The Random House Publishing Group, a division of Random House, Inc., in 2012.

Grateful acknowledgment is made to peermusic for permission to reprint excerpts from "Bésame Mucho" (Kiss Me Much). Original Spanish words and music by Consuelo Velázquez, English lyrics by Sunny Skylar, copyright © 1941, 1943 by Promotora Hispano Americana de Musica S.A. Administered by Peer International Corporation. Reprinted by permission.

Library of Congress Cataloging-in-Publication Data

Wolitzer, Hilma.
An available man : a novel / Hilma Wolitzer.
p. cm.
ISBN 978-0-345-52755-4—ISBN 978-0-345-52756-1 (eBook)
1. Widowers—Fiction. 2. Older people—Fiction. I. Title.
PS3573.O563A95 2012
813'.54—dc23 2011037248

Printed in the United States of America on acid-free paper

www.randomhousereaderscircle.com

9 8 7 6 5 4 3 2 1

Book design by Susan Turner

For Henry Dunow,
a most available agent and friend

An Available Man

1

Out of the Woodwork

Edward Schuyler was ironing his oldest blue oxford shirt in the living room on a Saturday afternoon when the first telephone call came. He'd taken up ironing a few months before, not long after his wife, Bee, had died. That happened in early summer, when school was out, and he couldn't concentrate on anything besides his grief and longing. At first, he only pressed things of hers that he'd found in a basket of tangled clean clothing in the laundry room. He had thought of it then as a way of reconnecting with her when she was so irrevocably gone, when he couldn't even will her into his dreams.

And she did come back in a rush of disordered memories as he stood at the ironing board. But he had no control over what he remembered, sometimes seeing her when they first met, or years later in her flowered chintz chair across the room, talking on the telephone and kneading the dog's belly with her bare feet—Bee called it multitasking—or in the last days of her life, pausing so long between breaths that he found himself holding his own breath until she began again.

Still, this random collage of their days together was better than nothing, and it was oddly comforting to smooth the wrinkles out of her blouses, to restore their collapsed bosoms and sleeves and hang them in her closet, where they looked orderly, expectant. And he liked the hiss of steam in the quiet house and the yeasty smell of the scorched cloth.

Now he lay the iron down on the trivet and, with Bingo, the elderly dog, padding right behind him, went into the kitchen to answer the phone. Without his reading glasses, which didn't appear to be anywhere, Edward couldn't make out the caller I.D. But when he said hello there was no reply, and he assumed he'd hear one of those recorded messages from someone running for something. It was late October, after all. Half his mail these days was composed of political flyers, the other half divided between bills and belated notes of sympathy. He was about to hang up when a woman's voice said, "Ed? Is that you?"

No one he knew called him Ed, or Eddie. Sometimes a telemarketer made a stab at sudden intimacy that way, but he was not a man who invited the casual use of nicknames. Even Bee, who knew him as well as anyone, and loved him, had always called him Edward. Her two grown children still kept their childhood names for him—Nick addressing him as "Schuyler" or "Professor," and Julie as "Poppy." Nick's bride, Amanda, said "Dad," a little self-consciously, while reserving the title "Daddy," as Julie did, for her own father.

"This is Edward, yes," he said into the phone. "Who is this?" and the woman said, "You don't know me, Ed, but we have a good friend in common."

He didn't say anything and she continued. "My name is

Dorothy Clark, Dodie to you. Joy Feldman and I went to school together."

Edward tried to imagine sweet, matronly Joy as a schoolgirl, but all he could think of was the Tuna Surprise casserole she'd slid into his freezer right after the funeral, and that days later he'd found a single hair at its defrosted center. Bee might have said, *Ah, the surprise!* He had a chilly premonition that this woman was going to try to sell him something death-related, like perpetual grave care, or hit him up for a contribution to some obscure charity in Bee's memory.

But her voice seemed to deepen a little with emotion as she said, in response to his silence, "You and I are in the same boat, Ed. I mean I'm recently widowed, too, and Joy thought . . . well, that we should probably get to know each other."

He wondered why Joy would have ever thought that, and then he understood, with a little shock of revulsion and amusement, not unlike the way he'd felt when he discovered the hair in the casserole. "I see," Edward said. "That was kind of her, but I'm afraid she was mistaken. I'm not really looking for . . . for any new friends at the moment." At the bird feeder tray right outside the window, a few chickadees settled and pecked.

"Oh, of course," Dorothy Clark said in a brighter tone. "Everyone has their own timetable for grieving. But when you're ready, why don't you give me a ring. I live in Tenafly, we're practically neighbors. I'll give you my number." There was a flurry at the bird feeder as a jay arrived, scattering seed and the chickadees.

"All right," Edward said resignedly, politely. He was polite to telemarketers, too, even those who took liberties with his name.

She was suspicious, though. "Do you have a pencil?" she asked. If he had a pencil, he might have noted the chickadees and the jay in his neglected birding journal, or tapped on the window with it to interrupt the bullying. But he said, "Sure, go ahead," and she recited the number slowly, twice. At least she didn't ask him to read it back to her.

He returned to the living room, but the glide of the iron over the worn blue field of his shirt was no longer soothing. His loneliness had been disturbed, and he wanted it back.

One evening near the end, he was reading at Bee's bedside, his free hand resting lightly on her arm; she seemed to be asleep. Then she opened her glazed eyes and said, "Look at you. They'll be crawling out of the woodwork."

"What will, sweetheart?" he'd asked, but she shut her eyes and didn't answer.

She had said many strange things during those last nights and days. "Oh, what will I do without you?" she'd cried out once, as if he were the one dying and leaving her behind. And there were drug-induced hallucinations, of small children standing at the foot of her bed, and mice scrambling in the bathtub. Maybe there were more vermin waiting in the woodwork of her fevered dream.

It wasn't until the second phone call, a few days after the one from Dorothy Clark, that he finally got Bee's meaning. This time the caller introduced herself as Madge Miller, a vaguely familiar name. She and Bee had been in the same book club a while back and she'd heard the sad news through a grapevine of mutual friends. She was just calling to commiserate, she said—what a terrible shame, what a beautiful, bright woman in the prime of her life. And maybe he'd like some company soon, for lunch or a drink.

Later that afternoon, Edward went into the kitchen and rummaged in what one of the children, in childhood, had aptly dubbed "the crazy drawer." Among the loose batteries and spare shoelaces, the expired supermarket coupons and the keys that didn't open any known doors, he found the chain that had briefly kept Bee's reading glasses conveniently dangling from her neck, until she caught a glimpse of herself in the mirror and declared that she'd rather go blind.

Now Edward untangled the chain and attached it to his glasses, carefully avoiding his reflection, which he imagined bore an unfortunate resemblance to his third-grade teacher, Miss Du Pont. His own students would have a field day. But he'd only use the chain at home, where he often mislaid his glasses, and at least he'd be prepared to screen any future phone calls from strangers.

2

Bachelor Days

For a very long time, following a disastrous affair, Edward believed he would never marry. He had gone out with many women, but like his father he'd fallen in love—in what promised to be a fatal and final way—with only one of them. Her name was Laurel Ann Arquette, and she'd taught French just down the hall from his lab at Fenton Day, a private school on the Upper West Side of Manhattan. Another teacher had introduced them at lunch on Laurel's first day.

He stood and said, "Hello, and welcome to perdition." The spoon he'd been stirring his coffee with clanged to the floor, making her laugh, a bell that chimed from the top of his head to the pit of his belly. Her abundant hair was prematurely white, silver really, and her face was actually heart-shaped. She was as slender as a schoolgirl, for whom she might be mistaken, if not for that hair and her knowing presence. "Edward," she said in return, as if she were naming or anointing him, and she let her hand be swallowed by his.

It was 1974. They were both in their mid-twenties then and each school day became an agony of hours until they could meet at his apartment in Hell's Kitchen and make raw and exhausting love. They were very prudent at Fenton, though, sitting discreetly apart in the faculty room, never even accidentally touching in the corridors, and resisting the temptation to exchange loaded glances.

But everyone, from the overstimulated students to the amused lunch ladies, knew anyway, somehow. One morning, he confiscated a note between two seventh-graders in his homeroom: "Does Dr. S. couche avec Mademoiselle A.?" *Oui!* Yes, he did, every chance he could, and he might as well have worn a sandwich board advertising his ardor. Even ripping up that silly note and frowning severely at the giggling transgressors didn't quell their excitement.

But once Edward and Laurel announced their engagement, right after their second spring break together, they became as boring to the students as their own parents, and somewhat less interesting to everyone else. Still, the engaged couple were consumed by their new status, and began to make wedding plans. He'd hoped for something simple, but Laurel wanted the whole show, in an almost unconscious act of defiance against her divorced parents, who had eloped to Maryland with Laurel already on board.

Edward thought she was conflating the lavishness of a reception with the success of a marriage, but he went along with her. She'd been such a miserable child, passed back and forth between her depressed mother and angry father like a hand grenade that might suddenly go off. Once, she told Edward, her parents had an argument that threatened to become physical, and Laurel, stepping between them, was accidentally knocked to the ground. She claimed her hair had turned white as a result of all that early tension. "You can't imagine," she said, and he couldn't.

His own parents had stuck it out, their early passion having metamorphosed into something lower-key but lasting, a soufflé collapsed into a comforting soup of days. They were as dazzled as Edward was by Laurel, and would have remortgaged their house in Elmont to buy her happiness, and thereby their son's. As it turned out, they only had to dig into their retirement fund to come up with the lion's share of the wedding expenses.

Edward swore that he would pay them back someday. There was nothing offered from the bride's side; money, squandered and lost, was one of the many contentions between the still-contentious elder Arquettes. Laurel had been estranged from both of them, and only after Edward urged her did she send them invitations.

Edward didn't want a church service—he wavered between atheism and agnosticism, between science and the unknown. But Laurel, a nonbeliever herself, insisted that they had to hedge their bets. When the arrangements began to get out of hand, they quarreled. "You don't care what I want," she accused him, unfairly, in the sweetly suffocating, refrigerated breath of the florist's shop.

She wanted a couturier gown and fountains of Cristal. She wanted to have tiny, speckled yellow orchids that might have been plucked from some mossy jungle placed at every table in the Rainbow Room, and there were too many tables. How could she complain about feelings of isolation and still list more than 150 friends who had to be invited? He'd only met a few of them.

He came back at her with, "You don't even *know* what you really want." But he gave in, finally, to everything, perversely pleased that she seemed more outraged than hurt by his resistance. She'd been hurt enough in her life. He wanted to protect and defend her, even before their official vows, to make up for her stolen happiness. And although he knew better—biology was his subject, after all—the heat between them seemed as if it might never die.

A week before the wedding, they lay in their usual post-sexual stupor. Edward was still marveling at her body, the bold and innovative ways she used it, the way she looked—those small breasts, as tender as if they'd only recently budded; the springy, surprisingly dark hair of her bush. Words from Human Anatomy 101 struck him with new poignancy. *Scapular. Clavicle.* She extricated herself, turning away from him, and, instead of her usual, throatily whispered "*Je t'aime*," or "Again, please," she said, "I almost got married once before, you know."

He hadn't known; she'd never mentioned it. His heart was just slowing, and he hoped she couldn't feel the way it began to leap against the curve of her spine. "To David?" he asked, as casually as he could. David had been her previous boyfriend. She and Edward, after they'd declared their love for each other, had exchanged romantic histories—it was a ritual of intimacy that was painful but necessary; Laurel said so. And everyone in her past, as in his, seemed ephemeral, anyway, like people encountered in a dream.

"No," she said, her voice slightly muffled by her pillow. "It was Joe."

"Joe? Who's Joe?" Edward said.

"This guy, Joe Ettlinger. Before I was with David."

"Are you making this up?" he asked.

"I'm sorry," she said. "I should have told you."

"Yes," he agreed. "You should have."

"I'm sorry," she said again, less distinctly.

"What happened?" he asked.

"We fell out."

"Over what?" Edward said, imagining rare orchids and sparkling Cristal at the heart of the story.

"This and that, I don't really remember. We just fell out of love."

He couldn't picture that kind of falling, a plunge out of love, like a film about diving played in reverse. "For good?" he said.

"Yes, of course," she answered, after a lengthy pause. "I'm almost asleep," she said then. "Let's stop talking now, okay?"

Despite that cautionary conversation, he was still taken by surprise when she didn't show up at the church the following Saturday. He waited for her in the vestry for what seemed like years, but was actually less than two hours. Mysteriously, she had decided to spend the previous night in her mother's apartment, which Edward had taken as a good omen. Peace on earth, goodwill toward everyone!

And there were her mother and his sitting in front rows on opposite sides of the satin-swathed aisle, the two of them looking sisterly in their elaborate hats, their long gloves and trembling corsages. But Mrs. Arquette said, when asked about it later, that she hadn't seen or spoken to Laurel in weeks.

Edward went into a kind of emotional hibernation after Laurel's defection, staving off sympathy because it embarrassed and pained him—as if someone were touching his fevered skin—and he managed to numb his own sense of anguished disgrace. At least Laurel had left Fenton as well as Edward. He kept telling himself he'd get over it; it wasn't a death, even if it felt like one.

That turned out to be true. Slowly, he began to recover, to see the world without her as an interesting place again, to even date a little. There seemed to be available, attractive women everywhere. And so he became a bachelor, that title nothing like the euphemism people once used for gay men such as Edward's uncle Lewis. Everyone had referred to Lewis, his mother's brother, as a "confirmed" bachelor, a man who adored women, really, but just couldn't be tied down. Lewis was called into service to escort homely cousins to their high school proms, and later as a "walker" for widowed and spinster aunts, but he'd never introduced the love of his life to anyone in the family.

Edward, on the other hand, assiduously played the field. Whenever a relationship threatened to become serious, he was the one to break it off, to move on. And he'd finally thrown away the letter Laurel had sent from Tucson about running into Joe Ettlinger accidentally, about the doubts and fears she'd been suppressing, and the sixth sense she'd had about Edward's own lack of commitment.

Maybe she was right, maybe he'd only been kidding himself. He had caught her out in several little senseless lies during their courtship that he'd written off to her "high-strung" nature, and refused to see her neediness or mood swings as pathology. And he had known all along that prematurely white hair was usually just a genetic tendency or some hormonal imbalance that reduces melanin, but he'd indulged her fantasies, and even entered them, letting desire trump science and just plain common sense. He was never quite that trusting or romantic again, until he met Bee.

3

The Beginning

She wasn't his type; he could see that right away. Even after all this time—almost fifteen years!—and how terribly Laurel had wounded and humiliated him, she had remained Edward's physical ideal. He chalked this up to some sort of brain thing, a primordial imagery beyond his control. Beatrice Silver was full-breasted, with curly brown hair; her hips, like her smile, were a little too wide. Childbirth must have altered her figure, of course. She was dancing the cha-cha with her little daughter—that was his first sight of her—at the wedding reception of a mutual friend, Sue Cooper, a colleague of Edward's and a former neighbor of Bee's. It had never occurred to Sue, a notorious matchmaker, to introduce them to each other.

One day, Bee would confide that she wasn't instantly attracted to Edward, either. He'd looked too standoffish, she said, too *patrician*, hanging back on the sidelines of the dance floor like that, with his hands in his pockets. Good looking, she conceded, like one of those fair-haired Fitzgerald heroes. But not hot-blooded enough, like her gorgeous, swarthy, rotten ex-husband, from whom she'd only recently been divorced. No more men, she thought, *cha-cha-cha!*

Edward still didn't enjoy going to weddings. He no longer had any conscious feelings for Laurel, not even residual anger or yearning, but the whole setup, of solemn vows and extravagant toasts—the pomp and the circumstances—always made him want to be somewhere else. And this was a Jewish wedding, where the bride and groom were lifted on tilting, teetering chairs above the chanting crowd, with only a skimpy silk handkerchief joining them—their brand-new union, their very lives, already seemingly imperiled.

Then there was all that communal dancing, wild and fast, to the piercing, joyful cries of the clarinets. Not Edward's sort of thing, really, although for some reason he found his eyes brimming with tears as the dancers sped by, faster and faster to the escalating music, like horses on a carousel. And then his hand was grabbed and he was pulled into the maelstrom before he could protest. No, he *did* protest: he was just watching, he didn't know the steps, but who could hear him in all that jubilant noise? And both of his hands were tightly clutched by then, on one side by the little girl who'd danced with her mother, and on the other by an older woman in a jaunty red hat, a kind of lopsided fez, who kicked up her heels like a chorus girl. They both held on as if he belonged to them, to Julie and her grandmother, Gladys, as he one day would.

Edward liked children—their natural curiosity, how truly funny and intuitive they could be, the elastic possibilities of their minds. Teaching had never been boring, even though so much of the core curriculum hardly ever changed. He might have had kids of his own if he'd married when he was younger—although Laurel wasn't keen about it—but he was in his forties now and didn't long for them, not anymore. At least his sister, Catherine, and her husband, Jim, who lived in San Diego, had made grandparents out of their mother and father.

And Bee's children—there were two of them, he soon found out—didn't immediately make him regret his own childless state. The boy, Nick, about twelve, Edward guessed, was seated at the almost abandoned children's table in the reception hall. Julie, who hadn't relinquished Edward's hand after the frenetic *hora* finally ended, pulled him in that direction; it might have been just another phase of the dance. "This is my brother," she announced, like a miniature docent showing off a prized painting.

Nick, his shirttails half out of his pants, his teeth caged in metal, ignored her. He was busy bombarding another boy, sitting across from him, with pellets of the ceremonial challah, which were quickly sent flying back. The whole table looked like the aftermath of a minor war. One chair had been knocked over. And there were spilled Cokes, beheaded centerpiece flowers, and bits of food all over the stained pink tablecloth, although some of the plates seemed untouched.

The band had now launched into something slow and romantic. "Bésame Mucho." *Each time I cling to your kiss I hear music divine.* One of Laurel's favorites, he remembered; did they still play that? He gently freed his hand from the girl's grasp, and her mouth dropped open in disappointment. God, was he expected to slow-dance with her now? Adopt her?

It was her mother who rescued him, coming up and telling Julie to bring her grandmother a plate of cookies from the dessert buffet. With a rueful backward glance at Edward, she ran off. In gratitude, and because she was already swaying to the music, he asked Bee if she'd like to dance.

"Don't worry about her," she told Edward as she turned to him. "You've just caught her on the rebound."

He didn't ask her then what she'd meant. It was only during their first date that he'd learn about Julie's father's desertion, Bee's work as a therapist at a community mental health clinic, and the challenges of being a single parent. That was when he opened his life story to her, as well, with unusual candor and ease.

But they didn't say anything else at all while they danced and danced at the wedding, the band flowing without pause from one ballad to another. Bee was surprisingly light in Edward's arms. Her face was glowing and her hair smelled damp and earthily sweet, like geraniums, he thought, or as if she'd just come in out of the rain. That was the beginning, with no apparent end in view: a needy young girl, a churlish boy, and a woman whose generous, swaying hips would soon cradle Edward in bed.

Their own relatively small and quiet wedding, seven months after they met, took place in the garden of her closest friends, the Morgansterns, under a canopy of wisteria. Edward had already given up his bachelor quarters in Manhattan and moved into Bee's Tudor-style house on Larkspur Lane in Englewood. Overnight, it seemed, he'd become a husband, a stepfather, a suburbanite, a mortgagor, a birder, and a commuter. He had never been so happy in his life.

4

The Messenger

Bee had brought up the subject of bereavement groups long before they'd even truly acknowledged their mortality, back when they still said things like "If anything ever happens to me," rather than "If I die first." In a joke that was popular then, a wife tells her husband, "If something happens to one of us, I'm going to Florida."

Then one night in bed, out of the blue, Bee told Edward that she didn't think he would be capable of grieving properly for her. He pretended to be insulted. "Why, I'd cry rivers," he said.

"Well, maybe," she conceded. "I've caught you tearing up during crappy movies. But you're so private, you'd wait until you were all alone, and you wouldn't let anyone really comfort you. It's not just you, all men are like that. You wear your genitals on the outside and your feelings on the inside—the exact opposite of women."

"*Vive la différence,*" he said, putting his arms around her.

But she pulled away. "You'd probably need to join one of those bereavement groups."

"I hate groups," he said. "Except for The Beatles and the Supremes."

"Edward, be serious," she said.

What had brought *this* on? Maybe it was just her habit of helping, an overflow from her work with troubled families at the clinic. But *they* weren't troubled. Only moments before her warm legs had been tangled cozily with his while they read the books now lying on the floor beside the bed, their places saved for the following night. They'd had an especially good dinner earlier with a nice Cabernet, and, with both of the children at sleepovers, had even made love in the living room before clearing the dishes. He wasn't going to let this unwelcome mood-shift take hold.

"I'll tell you what," he said. "I'll go first—age before beauty, et cetera. And you can grieve to your heart's content." He had been on the verge of sleep when she'd started the whole stupid conversation, and he put an end to it by turning off his lamp and kissing her good night. But he lay awake in the dark for a long time.

They were lucky, enchanted, even, and so were their friends. The years tripped by and several of their parents, including both of Edward's and Bee's father, succumbed to illness and old age, while they remained indestructible. Then a long-married couple in their crowd was killed instantly in a car crash. The first among them to go, as if they'd invented death the way they'd once invented love.

The spell was broken. Less than a year later, two other friends died, one right after the other. *Heart! Cancer!* Driving home from the second of those funerals, Bee said, "Our circle is getting smaller and smaller. Soon we'll only be a semicircle."

"And then a comma," Edward added. They smiled at each other, in a guilty rush of gaiety.

But those deaths seemed like tragic anomalies rather than the natural course of events. Bee and Edward were both still working; she was fifty-seven and he was sixty-two. Their sex life was more vibrant than anyone, including themselves, would have imagined. And her mother was alive and sentient, which preserved Bee's status as someone's child. This was only the late afternoon of their lives, and, despite the sorrow they felt, they could still make nervous comedy out of their friends' misfortune.

Soon after, when Bee's diagnosis and prognosis were delivered in what sounded like one choppy paragraph of doom read aloud from the *Merck Manual*—"Pancreas. Metastases. Stage Four. Months."—she and Edward simply throbbed with disbelief until they were given a second, identical opinion. Then they lay awake together in the menacing darkness. She murmured, "God," then "Wow. It doesn't seem real, does it?" And Edward held her and said, "No, no, of course it doesn't."

But it seemed shockingly real to him. He could picture the wild division of her cells, as if he were seeing them through the lens of his microscope. She was here in his arms, in their bed, and he could already imagine her absence from every room in the house. He remembered with horror when Nick was reading *Hamlet* in high school and had recited at dinner: "To be Bee or not to be Bee," and the way they'd all screamed with laughter. Julie, poor Julie, had snorted milk and had to leave the table. How would they tell her?

Edward ended up doing it by himself, after Bee had begged off. "I *can't.* Please. Not right now," she'd said, as if she had all the time in the world. So he called Julie, who had a share in an apartment in his old neighborhood in the city, and asked her to meet him that evening at Nick and Amanda's house, only a few miles from his and Bee's own. He advised them all on the phone that he needed to tell them something in person. "What? What is it?" Nick demanded. "What is it?" Amanda echoed anxiously on another extension. They often spoke to Edward or Bee in stereo like that.

"Let's wait until I get there, okay?" Edward said, already trying to mitigate what he had to say. But he couldn't help it—his tone was flat and somber.

Julie cried out, "You're not splitting up, are you?" She was five when her father had left, and she'd taken it harder than anyone, according to Bee. "No, never," Edward said, and her heavy sigh of relief shattered his heart. At least, he consoled himself, the child that he and Bee had wanted but failed to make together wouldn't have to be told.

Everyone wept that evening, except for Edward. Like those soldiers who are sent to deliver terrible news to families, his mission was to inform and give solace without breaking down. Bee was wrong about his ever needing a bereavement group; if he could do this on his own, he could do anything. Soon, eventually, he would even be able to tell Gladys, although he secretly wished she would die in her sleep before then, or "lose her marbles," as she was always threatening to do.

The worst moment came when Julie bleated, "Mom, Mom," sounding as plaintive as some lamb separated from the flock. Or maybe it was when Nick kept asking desperately hopeful questions about alternative treatments and experimental trials. Edward had searched medical websites in the middle of the night when Bee was finally asleep, seeking those same miracles despite everything he knew. He did his own weeping in private, too, just as she had once predicted, down in the sanctity of his basement lab, or in the shower where he used to belt out songs to the pulsing beat of the water.

On the way home from speaking to the children, he pummeled the steering wheel and moaned and yelled with the car windows rolled up. But he was able to compose himself before he approached their house, where Bee, with Bingo like a sentinel beside her, was waiting for him in the doorway.

Maybe, he thought later, Amanda's swollen silence was the worst thing, and the way she'd gripped Nick's hand, as if to keep him beside her, breathing, forever.

5

Lessons in Death

Bingo was almost fifteen years old when Bee became ill. He was the last in a long line of pets they'd acquired over the years, for the children's sake. True to that ludicrous cliché, Nick and Julie had promised—no, *sworn*—to care for, in turn, goldfish, turtles, a hamster, a lizard, and a couple of kittens. Bee believed that giving in to their pleas and pledges would make Nick more responsible and help raise Julie's self-esteem. Edward liked having animals around, but he thought of them more as first lessons in death. Most domesticated creatures had shorter life spans than humans, and then there were accidents.

He'd had a dog when he was a boy, a German shepherd mix called Schultz, after the neighbor who'd given him the puppy from his dog's litter. The canine Schultz had been hit by a car and killed after Edward's father had whistled for him across the street, and the entire family had suffered the loss. Bud Schuyler, talented whistler, especially of birdcalls, never whistled again. And Edward, who should have been walking the dog that night instead of being off somewhere with his friends—he and Catherine had also promised faithful care and feeding—shared his father's guilt. Sometimes he wondered if his interest in ornithology began back then, with the wonder of imitation birdsong and then its cessation.

Nick and Julie's pets had died, too, or mysteriously disappeared—the lizard and the hamster—one after the other. Edward remembered that Julie, a "minnow" in her swim class at day camp, came into the kitchen one morning in her Speedo and announced that Goldy was doing the sidestroke. She had poked at the floating fish gently with a pencil, trying to right it. "Do something!" she'd commanded Bee and Edward, as the truth began to seep in, and she wept enough tears that day to refill the emptied fishbowl. The first lesson.

Bingo had been adopted when Julie was twelve and in the midst of a social crisis. Her best friend had become someone else's best friend. She was positive nobody liked her; she *needed* a dog. Nick was a senior in high school by then, already moving away from home in his thoughts and plans, but in a rare gesture of solidarity he backed Julie up. Dogs were cool. They were funny and smart and they protected you. And sure, he'd help out whenever he could—he could teach their dog some neat tricks.

The whole family went to the animal shelter together, but Julie got to choose among all the frantically yapping, leaping, and wagging caged beasts. It was going to be her dog and, only peripherally, Nick's. Bee dropped hints about size and shedding and housebreaking. There was a two-year-old, purebred miniature poodle, a sedate and pretty little apricot-colored dog she'd tried to bring to Julie's attention. "Look, sweetheart, I think *she's* picked *you*!" Later, she would admit to having being shameless in her attempts to influence Julie's choice, but it didn't matter. Julie was smitten by a large mixed-breed puppy that wet himself and her with joy as she lifted him into her arms. Part beagle, Edward guessed, from the eyeliner and floppy ears, and part collie from its luxuriant, molting coat. God knew where the short fluffy tail came from.

Julie was allowed to name the dog, too, and Bingo was his name-o. What was wrong with Fido, Buster, or even Spot? If he ran away, as beagles were prone to do, Bee was afraid she'd seem like some crazy church lady with a winning card, scouring the neighborhood calling his name.

B-i-n-g-o! B-i-n-g-o! The song went mercilessly through her head and Edward's, as did the puppy's yowls of loneliness during those first nights in his new home. They tried all the old tricks to fool him into thinking he was nuzzled against his mother in the blanket-lined carton: a loudly ticking clock to replicate the maternal heartbeat; a heated, towel-wrapped brick; and even a stuffed Lassie preserved from Nick's babyhood that Bingo shredded in his despair.

Eventually, he settled in. When the novelty of feeding and walking him quickly wore off—Julie found both canned dog food and poop-scooping unbearably gross, and Nick went off to RPI—Bee and Edward took over. Bee's clinic was a five-minute drive from the house, so she came home for Bingo's middle-of-the-day walks. Edward took him out at night. After Julie left for Fairleigh Dickinson, Bee said that at least Bingo wasn't college material, that their nest wasn't completely empty.

When she was dying, the dog stayed close by her. Edward disapproved of anthropomorphizing animals. Some of them learned to live with us, but they still retained innate aspects of their own species. Stray dogs tended to find one another and move in wolf-like packs, and even well-fed house cats let out into the garden preyed on birds. He'd discouraged Julie from tying ribbons in her new puppy's fur, or polishing his toenails. When she lifted a silky ear and whispered "Who does Bingo love?" it was for her own assurance and consolation. Her familiar voice was what he responded to. He would have writhed in ecstasy if she'd recited the Declaration of Independence.

And reports of dogs howling at the moment of their owner's death seemed anecdotal at best. But there was something to the idea that they could sense and react to the moods of human beings. The household was tense with apprehension and sadness that centered on the sickroom—Bee and Edward's bedroom—where a hospital bed had been set up next to the regular bed, and where Bingo chose to hang out. The hospice nurses didn't object, even when he was underfoot; they seemed to find his presence there entirely natural. They often petted him as they went by, even if it meant washing their hands over and over again.

Nick rubbed Bingo, too, absentmindedly or as if for luck, and Julie still buried her face in his coat, as she had when he was a pup and served as her own personal comfort and confidant. And Edward could cry in privacy while the dog sniffed at every bush and scrap of grass in search of the perfect place to squat during their nightly walks. For a time, someone was always around to walk Bingo, which wouldn't be true, at least during the day, once Edward went back to school in the fall, and the rest of the family resumed their regular lives. He suggested that one of the kids might take him on.

But Julie couldn't keep him in the city because dogs were excluded from the lease for her apartment, and the woman she shared it with was allergic to fur and dander. Why didn't Nicky take him?—Bingo was his dog, too. Although Nick, as Bee had, worked close to home, and had a house with a fenced-in yard, he and Amanda didn't really want the responsibility of a pet. Their new marriage and their respective jobs used up all of their energy and time, and besides, Bingo had always been Julie's dog. What was that stupid joke? That life doesn't begin at conception or at birth, but after the children leave home and the dog dies.

Bingo was grizzled and arthritic and slightly deaf. Cataracts clouded his vision, and sometimes he lost his balance when he lifted his leg. He was very old, especially for a dog of his size, but he was far from moribund, from becoming anyone's lesson in death. In June, the month before Bee died, Edward found an ad in the local *Pennysaver* placed by someone offering to do odd jobs that included weeding, babysitting, and dog walking, all for a reasonable fee. He clipped the ad and threw it into the crazy drawer.

In the middle of August, he took the ad out and called the number listed. A woman answered the phone and said she'd come by that afternoon for an interview. Her name was Mildred Sykes and she was short and square, like a crude wood carving, and somewhere in late middle age. Bingo fell for her immediately. Not that he was a hard sell, but he took to Mildred as if she had sausages hidden on her person.

Her fee was as reasonable as advertised; she lived nearby, in one of those new, low-cost-housing units; and she was available every afternoon at the hour Bee used to leave the clinic and come home to walk the dog. An old boy like that, Mildred said, could probably use a midmorning walk, too. So Edward hired her immediately, without even checking the references she'd offered. He would make up a couple of extra keys—she could start after Labor Day. In the past, under other circumstances, he might have been more prudent, but right then it seemed as if he had nothing left to lose.

She asked if Edward needed her for anything else. She could

do some light housekeeping or cooking if he'd like, or help in the garden. But they'd had the same reliable cleaning service for years, food had become just a source of sustenance, and he depended on weeding and pruning to keep him occupied, something to do on those endless summer days besides his new hobby of ironing or just moping around. And outdoor work would help to sustain him during weekends once the school semester began.

"If you want me to, I could read your cards," she said. "Or do your numbers."

"Pardon?" he said.

"I'm mainly a psychic," she said. "You know, Tarot, numerology, auras. I do all this other stuff to fill in the hours."

"I see," Edward said, with a pang of regret. "Well, thank you, but right now I only need some dog care." Why had he said *right now*? He'd always believed that so-called psychics were deluded, demented, or simply con artists. And who in his right mind would ever want to know the future?

"That's fine," Mildred said, taking the leash from the broom closet doorknob. "Now, why doesn't Bingo show me some of his favorite trees?"

6

An Extra Man

After all his reluctance about going to the Morgansterns' dinner party, or anywhere else besides school since Bee's death, Edward was the first to arrive. The occasion, or non-occasion, as Sybil assured him—"The usual, just a few of us getting together"—had been called for seven o'clock and it was almost a quarter past, but there were no cars parked in the driveway or on the street right near the house, where the drapes were pulled open and the front windows blazed with light.

The porch lights were on, too, and the little hooded electric lanterns that lit the way up the leaf-littered path. Wood smoke was in the air and Edward, his Honda idling at the curb, saw Sybil and Henry move about their living and dining rooms, passing each other like the wooden figures in the Swiss clock on their mantel.

Henry's shingle swung and creaked in the wind. His medical offices, with their own entrance, and with cutouts of menorahs and Christmas trees taped to the windows, were on the side of the house. That was where Bee had taken Julie and Nick for checkups and childhood illnesses until they'd graduated from middle school and Henry's pediatric practice. Sybil, so efficiently in charge, was Henry's office manager.

Edward drove around the corner and parked midway between two streetlamps. In the relatively dark safety of the car, he contemplated continuing on back home, fixing himself a sandwich, and taking the dog out for a bonus walk. He was like a savage summoned into civilization, or someone suffering from a kind of behavioral amnesia. Maybe he'd forgotten how to be in company or eat with implements. Maybe he'd beat his chest and howl instead of shaking hands with the men and accepting the kisses of the women.

His hands, still holding the steering wheel, were trembling, and he was aware of his own heartbeat, the cooling tick of the car's engine. He could call them on his cell phone and claim a sudden illness, a stomach thing. There really was a vague cramping somewhere in his abdomen or chest. It was a sensation he remembered from his first days at a new school or a new job. He took the phone from his pocket.

But instead he called his own number and heard Bee say, "Edward and Bee aren't home right now. Please leave your name and number after the beep and one of us will call you back." Before long, one of their friends—probably bossy, outspoken Sybil—would challenge him about not having changed the message, and he'd have to claim that he'd simply forgotten and promise to take care of it.

In the meantime, though, he could still listen to Bee's voice in his ear and their names said together like that. Not that he did it often, just once in a while—from a private corner on school grounds or sitting in his parked car somewhere, like this. And he wasn't so far gone that he felt compelled to actually leave a message for Bee, although there were so many things he wished he could tell her: that the first African American president had been elected, that several of her clinic clients had sent Edward notes expressing their own sense of loss, that he would always feel grateful for the family she had given him.

"Edward and Bee aren't home right now . . ." Recording those outgoing messages had always been such a hilarious hassle. Bee had to revise hers a few times over the years: first to exclude Bruce, then to include Edward, and finally to leave off the children's names, one after the other, as they left home. Each time, something had gone wrong. Once, the doorbell had rung repeatedly in the middle of a taping. And the kids had started a screaming battle as soon as she'd started another. During the final recording, when she was joining Edward's name solely to hers, she'd said, "Bedward and Bee" at first and began to laugh until she got the hiccups. He ran off, laughing, too, to get her a glass of water, and then she made him leave the room so she could resume recording without cracking up again.

That's what he listened for mostly, and this time, too, a remnant of that laughter in her voice, a brief reprisal of their silly happiness that day. It didn't hurt anyone, he reasoned, and the message might even be putting off future phone calls from unknown, unattached women. He put the phone back in his pocket and considered what to do.

Edward had attended dozens of the Morgansterns' dinner parties, but he'd never gone there before without Bee and they had never been the first ones to arrive. Long ago, when the children were still at home, there were all the delays of saying good night—Julie was especially clingy—and the futile warnings about bedtime and homework and television repeated like protective mantras.

And once the kids were grown and gone, Bee had invented other delays: a misplaced earring or shoe, or the need to pee one more time, as if they were going into some third-world area without indoor plumbing instead of to an upscale suburban Jersey street so similar to their own. She'd insisted they were only "fashionably late" when they showed up last, after the other guests had made sloppy dents in the hummus, and the conversation was already heightened by alcohol. Bee loved plunging into the middle of a party, and Edward always followed in her wake, feeling his own natural reticence melt in the warm and lively room.

Now, hiding out in his car, he looked at his watch every few minutes until the half hour was reached, and then he drove back to the Morgansterns' street, where other cars were already parked near their house. He recognized Ned and Lizzie Gilbert's SUV, the environment-friendly Prius that belonged to the Jordans. Just a few old friends, as Sybil had promised in that cajoling telephone call. She had been Bee's oldest and closest friend, and she and Henry were like sturdy bookends of support throughout her illness and ever since.

"Edward, we *miss* you," she'd practically wailed on the phone, and he realized that he had been missing them, too, all these months, or at least the ordinary business of a communal life, of breaking bread with friends, and talking about politics and movies and neighborhood gossip.

So he grabbed the bottle of Chardonnay that had rolled around the floor of the passenger side while he drove, and went inside and accepted the minor clamor at his arrival, the velvet skim of the women's cheeks, the hearty grasps and back-patting of the men. But if they spoke of Bee, he believed he would not be able to bear it, and if they didn't, it might be equally terrible.

The recently dead were such a social menace. Their absence was as aggressive as the loudest voice in a room. You could not speak of them without sorrow, or ignore them without shame and even trepidation. They ruined the natural flow of conversation and the pleasurable balance of coupledom. It had been tolerable somehow during that unreal but official period of mourning, when they'd all come to him with their casseroles and consolation. But tonight was a kind of debut, or at least a reentry into the real world. Edward was on his own now; he would be the extra man in the room, the odd number at the table.

But when he glanced into the dining room, he saw that the gleaming Parsons table had been set for ten; its symmetry was shocking. And then the doorbell rang and Henry was greeting a woman Edward had never seen before. She'd come alone—the door was shut firmly behind her—and she carried a large ferny, foil-wrapped plant, which Henry took from her, along with her coat and trailing scarf, and he staggered a little under the awkward burden. Edward didn't offer to help, his automatic inclination, because he didn't want to be introduced to this stranger in the entry. It was only a fix-up, after all, and he felt the awful thrill of Sybil's betrayal.

Then Sybil herself was coming toward him, pulling the plant woman along by the hand. "Oh, Edward," she said, as if they'd just run into each other in the street. "I want you to meet my most favorite cousin, Olga Nemerov. Ollie, this is our old, dear friend, Edward Schuyler." The woman scowled at Sybil and then at Edward, who contained his impulse to scowl back as Sybil skittered away from them like a sand crab toward other guests.

Instead, he managed a stilted smile that this Olga Nemerov didn't bother to return. Was she really Sybil's cousin or merely some minor, sour character plucked from Chekhov? "Do you live in New Jersey?" he asked idiotically.

"God, no," she said, with what he perceived as a tiny shudder. She was a slight, bespectacled person in a prickly-looking tweed suit. Among the other colorful and scented women at the party, she was like a cactus in a rose garden. Bee would have intuitively shown up by now and rescued him.

"Well, it's not *that* bad," Edward said, thinking that it actually was that bad, that everywhere was. He wanted to ask her why she was so angry, before he realized that she, too, had understood why they'd both been invited and thrust together. "This wasn't my idea, you know," he said.

"My cousin is incurably romantic," she answered. "She's been doing this to me since we were teenagers."

And it never took, did it, Edward thought. "Sybil means well," he said, insincerely—another brilliant remark—and Olga actually snorted.

When Henry boomed that dinner was served and that everyone could sit anywhere, Edward and Olga quickly separated, as if they'd been demagnetized, and headed for opposite ends of the table.

During the rest of the evening, Edward felt as if he were under a light anesthesia, from which he was roused from time to time to exchange a few words with his neighbors, to eat a little of the food. He couldn't even bestir himself to become irate with Sybil for being so insensitive to him and disloyal to Bee's memory. It would have been useless, anyway. She would either baldly deny having tried to set him up, or scold him for yielding his zest for life, Bee's best and most contagious quality.

Finally, the ordeal was over. There were more handshakes and kisses, and farewells: "Good night, drive carefully, call me, good night!" Even Sybil's unsmiling cousin offered her hand at the door and Edward took it, surprised that it was soft rather than bristling with thorns. And then, mercifully, he was released back into his own care.

7

The Misery of Company

There was only one other man in the grief counselor's living room, and he looked up with something like relief in his eyes when Edward came in. A woman with a notebook on her lap smiled and said, "You must be Edward Schuyler. I'm Amy Weitz. Welcome, and take a seat." Five other women sitting there glanced at Edward with varying degrees of attention. The only remaining seat was between two of them on a deep sofa, where he slowly sank, as if into a downy trap.

As he'd told Bee, he wasn't partial toward groups of strangers. He wasn't a member of Kiwanis, the Rotarians, or even the National Education Association. And unlike Bee, he'd never joined a bridge or book club. They'd played bridge with their friends, and reading seemed to him like the last stronghold of privacy in a group-crazed society. Why had she ever thought he could abandon his natural reserve in a situation like this?

But Edward felt intolerably bad, and his friends kept clucking over him. At least there was school on weekdays, somewhere to go that was more or less programmed and predictable, something he had to get out of bed to do. When he'd first returned to Fenton in September, many of his students had looked at him shyly, almost fearfully. They knew about Bee; that kind of news spread easily in a school community, even during vacation months. Should they say something to him? What should they say?

He felt sorry for them in their awkwardness—everything was so much harder in one's early teens—so he spared them the remarks they dreaded as much as he did by jumping right into the work at hand. As they entered the classroom, he was writing on the blackboard in great, scrawling letters: "Welcome back! Start thinking again! Why is science important? What are the principles of good science?"

His encounters with colleagues were brief and manageable. Those he was closest to, Frances Hartman in math and Bernie Roth in English, had come to the funeral and to the house afterward, and had expressed their regrets about Bee and their affectionate concern for him. Now they took their cues from Edward, and although he caught some worried glances between them, they kept their conversations with him bearably neutral.

But weekends and evenings had become increasingly difficult. He didn't want company, and solitary pursuits like birding in the Palisades or performing lab experiments in the basement required energy he couldn't seem to muster. He'd declined all invitations since the Morgansterns' dinner—there were several during the holidays—and Henry told him that his withdrawal was unhealthy; perhaps he needed some outside help. And then his internist seconded the motion when Edward came to him for a prescription or two: something to help him sleep at night, something to keep him functioning better during the day. In addition to a mild sedative, Dr. Fiedler scribbled a couple of names on his prescription pad.

Amy Weitz, MSW, CSW, whose iron-gray hair and excellent posture reminded Edward of the teachers of his childhood, asked each of them to say who they were and why they were there. It wasn't like those 12-step programs where only first names and addictions are given, followed by a chorus of greetings. The prevailing mood in the room was like Edward's own—tentative and sad.

Most of them had lost spouses. The two women who flanked Edward, Claire Broido and Lucy James, were both recent widows whose husbands had succumbed, respectively, to a damaged heart and a major stroke. A third woman's husband had committed suicide. And the wife of the other man, Charlie Ryan, had died of lung cancer. But one of the women, who appeared to be in her early sixties, was mourning the loss of her aged mother, and another the death of her only child, an eleven-year-old boy.

When it was Charlie Ryan's turn to speak, he said, bitterly, "She didn't even *smoke*!" A murmur rippled through the room. There was a collective sense of outrage, in addition to the pall of sorrow, and Amy Weitz asked Charlie if it might be easier if there was someone or something to blame.

Charlie admitted that it probably would be, and Edward silently agreed. If you didn't believe in God, for instance, you couldn't rail against his injustice or his mysterious ways. Without faith or the tobacco industry, there was just nature and chance and everyone growing seasick in the same rocky boat. There was, in the end, only the mandate of biology. As he warned his new students, year after year, while they fiddled with their pens and looked out the window: everything that lives dies. But he didn't say any of that now. He just listened as the others told their torturous stories.

The almost elderly, unmarried orphan had always lived with her mother. And what could she say about a ninety-year-old woman who had died? That she was crippled by arthritis and nearly blind. That she had once been a dancer and had greatly loved her daughter, Helene, who was now clearly bereft. The mother of the dead child leaned over and patted her hand.

Then it was Edward's turn. He repeated his name and said, "I was married for almost twenty years. My wife's name was Beatrice—Bee. She died of pancreatic cancer." It sounded, to his own ears, like a paid death notice, with an eye to the cost per word. But he couldn't talk about Bee in more intimate terms here. Even if he were so inclined, it might take twenty more years to describe her, to convey a compendium of moments in their life together. And he wasn't petitioning for anyone's sympathy, anyway. He'd had lots of that from people close to him, and it was like a mild analgesic salve applied to a critical wound.

He was surprised by how few tears were shed at this gathering of the newly bereaved. He had feared outbursts of weeping and keening, an epidemic of despair. Maybe, like him, they were all cried out. Even Gabby Lazard, the dead boy's mother, was able to tell what happened without falling apart, although her eyes glistened while she spoke and others sniffled and blew their noses.

It was an accident, Gabby said. Her boy, Ethan, had been playing outdoors with a couple of his friends in their wooded suburban neighborhood. They were chasing one another around some trees when Ethan tripped and was impaled on the sharp arm of a fallen branch. His femoral artery had been punctured and he'd bled to death while the other boys ran to get help.

"Fucking trees!" Charlie Ryan blurted. "Pardon my French," he added softly, with a nod toward the women.

Fucking trees, indeed, Edward thought, *and fucking cancer, too.* After Bee died, he'd smashed dishes and kicked the stuffing out of her beloved chintz chair. But he'd had the chair repaired, and he found that anger, one of the five purportedly necessary stages of grief, only left him spent and shamefaced. What were the other stages? He could only remember two of them now: bargaining and acceptance, neither of which he'd experienced.

As if she had been reading his mind, Amy said, "Anger is one of the five stages of grief Elisabeth Kübler-Ross wrote about. You all might want to take a look at her book, if you haven't already. Or read Sherwin Nuland."

Like a dutiful, eager student, Helene took out a pad and pencil and made notes. Edward had read Nuland's book *How We Die* several years before, mostly out of intellectual curiosity. What still stuck in his mind was a single phrase: "The majority of people die peacefully." Had he misremembered or taken it out of context? In any event, that notion may have helped some survivors find their own peace. It didn't work for him. Nor did the word *closure* that a few of the mourners said they hoped to achieve. Edward believed that they thought of it as a door closing softly on their grief, but he was afraid it might shut out more than they'd bargained for, memories of love and pleasure as well as of loss.

The personal stories continued and expanded. Gabby told them that Ethan had been into Harry Potter, magic, and the band Green Day, and that her marriage had broken up after his death. In a way, she said, he had released her and her husband from a state of chronic unhappiness. The first signs of Oscar James's stroke was a drooping eye and a slurred complaint about a bad haircut. Only days after his death did Lucy realize he'd been trying to tell her that he had a bad headache.

Judith Frank, the widow of the suicide, said that she'd missed some vital signs, too. After years of depression, her husband's gloom had miraculously dissipated. It hadn't occurred to her that he'd become euphoric because he'd finally planned a way out. Claire Broido confessed that she had often secretly felt for Al's pulse while he slept. She said that she'd buried two husbands in ten years. Charlie, the class clown, muttered, "Remind me not to marry you," and there was actually a smattering of laughter.

No one spoke ill of the departed, who seemed to have all been good looking and generous to a fault, and Edward began to find some of the encomiums suspect. Didn't any of the husbands have a short temper, or leave the toilet seat up, or kiss his wife's best friend in the kitchen during a dinner party? Did Helene really never see her mother's love as a stranglehold that had deprived her of an independent life? And surely Judith Frank had to recognize the punitive aspect of her husband's suicide. The man had shot himself, at home, where she would be sure to find him. Even little Ethan must have committed some crime of childhood, like cruelty to an animal or bullying a classmate.

Which brought Edward to his own canonization of Bee, who'd had habits that irked him: the way she'd start reading something to him when he was trying to read, himself; the books she had always left lying open, facedown, sometimes cracking their spines; her enjoyment of some inane television shows. And what about her failed first marriage? He had only ever heard her side of that story.

Then, as if in another instance of telepathy, Charlie Ryan revealed that although his wife had never smoked, she often drank like a fish. And Lucy admitted that she and Oscar had been in marriage counseling because of his infidelity. Amy gently probed those sore spots, but sorrow and forgiveness seemed to triumph over disappointment and rage. Denial, Edward remembered, was another of Kübler-Ross's stages of grief, but this easy absolution of the dead wasn't what she'd meant. Maybe they got away with everything, he decided, simply because they'd gotten away.

Toward the end of the session, deathbed scenes were recalled—releasing a wave of withheld tears—and last words repeated, none worthy of anthology, but all precious to the teller. Bee had whispered, "Edward, wait," which he didn't share with the group. It might sound self-serving or like something he'd made up. And it was also what she'd sometimes said after sex when she wanted to keep him inside her. Instead, he told them that Luther Burbank's final words were "I don't feel good."

The ninety minutes passed more quickly than Edward had expected. The bereavement group had formed a kind of cautious community, the way his students usually did at the beginning of a new term. And he mostly liked the people in the room. He envied their openness and admired the respect they showed one another. But he still felt pretty much the way he had coming in: reluctant and skeptical and, most of all, alone. He didn't really see any point in coming back.

8

The Monster in the Basement

While Bee was still able to make sense, she'd told Edward many things: that she was afraid; that she wasn't afraid; that she was too old to die young, it wasn't even romantic; that she loved him; that she feared the darkness; that she feared the silence—but she wouldn't be able to sense them, right? She didn't know which was scarier: the absence of consciousness forever, or the haunting possibility of eternal consciousness. Sometimes she came awake and spoke without opening her eyes, as if to try out the darkness. Once she said, "Am I dead yet?"

He readied himself for an outburst of anger that never happened. So he became angry for her and tried not to show it in her presence. It was a hazardous balancing act; *they ought to give lessons in this*, he thought. Whenever he could, he went down to the basement to vent, or just to tremble with fury and terror.

This was where Bee's ex, Bruce, once had a woodworking shop, and Edward now had his home laboratory. There was a toilet and a slop sink down there, a metal cabinet for supplies, a small refrigerator for snacks and some of his specimens—"Now, don't become absentminded, dear," Bee used to say—and an old studio bed for naps or daydreaming.

Bruce's weekend hobby had produced various small household items, like fish- and frog-shaped trivets and a box for the television remote controls. He had taken all of his tools with him when he left, but not the long table that Bee had found on one of her flea market jaunts, and bought for him from a vendor who was moving to Florida.

Edward had appropriated it for his lab equipment. Once in a while, when Julie and Nick were still in school, he'd invited them downstairs to do simple experiments, for homework or just for fun. They sprouted lima beans in damp cotton, and grew bread mold that they examined under the microscope, along with hairs plucked from their own heads. It was during these sessions that Nick first let down his guard and began to communicate with Edward. Julie, he remembered, had freaked out at the magnification of her split ends.

After the kids grew up and moved out, Bee offered Edward the use of one of their bedrooms as his lab, but he preferred the quiet and seclusion of the basement. "It's more peaceful down there," he'd told her. "It's spookier, too," she said. "I just hope some guy with a bolt through his neck doesn't come thumping up the stairs one day." But it was always only Edward, rubbing his eyes, looking for her company, for a drink or a cup of coffee.

One Sunday night a few weeks after the bereavement group meeting, he went down to the basement after supper, hoping he could lose himself in work for a little while. The dog whimpered at the top of the stairs, which he couldn't manage anymore. Edward contemplated carrying him down, and then decided he'd think better on his own. He'd started an experiment just before Bee became ill, involving the growth of bacteria on a kitchen sponge. Although he'd lost track of the whole project, he saw that his samples had been preserved, and that his notes were still on the table.

But he couldn't concentrate. Bingo had stopped whimpering, but his toenails clicked as he paced the kitchen, waiting for Edward's return. And the house creaked and settled, like light, hesitant human footsteps above him, making him look upward for a moment. If only he believed in ghosts, or an afterlife, or anything besides the scientific evidence of decomposition. Despite the fears she'd expressed, Bee had chosen burial over cremation. "I don't want you to be stuck with my ashes," she'd told him, as if she were referring to a perpetual bad blind date. "And I don't want to be scattered all over the place, either. It sounds so . . . restless."

Now Edward lay down on the studio bed and closed his eyes. Why had he always associated silence with this part, *his* part, of the house? He'd turned on the dishwasher earlier, and water still gurgled through the pipes. The furnace kicked in and roared. And that subtle creaking continued from time to time. It was enough to wake the dead, he thought, and sat up in shock.

He took a package of cotton batting from the cabinet and tore off a couple of pieces. He rolled them into pellets and put them into his ears, pressing until he couldn't hear anything, not even the tapping of his own fingers on the cabinet door. It was as if he'd gone totally deaf.

Then he turned off the light switch on the wall near the steps. It was a cloudy, moonless night—the high, shallow windows appeared black—and the room was pitched into utter darkness. He had to grope his way back to the bed, and although he'd thought he knew the place by heart, he stumbled against a corner of the long table. He could feel it tremble, and the petri dishes and flasks must have rattled. But he didn't hear them any more than he heard the usual groan of the bedsprings as he lay down again.

For decades, in a unit on the senses, he'd shown classrooms of kids how their pupils contracted in brightness, and enlarged in the absence of light. They learned the role of vitamin A in night vision, the way the molecules in the rods inside their eyes split and then recombined. And how, after several minutes, they could begin to make out shapes and even details of their environment in the dark.

Now it was happening to him. There was the outline of the table, with its miniature skyline of test tubes and beakers. There were the skulking silhouettes of the furnace and the water heater, the dehumidifier in the shadowy distance. Edward pulled the folded blanket from the foot of the bed all the way up past his head, shutting his eyes once more, tighter this time.

Darkness and silence. But also *consciousness*, glorious consciousness, of darkness and silence, and of his own metabolism: the heat of his body beneath the blanket, his urgent pulse and anxious breathing. His eyelids fluttered behind their blindfold, and all of his muscles seemed to flex involuntarily; he was a veritable machine of motion. And his brain teemed with stored sounds and images. Bee!

Edward threw off the blanket and opened his eyes. While they readjusted, he pulled the cotton wads out of his ears and got up and stretched, easing a slight cramp in his left leg. His real bed was a lot more comfortable. The book he'd been reading earlier, on Darwin and Lincoln, was waiting on his night table. He looked at the luminous dial on his watch; the dishwasher would be ready to be emptied by now.

Then there were three sets of exams to go through and grade, the lesson plans to prepare for the following week. He was thirsty, as if he'd been running for miles. And he remembered that Sybil had left a message earlier: "Edward," she'd said, "why in the world do you still have Bee's voice on this thing?" He hadn't called her back, but he knew that he had to change the outgoing message on his voice mail. He tidied up the remains of the abandoned experiment, and soon he was lumbering up the stairs, half monster, half human, returning to the noise and light of the living world.

9

Science Guy

"Professor, hey, I'm glad you're home. I wanted to give you a heads-up about something." It was Nick, on the telephone, as soon as Edward walked into the house after work.

"What's going on?" Edward asked. His manner was carefully casual, but he felt a pang of foreboding. He'd suddenly remembered other phone calls from Nick, or about him—from school and once from the police—when he was a teenager and Bee and Edward were newly married. It was hard to believe how sullen and unapproachable the boy was back then, the way he'd always said "*What*" if you so much as glanced in his direction, a flat, belligerent statement rather than a question. Edward, having won Bee, but still courting the children, had come to his defense. "It's only adolescence," he assured Bee. "It's boys. I was like that, too," he said, although he hadn't been. "He'll outgrow it," he ventured, without real certainty.

But Nick *had* outgrown it, whatever it was. He was a man now, married, and a highly paid software designer, tamed at last by maturity and the quicksilver magic of love, for Amanda, for his mother and sister and grandmother—even for Edward.

On the phone, Nick said, "It's the girls. Man, I'm sorry, but they've taken this ad out about you." Before Edward could respond, he went on. "I tried to stop them. I told them it was a stupid idea and they had no right . . ." Now he sounded like the younger Nick who was never at fault for anything, from skipped classes and failing grades to vandalized mailboxes and the stash of weed in his own smelly sneaker. But this wasn't about Nick; apparently it was about Edward. Something to do with an ad.

"What ad?" Edward asked. "What are you talking about?"

"That literary paper you subscribe to, *The New York Review*?"

"*Of Books,*" Edward finished lamely. "What about it?" But he already knew. Those personals that Bee had gleefully insisted on reading aloud to him, along with a running commentary. "Listen to this one. 'Sensual, smart, stunning, sensitive.' Oh, why do they always resort to alliteration? 'Julia Roberts look-alike.' In her dreams, maybe. And this one's a music lover! Well, who doesn't love music, besides the Taliban? 'Searching for that special someone to share Bach, Brecht, and breakfast.' When they'll probably eat bagels, bacon, and brussels sprouts."

Pretty, petite, passionate. Witty, wise, wonderful. Wasn't anyone ordinary, a little flawed? Bee wanted to know. Homely and shy, with a stammer, perhaps, or a glass eye? "Well, who places those ads? And who answers them?" Edward once said, irritably, rattling his newspaper—once again he was trying to read while she read to him. "Why, lonely people, Edward, that's who," Bee said, in tones of gentle reproach, as if he'd been the one making fun of them.

Now his blood seemed to thicken and slow with dread. The "girls," Amanda and Julie, had joined that furtive cabal of matchmakers: Sybil and her oddball cousin, Joy Feldman with her recent hints about online dating, all those phone calls from strangers streaming out of the woodwork. "What does it say?" he asked Nick.

"I've got the paper right here. Should I read it to you?"

"Do you mean it's published already?"

"Well, yeah," Nick said. *Duh, Professor.* "Manda showed it to me this morning. Believe me, I wish they'd listen to reason."

Edward glanced at the mail he'd tossed onto the kitchen counter when he'd answered the phone, and there among the envelopes was that familiar thick, folded wedge. He and Bee had had an on-again, off-again subscription for years.

Off, when they both complained about having much too much to read and admitted that they were merely skimming most of the essays. On, when they became hungry for literate writing, for opinions that sustained or argued with their own, or when they simply feared the threatened loss of the printed word. Bee used to inhale the inky fragrance of the *Times* in the morning before she started reading it, with an expression that was already nostalgic.

In the months that he'd been alone, Edward read while he ate his supper—sometimes with the television set mumbling in the background, for noise, for company—and at bedtime, and in the middle of the night when he came abruptly awake as if his name had been called. He went through everything in the *Times* and *The New Yorker* and the *NYR*, except for the personal ads in the latter, which didn't interest him in the first place, and reminded him of Bee's wicked delight in them.

"No," he told Nick, as offhandedly as he could. "I have my copy here. I'll take a look at it later."

But he didn't even remove his jacket before he reached for his glasses, grabbed the paper, and dropped into a chair at the table. His eye was caught by some of the headlined names on the cover—Tony Judt, Freeman Dyson, Elizabeth Drew, former seductions—but he quickly turned to the back pages, where phone sex was advertised in discreet code, alongside rentals in Tuscany and the Loire Valley, and offers for the editing of manuscripts by acclaimed authors.

Jesus, there it was, crammed between ads for two divorcées of competing charms.

> **Science Guy.** Erudite and kind, balding but handsome.
> Our widowed dad is the real thing for the right woman.
> Jersey/Metropolitan New York

Balding! He ran one hand over his slightly thinning hair and squinted at his reflection in the toaster. He wasn't about to resort to a comb-over yet. And *handsome* was another overstatement, of course. But would people still recognize him somehow, anyway? *Science Guy* could refer to anyone from Bill Nye to a Big Pharm researcher to some loner in a remote weather station. The term sounded suspiciously like one Nick had come up with, despite his self-proclaimed innocence and indignation. *Erudite* must have come from Amanda—it was a word she used—and *kind* from Julie. A collaboration, then. He'd kill them all.

He read the ad again, with slightly less agitation this time, parsing it for meaning with what he imagined would have been Bee's point of view, thinking, with a jolt, that she could have contributed *the real thing* herself. She had told him, more than once, that his best quality was his authenticity. "You are what you are," she'd said in a kind of cockeyed parody of Popeye.

No phone number or email address was given, thank God,

just the number of a post office box. They'd probably had to pay extra for that; good money after bad, as Gladys would say. And they hadn't mentioned how old he was. People's ages were usually included, or hinted at, which used to be only more fodder for Bee's disdain: *fiftyish*, she was certain, meant at least sixty, and *young at heart* could be anywhere from seventy to senility. Men, no matter how old, she'd pointed out, were always in the market for women of childbearing age. "*You* men," as she put it to Edward, leaning over to poke him for emphasis, as if he'd placed one of those ads, himself, as if he was in the market for anyone at all.

He made himself look at a few of the other ads, most of them from women, single or unhappily married, using the language of high-powered salesmanship. If they were all that great, why did they have to advertise? And if they weren't, then why did they exaggerate like that? *Because they're lonely*, a voice in his head murmured.

At least the kids hadn't gone overboard about him, he'd give them that. *Balding* would surely be off-putting to many women, evoking visions of Mr. Clean sooner than Sean Connery. And *erudite* could easily be read as stuffy, couldn't it? He probably *was* a little stuffy, even when he was younger. Once in a while, Laurel used to say, "Oh, Edward, lighten up!" That still rang in his ears sometimes, like a schoolyard taunt.

In a couple of the other ads, placed by men, one declared himself a physician in his forties, a world traveler and a gourmet, and the other a "retired millionaire." So why would anyone choose to pursue Science Guy, a man who ironed women's blouses for recreation, an aging, balding middle-school teacher with a basement laboratory, to which he'd often retreated to cry like a baby, or to fantasize about cloning his dead wife from the DNA in the hairs still trapped in the bristles of her brush?

10

Dating After Death

There were forty-six replies waiting for Science Guy in the post office box. Bee's children were thrilled, and Edward simply bewildered. He didn't think the person depicted in the ad—*him*—had sounded particularly appealing; he could only imagine how many responses that bon vivant of a doctor and the retired millionaire must have received.

Julie called Edward from the law office where she worked as a paralegal to whoop and cheer at the count, as if she'd just heard favorable election results. He tried to reconcile her wild enthusiasm with how inconsolable she'd been less than a year before at the death of her mother, and the many bouts of gloom in between. He'd spoken on the telephone with both Julie and Amanda after he'd seen the ad, chiding them for their impulsive act, which, he pointed out, was ill conceived, if well intended. "We don't want you to be alone, Dad," Amanda said. And Julie said, "Mom would have approved, I just know it." What was she talking about? Bee had been proprietary when it came to Edward, even a little jealous.

She hadn't liked the way Lizzie Gilbert always kissed him (and all the other men in their crowd) on the mouth in greeting and farewell, although Ned never seemed to mind, or even notice. But Bruce Silver, Bee's first husband and the father of her gung-ho children, had screwed around. It was a violation, she'd told Edward, that she had foolishly tolerated for a while, but never would again.

When Bee and Edward wrote new wills, about a year after they married, their lawyer half-jokingly mentioned something called the "Floozie Clause," to protect the children's inheritance against Edward ever remarrying unwisely and in haste. He'd laughed, but she had not, although she decided against the clause. And he remembered her once reading aloud to him about a woman urging her husband to marry again after her death, but forbidding him to ever sleep with his new wife. Bee hadn't found that hilarious, either. She might have preferred him lying down beside her in the earth to his starting up with a bunch of strange women.

Amanda and Nick had had the *NYR* letters forwarded to them, and they hand-delivered them to Edward that evening. Nick upended a grocery sack onto the kitchen table while Amanda opened her arms like a magician's assistant and said, "Ta *da*!"

Several of the envelopes fell onto the floor and slid away in different directions. Bingo sniffed and poked at a couple of them with his snout—nothing to eat—while Amanda scurried around the room, picking them all up and throwing them back onto the pile on the table. Then she ran her hands almost sensuously through them, sending some of them back onto the floor.

Edward was reminded of those movies where the bank robbers lie in bed in a state of delirium, covering themselves with stolen bills.

"Wait a minute," he said. "Hold it. I don't get this."

"What don't you get, Schuyler?" Nick said. "You're the man."

"An *available* man," Amanda added. "Go ahead and open one. Please."

He cleared his throat. "Listen," he said. "I'm sorry, but I'm not ready for this. And the whole thing's just not my style."

"It's only a civilized, practical way to meet new people," Amanda said in that pedantic tone she sometimes affected, the way she probably spoke in her motivational talks to young women in the workforce. "It's not like we're suggesting you speed-date or anything."

"But maybe Julie should try that," Nick said.

Two young teachers at school had discussed speed-dating one day in the faculty lounge, to Edward's fascination and horror. As far as he could tell, it was a version of musical chairs in which one was supposed to find love in addition to a seat.

How could he explain to Nick and Amanda that even the word *dating* was a little abhorrent to him? Their eagerness touched and troubled him at once. He never doubted their benevolence, but they were so pleased by their own marriage that they probably wanted to spread the word, like missionaries pushing religion on people they considered barbarians. The main thing was that he didn't *feel* available. The ghost of his marriage still inhabited the house, even if Bee herself was missing.

He knew he should have disposed of her clothing by now—at least he'd given the few valuable pieces of jewelry she'd owned to Amanda and Julie. Amanda was wearing the rose gold Victorian slide bracelet right then. But it wasn't just Bee's personal belongings that tugged him backward. All those commonplace domestic artifacts—dishes, lamps, pillows, books—were compelling souvenirs of the daily life they'd shared. How could he even think of someone else when he was constantly reminded of what he'd had and lost?

He supposed that Julie had merely caught the proselytizing fever from Nick and Amanda. At twenty-seven, she was still somewhat child-like and dependent, and her own love life always seemed to be in crisis. She called Edward more often than he suspected most women of her age called their biological fathers, giving him a rundown of her days, seeking his advice and, he was certain, his approval.

Bruce Silver, who sold paper for a living, had married again, twice, and had a brand-new family now, those kids more than twenty years younger than Nick and Julie. His contact with his older children was sporadic, and not always pleasant. Recently, he'd accused Julie of being moody when she was sad in his company. Edward had to talk her up after that encounter. Bruce hadn't even come to Bee's funeral, although Julie kept looking toward the entrance of the chapel for him until the service began.

And then there was the matter of Gladys. Her husband, Jacob, her first and only sweetheart, had died about ten years before. When Edward finally worked up the courage to tell her of Bee's, her Beattie's, fate, she'd swooned into his arms like some felled, boneless creature. But despite the natural laws of succession and her frequently expressed wish to die, she continued to survive her daughter. "That Mother Nature," she said wearily to Edward, "is a real bitch." His devotion to Bee's memory, he was certain, helped to sustain her.

Lately, there was some noticeable decline on her part, the usual failures of hearing and vision and balance that come with great age. The jigsaw puzzles she was addicted to required a magnifying glass now, in addition to her spectacles. She was almost ninety-two, after all. But she wasn't quite "the Wreck of the Hesperus" she claimed to be. And her mind remained astonishingly acute. She reported that when she'd told her doctor she was losing it, he said that she'd likely had too much to begin with.

Bee had tried vainly to get her to move from her co-op apartment in Teaneck into an assisted-living facility. Now Edward took up the cause, urging her to consider someplace nearby with planned activities and the company of her peers; she had outlived most of her friends as well as her only child. Gladys shuddered at the idea of organized senior recreation, which she summed up as "sing-alongs in hell." And even old people, she said, didn't really want to be with old people.

"I'm leaving here feetfirst, honey," she told Edward, "and not a minute too soon." Lately, she called everyone "honey," from the mailman to her grandchildren, in preparation, she said, for when she'd have forgotten all of their names. But Edward knew that she secretly took pride in her excellent recall, even as it caused her psychic pain. Just recently she'd said, "If only I could forget, just a little."

"Dad, Dad," Amanda said. "You're not listening." She was holding up a fan of envelopes. "Pick a card, any card." Her eyes were shining with merriment, the bracelet winking from her wrist.

Edward reached out and plucked an envelope from her grasp. When Nick and Amanda continued to gaze at him expectantly, he took a paring knife from the rack on the counter and slit open the envelope. There was a rush of a sweetly floral scent, as if he'd pulled the stopper out of a perfume bottle. "Ooh-la-la," Amanda said, and Edward forced himself to smile at her before he put on his glasses and opened the folded note.

"Dear S.G.," it said. "Your ad intrigued me. I am widowed, too, and my late husband was also a man of science, with his own pharmacy until Duane Reade took over Hackensack and the world. I know that dating after death isn't easy, but we should give it a try, no? Sincerely, Eleanora Perkins."

There was a snapshot in the envelope, too, taken from a distance, of a woman standing near a tree, with a house in the background. Amanda took it from him. "I can hardly make her out," she complained, squinting at the photo. "Why didn't she just send an aerial view?"

Nick took the magnifying glass from the pencil holder on the counter and peered through it at the photo. "Not bad," he said. "Late fifties, I'd guess."

Amanda grabbed the magnifying glass. "Hmm," she said. "Nice legs, actually. And that doesn't look like the state loony bin behind her. Dad, I hope you're not going to wear that dorky eyeglass chain on a date."

They continued to comment, but their voices seemed to recede into the background, dimmed by the refrigerator's hum, the distant sounds of traffic on the turnpike, and the mating call of some denizen of the woods behind the house. *Dating after death*, Edward thought grimly, *that's a good one.*

11

Love Letters

Hi!
My name is Kristi Womak and I caught your ad at the dentist's. My Mom is widowed, too, although she was divorced first (long story!). Anyway, your kids put in that ad for you and I'm answering it for my Mom. So this is sort of like Sleepless in Seattle + You've Got Snail Mail! (lol) One question—did you go bald early? Mom is only 39 and she doesn't want to date anyone old (no offense if you are). Her name is Mary Lynn, not Marilyn, which she hates when you make that mistake. Anyway, you can call—

Dear Mr. Science Guy,
We have many beautiful Russian brides waiting to meet you. You can view them online right now—15,000 choices for only 98 USD—

Dear Bill Nye,
I'm one of your biggest fans, and I could hardly believe that someone as famous as you has to advertise—

Hello there, handsome,
I am your fabulous, fiftyish fantasy—

When the doorbell rang, Edward tossed the newly opened letters into the trash and shoved the others into the crazy drawer in the kitchen. Then he went to let Sybil, Lizzie, and Joy in. They'd come, at Sybil's suggestion a few days earlier, to help him dispose of Bee's belongings. "Don't you think it's time, Edward?" she'd asked—a diplomatic rhetorical question. But he could imagine her telling Henry that Edward was becoming morbidly attached to artifacts, straight out of "A Rose for Emily," and she didn't even know about the ironing.

And now there she was, armed with two sidekicks and a stack of cartons. "Your cleaning brigade has arrived!" Joy announced gaily in the doorway, as if the three of them were really there to mop up after a wild party. It was only nervousness that made her blurt things out like that, Edward knew. She often put her hand over her mouth right after she spoke, as if to stem the flow of any further faux pas.

Edward squeezed her arm. "Thanks for coming," he said. "All of you must have better ideas than I do about this stuff." *This stuff.* He could have clamped his hand over his own mouth. Instead, he took the cartons from Sybil and led the women upstairs to the master bedroom, where he flung open Bee's closet. "I guess we can start here," he said, and Joy burst into tears.

"Sorry, sorry," she said, fluttering her hands helplessly before dabbing at her eyes. "It's just—"

"We *know*," Sybil said, slapping Joy sharply on the back, as if to dislodge a fish bone from her throat. Then she began pulling hangers off the rack and laying Bee's clothing out across the bed. The long gray velvet skirt, the pale green silk suit she'd worn to Nick and Amanda's wedding, the blouses Edward had so carefully ironed falling into a limp, shapeless heap. The other women quickly joined in, Lizzie piling shoes on the floor next to the bed, and Joy gently placing one of Bee's favorite dresses—with a pattern of violet sprigs—on top of the blouses.

Edward opened the drawers of her dresser and added underwear and panty hose and nightgowns; they slithered so easily through his fingers. From the corner of his vision, he saw Lizzie briefly hold the violet-sprigged dress against her body while glancing into the full-length mirror inside the closet door. "If there's anything anyone would like to have . . . ," he began, and then abruptly stopped. He'd had a vivid image of a future dinner party where every woman showed up wearing something of Bee's.

"No," Sybil said, yanking the dress from Lizzie's hands. "No. Bee would have wanted it all to go to some charity. She said something about it once, don't you remember, Edward? We'll put the boxes in the garage and you can arrange for a pickup. Maybe we can get them to that flooded area in the Midwest . . ."

"Yes, perfect," Edward said, his motives less altruistic than Sybil's. He just wanted everything to be taken as far away from there as possible.

When they were done, he opened the drawer in the dresser where Bee had kept her costume jewelry in a tangled mass, like a child's dress-up treasure box. "I know she would have liked each of you to have something of hers as a keepsake," he said.

It would be tolerable, he'd decided, to spot one of her Bakelite bangles in a crowd one day, or a string of glass beads that actually might have belonged to anyone. Most of them *had* belonged to someone before Bee. She'd loved to shop at flea markets and garage sales, sometimes speculating on the previous owners of her finds as possible kindred souls.

Each of her friends chose a single piece of jewelry and the rest went into one of the cartons destined for distant strangers. The four of them carried the cartons into the garage, and Sybil gave Edward a list she'd prepared of organizations that might pick them up and distribute them. Edward felt oddly lighter and heavier at the same time.

After the women were gone, he resisted the impulse to go back upstairs and look at the empty closet and drawers. He walked the dog, who'd been confined to the kitchen during the purging, and then Edward went in there and poured himself a stiff shot of vodka on the rocks. He sat on a stool at the counter, sipping his drink and looking through the newspaper he'd already read that morning.

The war, the war. Stalemates in the Middle East and in Congress. There were photos of the flood-ravaged towns Sybil had referred to, where Bee's clothing would probably be worn in some makeshift shelter rather than at a festive dinner party. Bloomingdale's was having a white sale. Some eighty-nine-year-old musicologist had died following a fall in his home. It was Saturday and the crossword puzzle looked daunting. Edward put the paper aside and opened the drawer where he'd stashed the letters. There was still time to open a few more before he'd have to start thinking about dinner.

Some of the women sounded nice—quietly friendly, and funnier and more modest than most of those who had placed ads. Lonesome, the way he was. A couple of them seemed slightly insane. He began to put the letters into piles, the way he did sometimes with students' papers before he graded them: the brainy ones, the hopeless cases, and those that fell somewhere in between.

He opened a can of clam chowder and poured it into a pot. There was a desiccated-looking bagel in the freezer that might be toasted back to edibility. He wasn't hungry exactly, just kind of restless. How good it once was to prepare dinner for two, to chop onions on the cutting board while Bee shelled the peas and the broth simmered. To set the table, each place mat a mirror image of the other.

He saw that they'd forgotten about Bee's aprons, still hanging on magnetized hooks at the side of the refrigerator, but they were unisex, really. He tied one around his waist and turned on the heat under the soup.

For over a year Edward hadn't felt sexually aroused, as if a vital wire between his brain and his penis had been severed. He'd tested himself a couple of months ago with a porn site on the computer, and those women with their absurdly enhanced breasts, their staged expressions of lust, and the choir of moans that might have come from a horror movie all left him unmoved. Now, standing at the stove stirring the soup, he became aware of a halfhearted erection.

What kind of sicko was he that the discarding of Bee's clothing, or scanning the desperate letters of women he'd never met, or the sea-smell of the canned chowder could turn him on, even weakly, after such a long dry spell? Then he thought of the three women he knew well who had been in his bedroom only hours ago, with their rustling skirts, their hair, and the fluty chorus of their voices. And he remembered how they'd each embraced him at the garage door before they left, Lizzie going last, after the others had turned away, and that she'd kissed him fully and lingeringly on the lips.

12

First Date

In the darkened AV room, Edward kept telling the kids to settle down. But the title of the video, *Our Sexual Selves*, had been paused on the big plasma screen as they'd come in, sending a ripple of nervous excitement through them, like a wave undulating through the fans in a baseball stadium. There was a lot of laughter and shoving as they scrambled for seats, and pens and pencils clattered to the floor.

It was always like this. The videos had changed over the years, growing more explicit in content and language, along with the sophistication of the students, but their reactions remained the same. Most of the boys had gravitated toward the left side of the room, the girls to the right. They could have been Democrats and Republicans, divided by ideology and an aisle. But the two groups in front of Edward were likely to find common ground a lot sooner. Some of them, he was pretty sure, already had.

The voice-over on the video was female and friendly, as opposed to the god-like authority of those sonorous male voices in the "sex education" films when Edward was a teenager. One of them, he remembered, was called *How We Got Here* and might have been about Christopher Columbus, or immigration, rather than human reproduction. The first image on the screen then was of a boy and girl shaking hands. The only thing missing in that sanitized version of their supposed attraction was gloves.

The narrator intoned that Tommy and Jane were friends, and that friendship sometimes blossomed into love (an older T. & J. *holding* hands), and love into marriage (rice being thrown at the newlyweds). As Edward recalled, those were the final postnatal human beings in the film, until the cute little baby in Jane's arms at the end, with Tommy grinning beside them. The rest were medical text illustrations of gonads and ovaries; the age-old story, illustrated with arrows, of the sperm's journey toward the waiting egg; and the gradual development of the folded, big-headed fetus. No penises, no vaginas, and definitely no foreplay.

There was enough, though, to arouse disgusted and titillated cries from the adolescents in that 1950s classroom: "Eww!" "Gross!" "Whoo-hoo!" Mrs. Grady, Edward's eighth-grade hygiene teacher, had to rap on her desk with a ruler, calling, "People, people!" as if to remind them that they belonged to a civilized species. Maybe it was only their imaginations and hormones at work. Edward wondered if just the sputtering sounds of an old movie projector could provoke an erotic charge in him.

Our Sexual Selves had the soft-porn look of a music video. It began with a blast of rock music to which a group of male and female dancers in body stockings stomped and shook. Sex, the female voice said, as the relentless beat continued in the background, is everywhere in our culture. This was followed by clips from romantic scenes in movies and TV shows, glimpses of nude Roman statuary, suggestively clad fashion models shimmying down a runway, and even a brief view of an ordinary young couple making out on a park bench. One of the boys in the classroom cried out, "No, stop!" in falsetto, as one of them invariably did, to the cheering of his buddies.

Of course the video's focus, like those of the 16mm films of Edward's schooldays, was on reproduction, the blending of genetic information—nature's raison d'être for sex. And words like *scrotum* and *testes* were still good for a laugh.

While stopping short of advocating abstinence, the narrator told her audience that although desire was a normal, healthy part of growing up, it was best to engage in sexual activity when one was mature enough to make wise decisions. The girls trilled and buzzed about that. The boys booed heartily, of course. *Tell it to their testosterone*, Edward thought. And at lunch in the faculty room afterward, when he recounted the video's caution against mindless sex, his friend Bernie said, "Hmm, mindless sex. Isn't that a redundancy?"

Later, at home, Edward prepared for his first date in what seemed like a millennium. He showered and shaved and polished his shoes. He used the electric toothbrush, which he hadn't done for such a long time that his gums bled a little. Then he tried on a couple of sports jackets before deciding on one. No tie, though. The restaurant he'd chosen was supposed to be very good, but casual. Bingo seemed to have picked up on his mood, moving anxiously behind him from room to room. Mildred was going to take him for his walk later, relieving Edward of a curfew.

Almost fifty years before, when he was getting ready for his very first date, which consisted of changing his T-shirt and taming his unruly blond hair with water, his mother and father were at home but keeping their distance. Back then, he was going to take a girl named Rachel Granby to a school play, a kind of evening version of their daytime lives.

Tonight, he was meeting someone called Karen Leslie at the Paper Moon in Short Hills. She was one of the five correspondents whose replies to the ad he'd held on to. She'd declined his offer to pick her up—either a sign of her independence, or a defense against some potential serial killer knowing where she lived.

After her letter, their communication had been through email. She was fifty-four, she'd informed him, a Jerseyite, too, who worked in finance and had been divorced for a long time. He liked the specificity of her age, her laid-back tone, even the odd fact that she had two first names. *Relax*, she seemed to be saying, *this isn't going to be a big deal.*

He realized that he wanted the company of a woman—a shared meal and conversation—but beyond that, he told himself, he had no plans, no intentions. The near future was a peaceful blank. He tried not to think about Bee, about the past, about anything at all. But his mind kept returning to the video he'd shown at Fenton that afternoon with its underlying message that sex was for procreation, not recreation.

All those years ago, when he'd sat next to Rachel in their junior high school auditorium as the houselights dimmed, he was excruciatingly aware of their elbows almost touching on the armrests. Did the hair on his arm actually stand up to graze the amber down on hers? She had breasts as tiny as teacups he could sip from. He'd felt swamped by a surfeit of that normal, healthy desire. What a dirty biological trick it was to inflame barely socialized kids with such burning lust.

Karen Leslie was sitting at the bar in the Paper Moon, drinking a martini, when he got there. He knew who she was by the way she turned to look at him, raising an eyebrow in appraisal. Her crossed legs were long and muscular. He went over and shook her hand, like a business acquaintance, like Tommy in the sex ed film of his youth.

She was good looking in a hard-edged, female-action-figure sort of way. Walking behind her and the hostess to the table, Edward realized that the two women were almost interchangeable, with their artful makeup and twitching short black skirts. They had the same self-possessed carriage, too, but only one of them was carrying menus.

They sat down and Karen said, "So, who are you?" The question caught him by surprise. He'd already told her about himself in their email exchange: his marriage and widowhood, his job, the stepchildren—but maybe all that was only the dating equivalent of giving his name, rank, and serial number.

He'd grown to be, post-Laurel, fairly confident with women, whether or not there was sexual tension between them. There was tension at this table, but he wasn't sure of its nature. Suddenly he wasn't sure of anything, least of all what he was doing there. *I'm heartbroken*, he might have said, *and I'm horny*. There was an icebreaker for you.

Instead, he caught the eye of the waiter and ordered two martinis. In his head, Bee whispered: *You are what you are*, *Edward*, as if she were giving him dating pointers from beyond. "I guess I'm just a guy trying to make a good impression," he told Karen Leslie. "What about you?"

"Let me see," she began. "I'm a fiscal conservative; I've been divorced twice. My older son doesn't talk to me. Should we look at the menus? I'm starving."

"Sure," he said, but she had already raised and opened hers, so that her face was hidden. He could still see the pale shadow of her cleavage, that sweet place. Her fingernails were long and crimson. This was a mistake; he didn't like her—she was cold and tough—and yet he wanted her. Or the hostess. Or another woman, blond and chubby, sitting at the bar clinking glasses with a friend. Jesus. It was an even dirtier trick to allow those long past the age of procreation to want to go on fucking, maybe forever, even without the gentling grace of love.

"I'll have the striped bass," Karen Leslie said.

They got through dinner discovering that they didn't care for any of the same movies or music or books. If they were a couple, Edward thought, they would always cancel out each other's vote. And if one of those matchmaking services had set them up, they'd have just cause for a refund, if not a lawsuit.

But his own cynicism disturbed him. Bee used to say that he had a gift for bringing out the best in people, a natural empathy. Had he lost that when he'd lost her? "What happened between you and your son?" he asked Karen.

"He's decided to be gay," she said.

"That's not really a decision," Edward said.

She clicked her fingernails against the side of her espresso cup for a moment, and then she said, "You don't do this very often, do you?"

"Have dinner?" he said. "Nearly every night."

"Funny," she said mirthlessly.

So he'd blown it. A least they'd come to the restaurant in separate cars and could part ways in the parking lot without too much discomfort.

When he'd walked Rachel Granby home from their date, he'd ventured to take her hand and she let him, after moving a balled-up Kleenex to her other one. The play had been *Our Town*, that perennial favorite of the school's Drama Department, and Rachel had snuffled and wiped her eyes throughout the performance. Edward had to swallow several times, but managed to hold back his own tears. Love and death, that incomparable duo; a good-night kiss seemed built into the scenario. He remembered to moisten his lips, while Rachel dried hers with the back of her hand. Then he moved closer and she met him halfway.

In the parking lot of the Paper Moon, Edward walked Karen Leslie to her BMW. "This was nice," he found himself saying as she pressed the remote to unlock the doors. The headlights blinked and the horn beeped, and he leaned over to kiss her cheek. He almost lost his balance when she grabbed the lapels of his jacket and pulled him toward her, crushing her mouth against his—tongue, teeth, pelvis, the works.

Then she released him just as quickly, slid into the driver's seat, and asked if he wanted to get in beside her or follow her home. Edward stood there, regaining his breath, his equilibrium. First Lizzie's furtive smooch in the garage, and now this—Bee's reluctant prophecy for him coming true. So why didn't he feel elated, at least below the belt? He patted the roof of the car and said, "Karen, thank you, but you're right, I am still new at this. And I'm not quite ready yet." When she slammed the door and sped away, he inhaled a lungful of exhaust as if it were pure oxygen.

13

What I Did on My Summer Vacation

Even as a child, Edward, who enjoyed school, had looked forward to the freedom of summer. By May, he was already distracted by the balmy air and the occasional housefly or gnat that drifted in through the open classroom windows, by the promise of all the unstructured days that lay ahead. His father had worked for the post office and always took his two-week vacation time in July. The family would go on a short trip somewhere—to camp out up at Lake George; to visit a historic site, like Colonial Williamsburg; or to stay at a small hotel in upstate New York. Edward had shown an early propensity for science in school, but his love affair with nature began during those summers, with the discovery of nearly invisible life among the blades of grass, and the mysterious humming and chirring from the trees and ponds at night.

As a young teacher, he'd gone off to Europe in the summertime, like most of his colleagues. He and Laurel had planned a monthlong honeymoon in Venice and Trieste; she'd littered their apartment with travel guides and brochures. His honeymoon with Bee was a three-day weekend in Provincetown, while Gladys took care of Nick and Julie. Every year after that, until Bee's illness, they'd rented the same house on Lake Tashmoo, in Vineyard Haven, for the month of July.

Now those intoxicating spring breezes and yet another generation of insects floated just outside the closed windows of Edward's air-conditioned classroom at Fenton Day, and his students were already glancing away from the lesson on the blackboard toward escape. But so much leisure time—that bonus of teaching envied by other, much higher-paid professionals—loomed as a threat to the sanctity of Edward's daily routine. And summer itself was booby-trapped with memories.

July 8 would be the first anniversary of Bee's death. In the bereavement group, Amy Weitz had warned against the particular pain of holidays and birthdays and anniversaries. Somehow, Edward had gotten through Bee's birthday in September with the diversons of the new school term, and the winter holidays seemed like a blur in retrospect, an emotional snowstorm through which he'd somehow found his way.

But how would he get through ten long weeks without any plans? He couldn't go back to the Vineyard without Bee, to the borrowed house they'd both loved, and face fresh condolences from their neighbors there. And he didn't think he could occupy himself at home; he certainly wasn't eager to try dating again anytime soon. So he went to the guidance office at school in early May and found a private tutoring job two days a week with a seventh-grader who wasn't in any of his classes.

Nathaniel Worth was failing science and falling behind in almost everything else. According to his guidance counselor,

Jenny Greene, Nathaniel had been a "late surprise," born when his parents were in their mid-forties. His older brother and sister had both breezed through Fenton years before, earning him an automatic place there. He'd been tested by a psychologist and a learning specialist, and was deemed intelligent but with low self-esteem, and with issues about his organizational and social skills. He didn't have many friends, Jenny said, and had been nicknamed, with the cruel marksmanship of children, "Worthless." There was some concern that he might fall somewhere on the high-functioning end of the autism spectrum.

The Worths lived across town from Fenton Day in an imposing prewar building that faced the East River. Margo Worth came to the door when Edward arrived for her son's first tutoring session. She led him through stately rooms to what must have been a study or an office, where Nathaniel sat at a large, gleaming desk, gnawing like a beaver on a yellow pencil. Kids always looked smaller to Edward outside of school, and this scrawny boy was dwarfed by the desk and the leather executive's chair on which he was perched. His summer buzz cut made his ears stand out.

In a quick survey of the room, Edward saw law books on the shelves, punctuated by trophies of some kind, and a couple of seascapes that he thought might be by Winslow Homer. The rug under his feet was Persian and beautifully worn. Jenny had told him that both Margo and Johnson Worth were corporate attorneys.

"Here's Dr. Schuyler," Margo Worth said. "Take that thing out of your mouth and say hello." Nathaniel let the ravaged pencil drop from his teeth onto the surface of the desk, and, without looking up, lifted his hand in a brief, languid salute—a wary Indian greeting the white stranger.

"Hi, Nathaniel," Edward said. "It looks as if school has followed you home." He put his briefcase on the floor. "Would you like to work in here?"

The boy's head and shoulders twitched in something between a shrug and a nod; maybe he had a tic, or had simply taken a vow of silence.

"Where are your manners?" his mother asked, and Edward said, "Thanks, this looks fine," as if he were the one she'd been scolding.

As soon as she left the room, Nathaniel retrieved his pencil and put it back in his mouth. There were yellow flecks of wood on his lips, and Edward imagined that he must have been tasting graphite by then. "You were in Mrs. Wheeler's class this year, weren't you?" he asked, as he reached into the briefcase for study materials.

The boy removed the saliva-slick pencil. "Yeah," he said in a voice that sounded as if it needed oiling.

Maureen Wheeler was considered a tough, humorless teacher, given to sarcasm and onslaughts of pop quizzes. Her lab was referred to, by students and faculty, as "the dungeon." She was famous for ignoring raised, even frantically waving, hands, and for asking students if they were sitting on their brains. Through the sadism of chance, shy underachievers like Nathaniel often landed in her classroom, and the school's policy was to categorically deny parental requests for transfers. Not that Edward was aware of the Worths ever requesting one.

He sat down on another, smaller chair, across the desk from Nathaniel, as if he were applying to him for a job. The idea made him smile, but the boy had dropped his pencil again, and was under the table, retrieving it. *What I did on my summer vacation*, Edward thought glumly before shuffling through his papers. He'd been given copies of some of Nathaniel's failing tests, but hadn't brought those with him. Instead he had the worksheets for the material Maureen Wheeler had covered the previous term, including the life cycles of butterflies, mosquitoes, and earthworms.

She was one of those teachers who concentrated on the memorization of facts, many of which seemed to slip from Nathaniel's head almost as soon as he read or heard them. Edward handed him a page to study and then asked a few questions about it. The boy appeared to merely scan the text, and his answers were mostly wildly improbable guesses, delivered without affect or hope. After about ten minutes of this futile exercise, Edward gathered the papers and returned them to his briefcase. He sat back and said, "So, what do you like to do for fun?"

Nathaniel seemed to consider this question as tricky as the ones about larvae and pupae. He swiveled back and forth in the leather chair and finally said, "Stuff. I don't know."

He was such a lackluster child. Asperger's? Edward wondered. Depression? "Do you have any pets?" he asked. He was thinking of bringing Bingo along for their next session.

"Uh-uh. I'm allergic."

Of course, Edward thought. "Do you want to take a walk?" he said. "Should we go ask your mother?"

Permission was granted for a "local field trip," and Edward had Nathaniel lead him to the nearest supermarket, where he bought a covered plastic food container, a bottle of water, and a jar of mustard. He swiped a couple of plastic spoons from the deli counter, and they headed for Carl Schurz Park at the river's edge.

In a shaded grassy spot several feet from one of the footpaths, they crouched, looking for wormholes. Edward instructed Nathaniel to squirt some mustard onto a plastic spoon, to which he added a spill of water, then stirred. They poked the solution into one of the holes and in moments a worm came crawling out, and then another. Edward had a moment of vertigo, but Nathaniel seemed to come to life. "Hey!" he said, almost shouted.

"Yeah," Edward said, "they like their hot dogs plain." The kid frowned, puzzled, and Edward said, "That was only a joke. They're actually vegetarians. The mustard just irritated them, so they came up for air. Want to do it again?"

When there was a whole congregation of wriggling worms, Edward began punching small airholes in the lid of the plastic container with his pocketknife, and he told Nathaniel to gather up some of the grass. They put three of the fatter worms into the container, along with the grass and a few spoonfuls of earth, dampened with water, and covered the makeshift terrarium with the punctured lid. Nathaniel carried it carefully back to his apartment as if he were bearing something sacred to an altar.

As Edward had expected, Margo Worth wasn't thrilled by this addition to her household, but she succumbed to his argument that it was a learning experience for her son, and to his assurance that the worms were securely ensconced. Nathaniel put the container on a shelf in his room, and Edward said, "Well, now you have some pets that won't shed." Then he dug a fact sheet about earthworms out of his briefcase, which would serve as a guide to their care and feeding. When Edward left, Nathaniel was busy reading it and barely looked up as he waved good-bye.

14

Smoke and Mirrors

Bee had loved parties, and the Gilberts' annual August barbecue was particularly festive, with a rented tent, live music, and even a small wooden dance floor. They always seemed to invite everyone they knew. Each year Ned concocted some exotic cocktail, like blood orange margaritas or blue martinis, and the caterer brought portable grills and people to man them.

Edward hadn't attended the previous barbecue, so soon after Bee's death, but this time he had no excuse, although he still felt conspicuously alone in a crowd of couples, and leery of another awkward fix-up. That evening, after he'd showered and shaved, he went into his garden, which he'd begun taking care of again—his other summer project besides Nathaniel—and picked a lavish, fragrant bunch of lavender, roses, and astilbe to bring to the party.

It was coals to Newcastle, of course. The Gilberts' own garden had been lushly planted as usual, and every table under the tent held a summery floral centerpiece. Still, Lizzie made a fuss over Edward's bouquet and extracted a promise that he'd save a dance for her. He'd offered his cheek for her hello kiss, but she managed to catch the corner of his mouth. In his head, in his memory, Bee smiled knowingly.

The trio was playing "Smoke Gets in Your Eyes" as Edward walked across the lawn toward a cluster of friends, although the barbecue smoke drifted discreetly away from the guests. Sybil was holding a glass of this year's special cocktail, something emerald green, and a little of it sloshed onto Edward's neck when they hugged. "Ooh, sorry," she said, dabbing at his neck with a cocktail napkin, and Edward said, "It's nothing, just a little frog juice."

"Tastes more like mouthwash," Henry said, setting his own glass on the tray of a passing waiter. "So how's that boy you're torturing?—whoops, I mean tutoring," he asked Edward.

"Nathaniel? He's coming along, learning stuff. He makes eye contact now and even smiles once in a while."

"And the worms?" Sybil said.

"They don't smile. And they don't even have eyes."

"Really?" Sybil said. "How can you tell which end is which?"

"You run your finger along the body. It's smooth from front to back, and bristly in the other direction. The kid discovered that by himself, and announced it like a news bulletin." Nathaniel had read up thoroughly on his new pets, going onto the Internet after he'd exhausted the information on the worksheet.

"Did he name them?" Sybil asked.

"Yes, and I think he's got a sense of humor. When he found out they're hermaphrodites, he came up with names like Billy Sue."

Coaxing the worms from the earth that day in the park, Edward had a terrible flash of Bee lying underground in their company. Only the boy's sudden interest in what they were doing kept Edward engaged, too, and stable. *It's not Bee anymore*, he reminded himself whenever he had such graphic, morbid thoughts, which didn't always help.

Now the musicians picked up the tempo, and Sybil asked Edward to dance with her. "Take my wife, please," Henry said, and off they went to the dance floor under the tent.

"How's Masha?" Edward asked as Sybil came into his arms.

"*Who?*"

"Your cousin, the one at your dinner party last year." Why had he brought her up? He'd already cased the crowd and hadn't noted any suspicious-looking female strangers.

"Do you mean Olga?" Sybil said. "She's fine. She's in the Netherlands for a few weeks, doing research with a colleague, someone she's seeing, actually."

"On what?"

"Her specialty, medieval tapestry. Didn't she mention it?"

"I don't think so," Edward said. All he could remember was the shock of the situation, that woman's surliness and his own misery.

He swung Sybil out and reeled her back in. "You're such a good dancer, Edward," she said. "Henry always tramples my toes."

"My pleasure," he said, happy that she'd changed the subject. "You are the proverbial feather."

There were no place cards on the tables, and Sybil invited Edward to sit with her and Henry and a few other neighbors he liked. When Lizzie came to claim him for their dance, the band was playing a medley of romantic standards. All around them, couples moved together slowly, closely entwined. Lizzie held out her arms, and she and Edward joined the other dancers. She was a pretty woman, which even Bee had grudgingly admitted, saying that Lizzie wore her age well, that she had good bones and great skin.

That night, she wore a flowing white dress, and her dark hair was pulled up into a loose knot studded with tiny fresh flowers. She put her cheek against Edward's as they danced. Hers was flushed and warm, but her hand in his was cool. He was sharply aware of her body pressed against his and, in the background, of Sybil looking their way, while Ned hovered over another table of his guests, drinking and laughing.

Then the band swung into a fast, loud number and Edward let go of her, saying, "Whoa, that's heart attack music. I'd better sit this one out." Lizzie laughed and wiggled her shoulders and hips to the new, frenzied beat, reaching for his hand again. "Oh, come on," she said. Like Laurel persuading him to lighten up. But he said, "Sorry, Lizzie, really," and then another man came up behind them and danced her away.

Edward was sweaty and short of breath when he got back to the table. He could smell the smoke from the barbecues now, and the air seemed hazy. Maybe the wind had shifted. Maybe he actually *was* having a heart attack.

"Well, here's our dancing fool," Sybil said, but she was looking at him fondly. And Joy, who was sitting next to her, said, "Edward, the buffet is ready. Would you like me to fix you a plate?" Henry passed him a glass of water. Soon he felt well again, cared for, and safely returned from behind enemy lines.

Later, just before he was ready to leave, he went inside the house to use the bathroom. The one downstairs was occupied, so he went up to the second floor and knocked on the closed door of the bathroom near the landing. Someone, a woman, called, "Who is it?" and he said, "Edward. Take your time."

He was about to move a couple of feet down the hallway to wait when the door opened and Lizzie was standing there, barefoot and smiling. "Where've you been?" she said, and when he stepped inside she locked the door behind him.

"Liz—" he began, and she said, "No talking," like a strict teacher to an obstreperous pupil. He didn't want to talk, anyway; that was only his final, pointless defense against the rough hunger that overtook him. For once, his mouth sought and found hers.

There were facing mirrored walls in the small room, throwing back multiple images of Edward and Lizzie kissing and writhing against each other, silent except for their strenuous breathing. Like an orgy of quintuplets. He saw his own crazed eyes staring into his own crazed eyes and almost laughed, but it came out in a groan.

Someone knocked at the door. She put her hand to his mouth. "Shush," she whispered, the word itself a little blast of liquid heat in his ear. "They'll go away."

There were a couple of sharper raps on the door, and it was as if someone were rapping directly on his head to bring him around. He pulled away from Lizzie, sick with desire and regret. "We can't," he said as softly as he could.

"What?" Her voice was too loud. He thought she was going to hit him. "Why not?" She wobbled a little, and he noticed that her tongue was green—those stupid drinks. He wanted to put his hand over her mouth, but she might have bitten him.

"You know why," he whispered. "Ned. He's my friend . . . oh, shit. We just can't do this, Lizzie."

The knocker hadn't gone away. There were no footsteps on the hardwood floor, and Edward could sense a listening presence. Maybe it was Ned, himself. Or Sybil, or Henry. Bee's ghost would have simply floated through the closed door. Jesus, what had he been thinking? But of course he hadn't been thinking at all.

Lizzie sat slumped on the closed toilet seat. Her anger seemed to have dissipated, and he expected her to wait quietly with him until whoever was outside gave up and left. But then she stood, made a few fast, blind adjustments to her dress and hair, and flung the door open. The young waiter standing there watched her stride past him before turning to offer Edward a sly, loaded grin. "Hey, sorry, man," he said, "but nature calls."

Edward took one last look at his disheveled self in the mirror, tucked in his shirt, and wiped the lipstick from his face with a Kleenex that he then tossed. "It's all yours," he said, going out onto the landing. And after a decent interval he went down the stairs.

15

Patterns of Evolution

"Poppy? I didn't wake you, did I?"

"No, no," Edward said. "I was just lying here." He'd been dreaming about Bee for the first time since her death, or at least the first time that he could remember. She had been standing on the stepstool in the kitchen, holding a swaddled baby, the one they hadn't conceived during the first year of their marriage, though not for want of trying. Bee's balance seemed precarious, and he was hurrying in to steady her, or to catch her if she fell. Then the phone rang, in the dream and in reality. Had he reached her in time? He didn't know, and now even Bee's image was evaporating, and he was lying on her side of the bed talking to Julie on the phone.

"So, Todd and I went to this club last night?" she said. So many of Julie's statements seemed to be questions, as if she wasn't sure they were true. "And he kept looking at this cocktail waitress? So I said maybe he'd like to be with her, and he said, 'What is your problem?' "

Julie's ongoing problem, Bee had always maintained, was the fear of abandonment that colored most of her relationships. When she was a schoolgirl, she'd agonized over her friendships with other girls. They had all moved in cliques that appeared to arbitrarily take her in and toss her out. Edward had often observed the same phenomenon at Fenton. Bee was right when she said that girls of a certain age were mean, even viciously cruel to one another, in their precipitous climb toward womanhood, their vying for the attention of boys. And the boys, both Bee and Edward agreed, were mostly senseless thugs fantasizing about blow jobs. How did anyone survive?

In Julie's case, not all that well. She'd been in therapy a couple of times but quickly dropped out, using one excuse or another: It was a total waste of time, she had better things to do, it was too hard talking to a stranger. She preferred getting help closer to home. And her mother had been her mainstay—listening, commiserating, counseling—the one girlfriend who would never kick her to the door.

Edward felt like a substitute teacher, a babysitter, really, who didn't know the curriculum but valiantly tried to fake it. What if he turned the tables on Julie and said, *So, I went out with this woman I met through that ad? And she was like those mean girls at school? But I wanted her anyway, and then, when I could have her, I said no, thanks. And wait, that's not all—a couple of months later, I nearly screwed my friend's wife. What is my problem?*

Of course he didn't. And unlike Julie, he'd outgrown or cast off his problem, falling back into the chaste, secure routine of school and home, while time flitted by the way it did in that affecting Kurt Weill ballad: *September, November* . . . He said, "Jules, Todd is a jerk." This opinion, rendered before, was based on previous reports from Julie that Todd had complained that her breasts were too small, or that he'd advised her to get over herself.

"I *know*," she moaned. "I'm like this *magnet* for jerks."

He couldn't disagree with that; Todd was just the latest in a series of losers in Julie's life. "Pretty women often are," he said.

"I wish my face was more symmetrical," she said. "I wish my boobs were bigger."

I hate that word, Edward thought. *Todd is a boob. Your father is a boob. They're a real pair of boobs.* His stomach growled, and he looked at the clock. Not even eight thirty, and it was Saturday. "Well, you can't have everything," he said, which seemed to stop Julie cold. Her mother would have gone on reassuring her, he knew.

But Edward felt weary, as though he hadn't slept at all. He tried to imagine how his dream might have continued had he not been awakened, and if it would have offered some consolation, or insight into the mystery of non-being. Well, he'd never know. "Listen," he said into the phone. "I'm going to Greenbrook later to check up on the birds. Do you want to come?" It was a perfunctory invitation. Julie didn't "get" birding, although the stillness and the patience it required might be good for her. It might even take her out of her own unhappiness for a while, as it did him.

"No, thanks," Julie said. "But have fun," she added doubtfully.

Bee hadn't truly gotten birding, either. They didn't do everything together, as other couples professed to do. She hadn't gone to nature preserves with him, and he'd never joined her on her flea market treasure hunts. It was the coming together after their separate outings that had been so pleasurable. Sometimes he wondered how Sybil and Henry could spend almost all their time in each other's company. Or how Ned and Lizzie worked out their "don't ask, don't tell" protocol. And how did Bruce Silver manage to sleep at night?

Before they hung up, Julie asked Edward if he had any social plans for the rest of the weekend, an only slightly veiled allusion to the personal ad, and Edward admitted that he hadn't made any. "I have some papers to grade," he told her, as if that were a project requiring days to complete. The truth was, he didn't want to be with anybody, least of all any of the prospective dates waiting for him in the crazy drawer. Yet he hadn't gotten rid of the letters.

There were no organized nature walks nearby in the sanctuary, and no other birders in sight. It was a dank, cold November morning, as Edward noted in his journal, with the promise of winter in the air, and in the thinned-out foliage of the oak forest. It had rained the night before, so the ground cover of leaves hardly crunched beneath his boots. Through his binoculars, he spotted a pair of yellow-rumped warblers on a high, bare branch. No melodic warbling this time of year, though; only their soft, mechanical chipping. You could count the bars.

Bee once read aloud something Emily Dickinson had said to a friend: "I hope you love birds, too. It is economical. It saves going to heaven." Maybe he should have urged Bee to come here with him, just once. It was beautiful, with the Hudson rushing past hundreds of feet below. But he'd always prized his solitude in the forest, as opposed to the loneliness he felt now at home.

There was only a little visible activity in the trees: some winter wrens and white-throated sparrows. A single dark-eyed junco. The improbability of animals, as someone once observed. Edward recorded those sightings in his journal, along with the variety of spongy mushrooms pushing up among the fallen leaves. He'd dressed warmly, but there was some wind now, and the damp chill permeated the layers he wore. *Getting older*, he thought, and in a rare instance of registering personal data, he wrote that down, too. He'd leave soon, and maybe he would call Julie back after he'd graded his papers, and take her someplace festive for dinner.

As he looked down once more at the river, he sensed a dark cloud descending—a storm? And suddenly there was an enormous flock of European starlings—hundreds and hundreds of them flying in formation, putting on a private air show as they circled above him. It was thrilling; he'd forgotten about the rapturous quality of nature in his pursuit of quietude. Edward watched until the starlings changed direction and flew off into the distance. Then he walked back through the woods toward the parking lot.

When he got home, Bingo was still out with Mildred on their afternoon walk. Edward picked up the telephone in the kitchen, but instead of calling Julie, he called Bruce Silver, whose number he'd found in Bee's Rolodex, the unfinished business of their children still between them when she died. Bruce answered the phone himself. Edward could hear a television playing in the background—cartoon squeals—and the voices of young children. "This is Edward Schuyler," he said. "Bee's husband."

"Hold on a minute," Bruce said, and then he shouted, away from the mouthpiece, "Turn that down, will you? I'm on the phone! What can I do for you, Ed?" he asked.

"Nothing," Edward said. "But you can do something for your daughter, for Julie."

"What? Is she okay?"

"Yes," Edward said. "She's fine. She misses her mother."

"I know," Bruce said. "Tough break."

There it was, like the sparest of elegies, after fifteen years of marriage and two kids: tough break.

"Why didn't you come to Bee's funeral?" Edward asked. "The children expected you."

There was a pause in which he could hear Bruce breathing, maybe even thinking. "I wanted to," he finally said. "I intended to. But it was . . . awkward, you know. All her friends, her mother. They blamed me for what happened between Bee and I."

Between Bee and me, Edward immediately, pedantically thought, but stopped himself from saying. "Well, whose fault was it?" he said.

"I don't like to assign blame," Bruce said. "It's complicated. Things happen in a marriage."

Yes, Edward said to himself, *one person dies.*

"So what about Julie?" Bruce asked.

Edward was going to say that Julie was fragile, that she needed Bruce, had always needed him, and especially now, in her mother's absence. That all of her relationships were tainted by his failure as a parent. But if the man had to ask, he wouldn't really understand. That boob. That clueless prick. "Call her once in a while, she misses you, too," Edward said.

"Sure thing," Bruce said, sounding relieved. "Will do." At least Edward had not asked him to behave like a father.

Mildred and the dog came back to the house soon after the phone call. It was drizzling by then, and Bingo's coat and Mildred's rain bonnet were both wet. While she was rubbing the dog dry with an old towel, Edward invited her in for a cup of tea. "Do you want me to read the leaves for you?" she asked, with a flicker of hope on her face. "On the house?"

"No, thanks," he said. "I'm afraid I'm not into the occult." His polite word for hokum. "And besides, I only have tea bags."

The essays Edward graded later were about the patterns of evolution. His brightest student, an eighth-grader named Shelby Marks, had written, in conclusion, "We humans always think in terms of our own survival. We truly can't imagine that, like most species that have ever lived on earth, we, too, might become extinct someday. The others died out because they couldn't adapt to the changing environment. Poor us!"

"Indeed!" Edward wrote under that last line, before scrawling a big, red A at the top of the first page. Then he thought, in a flash of spiteful satisfaction, of Bruce Silver, still selling paper in a digital age.

16

Second Date

Edward was looking in the crazy drawer for a rubber band when he came across the letters in response to the personal ad. Not that he had forgotten about them. He'd only kept them tucked away, out of sight, while he tried to keep his increasing loneliness out of mind. Now he laid the letters out on the kitchen counter and contemplated them, while he flexed the rubber band over and over again until it shot from his fingers across the room.

Roberta Costello was an amiable woman, practically the antithesis of Karen Leslie. Edward had chosen her letter because it exuded warmth and an appealing modesty. "Hello!" she'd written. "Am I the zillionth woman to write to you? I hope not." She described herself as a widow, "average" in most respects, including her height and weight and even her looks.

She was actually quite pretty, with graying black hair and

dark eyes. And she gave him a big smile and a little hug when he picked her up at her town house in Teaneck, not far from the restaurant she had suggested for Sunday brunch. "The best omelets in the world," she'd promised. "We always went there."

Although Edward had made a reservation, it wasn't honored. The place was mobbed when they arrived, and they found themselves in the midst of a noisy, impatient crowd of couples and families waiting for tables. Bee, Edward remembered, had resisted the popular restaurant brunch, which she claimed was "just breakfast, only later, and in public." She'd preferred eating eggs in their bathrobes, exchanging sections of the Sunday paper across the kitchen table. This was just the sort of scene she had probably wanted to avoid.

"Shall we try going somewhere else?" Edward asked Roberta. A baby was crying nearby, and he had to shout a little to be heard.

"Well, if you want to," she said, but he detected a note of disappointment in her voice. So he didn't offer the next suggestion that came to mind—that they stop at a deli and buy all the ingredients for a meal and bring them back to her place. She might have taken it as an inappropriate move on his part, when what he really wanted was a quiet meal in a domestic setting. He would have even done the cooking, as he'd often done on Sundays at home.

When they were finally seated and handed menus, the waitress greeted Roberta as if they were old friends, and she gave Edward the once-over, which felt like a severe assessment. "Did I pass muster, do you think?" he asked after the waitress left, and Roberta smiled and said, "Oh, Wynona's just being a little protective. Vince was a big favorite around here."

Roberta had been widowed about the same time as Edward, but her husband had lingered for two years, breathless from emphysema, she said, and mad as hops. Edward imagined that he might have taken his anger out on Roberta—there was a resigned weariness about her, in the corners of her eyes and mouth, whenever she forgot to smile. But she said that he'd only railed against his bad luck, his lifetime smoking habit, the crappy, poisonous air in industrial New Jersey.

He had worked, she told Edward, as an account executive at an oil refinery in Linden, having risen up through the ranks from the pipelines on merit and perseverance. Roberta had been an adjuster for a large insurance company, work she'd once enjoyed. But she had retired soon after Vince died. He'd left her well provided for—his main concern—and she had lost interest in her job, anyway.

Edward was grateful that he had stayed on at Fenton. At first the mere routine of going to work had helped to sustain him, but now his old excitement about teaching had revived. Even the mild spark he'd struck in Nathaniel Worth during their tutoring sessions had provided some gratification. He told Roberta that each new crop of students was a challenge and a joy. *Tabula rasa*. She said that she had grandchildren about to start school; she hoped they'd find dedicated teachers like Edward.

After their omelets were served, she said, "Vince always had the western with a side of sausage," and her eyes filled with tears. Edward put his fork down and touched her hand. "It's hard, I know," he said. And he did know. The stages of grief weren't so neatly arranged or easily disposed of. And as that pharmacist's widow had said in her letter, dating after death wasn't easy. But why had Roberta responded to the ad if she didn't feel ready? Or even read the personals in the first place.

Yet who was he to talk about readiness? On New Year's Eve, he'd finally agreed, under pressure from Sybil and Henry, to drop in on their supper party, arriving alone on the late side and fleeing before midnight, like Cinderella, without leaving behind what he'd thought of as his glass heart. At least Lizzie hadn't come on to him again.

"Very hard," Roberta agreed. "We were married for thirty-four years, six weeks shy of thirty-five." She fumbled in her purse, for a Kleenex, Edward assumed, but she pulled out a cell phone instead. Was she going to leave, call for a cab?

She fiddled with the phone for a moment and then passed it to Edward. "Our wedding," she said. He stared at a photo of a younger Roberta, swathed in white, gazing up at a tall guy in a tux.

"You were a handsome couple," he said, passing the phone back to her. She fingered some buttons and handed it back to him. "Our kids," she said. Edward saw three children sitting under a beach umbrella, everyone and everything in faded colors. "They're much older than that now, of course," Roberta said. "But they all live in different states, so I like to remember when they were little and everybody was together." She asked how many children Edward had.

"Two, plus a daughter-in-law," he said. "They were Bee's, my wife's, kids, but I inherited them."

"Tell me about your wife," Roberta said huskily, leaning toward him, and he was struck dumb, sideswiped by emotion. "Do you have any pictures?" she asked.

Edward had never kept photos of anyone on his cell phone or in his wallet. "No," he said. He looked down at his plate, where the folded eggs were congealing next to an orange slice. "Not on me." And then, suddenly, there was a whole slideshow of pictures going through his head. *Help me*, he thought, and Bee said, *Don't say I didn't warn you!*

"What can I say?" he told Roberta. *That she was my one true love? That she hated brunch?* "We had a very good life together," he said.

"Oh, we did, too!" Roberta said. "We met in high school, we were high school sweethearts." And she went into a précis of the years since then. Edward only took in the highlights of what she was saying—college, the army, first apartment, first baby—before he stopped listening. He pushed his food around on the plate, the way Nick used to do, hoping it would somehow disappear. Roberta seemed to come out of her reverie. "Don't you like what you ordered?" she asked.

"It's fine," he said, taking a bite of toast and washing it down with a swig of coffee. "I'm just not as hungry as I'd thought."

She sighed. "I guess I'm used to a man with a big appetite," she said. "Vince always cleaned his plate."

Edward was reminded of the bereavement group, where the dead were praised for everything from good penmanship to good teeth before the survivors' defenses gave way, and they admitted to their loved ones' human flaws. He waited for something similar to happen to Roberta, but it never did. It was like attending a memorial brunch for someone he'd never met, alongside the not-so-merry widow.

He tried to change the subject without making too great a leap, and he mentioned a book he'd read about disturbances in the food chain as species were facing extinction. It seemed to work. They talked about books for a while—she belonged to a reading club—and then Edward brought up his birding. "Birds!" she exclaimed. "I love them, too!" She pulled out the phone again and showed him a close-up of two budgies in a gilded cage. "That's Alice and Petey," she said. "I've taught them to hop right onto my finger."

She held her left hand up, perch-style, and Edward noticed that she was wearing a wedding ring. He tried to remember when he'd stopped wearing his. Not long after he had given Bee's clothes away. And right after Sybil had chided him about it, he'd erased Bee's message from their voice mail by taping a new one over hers. "This is Edward Schuyler," he said into the mike. "Please leave a message."

When he played it back, he sounded affectless, almost robotic. On the second try, he coughed and had to do it all over again. The whole process seemed haunted by the past, but at last he got it right. Two days later, Julie called him. "What happened to Mom's message?" she asked before breaking into tears. It seemed that she'd been calling the number, the way he had, just to hear her mother's voice. "Dear, we have to let go," he said, as much to himself as to her, and then listened in silence while she wept.

"And I've taught them to talk, too," Roberta was saying proudly, startling him back into the moment. "Petey is up to six words now." *No bird imitations, please,* he silently begged. *And no more pictures.*

As he drove Roberta home, he remembered Karen Leslie's unexpected, almost violent kiss in the parking lot of the Paper Moon. He was pretty sure nothing like that would happen this time, nor did he want it to, but what if she asked him to come inside, out of simple courtesy? Edward was courteous, as well, and he wouldn't want to hurt her feelings. But he didn't think he could chance it. She might have a shrine to her dead husband in there, replete with flickering votives and a whole gallery of photos. And he didn't want to see or hear her caged birds, positive now that *Vince* was one of the six words in Petey's vocabulary.

He needn't have worried. When he escorted Roberta up the steps to her town house, she said she'd had a wonderful time, flashed a brave smile, and gave him another little hug. Then she went inside, shutting the door firmly behind her.

17

What Women Want

"Never again," Edward said. He was in another busy restaurant, this one a long, dim room on Columbus Avenue, filled with the vibrant conversation of adults recently released from the company of children. Bruno's was more of a bar, really, but they served halfway decent food from a limited menu, and this was where several members of Fenton's faculty, and the faculties of a couple of nearby public schools, often hung out on Friday afternoons and evenings.

When Bee was still alive, Edward had only occasionally joined them; he'd preferred to start the weekend back in Englewood with her. And for several months, those dark, antisocial months after her death, he still hardly ever showed up at Bruno's. But gradually he was lured into that after-school ritual, and the company of other people who weren't in a hurry to get home, either.

He was sitting in a booth, sharing a pitcher of beer and a bowl of popcorn shrimp with Frances Hartman and Bernie Roth, in whom he'd begun to confide a little about his adventures in the dating world. They were both unattached. Frances, in her early or mid-fifties now, had been married and divorced years before and seemed to have sworn off men recently. At just past sixty, slight, dapper Bernie had managed to remain single, and had a reputation for superficial, short-lived affairs—something like Edward's love life between Laurel and Bee. Bernie's crack about mindless sex probably had an element of personal truth in it.

Edward didn't offer any information to his stepchildren about the dates that had evolved from the ad they'd placed, even when they hinted or asked outright, except to say that there was nothing to report. And he chose not to talk to the friends he'd shared with Bee about any of it, either. His reticence also extended to Gladys, who, he was sure, would be terribly hurt by his attempts with women, even though they had failed.

"Never say never," Frances told Edward.

"Your problem, my friend," Bernie said, "is the whole meal deal—the commitment to spending hours with someone you've never met. What's wrong with just a drink or a cup of coffee?"

"You're a cheapskate, Bern, and a drive-by lover," Frances said. "Edward is a gentleman, maybe the last of his kind. Inviting a woman to dinner is a sign of good faith."

"Is *that* what women want?" Bernie asked. "Signs? Gentlemen? A free dinner?"

"Don't start," Frances warned.

Bernie was of the opinion, often and freely given, that what women really wanted was the same thing he and most other men wanted—a little companionship and sexual pleasure. On the European plan, which might include breakfast.

"I can't get used to the way people meet now," Edward said.

"It seems so programmed, so, I don't know . . . *desperate.* We used to leave things to chance, didn't we?"

"Some enchanted evening," Frances sang, hoarsely and slightly off key, "you will see a stranger—"

"Across a crowded Internet," Bernie croaked. "You can't stop progress, darling," he added when she made a face. Although most of his own brief relationships began in bars.

"Progress!" Frances said. "It's a business, and the death of romance."

"Yeah," Bernie said. "And the death of printed books and retail stores and—"

"I met Bee at a wedding," Edward said. "We danced. I didn't have to send her a CV." *Bésame, bésame mucho. Hold me, my darling, and say that you'll always be mine.*

"You fell in love," Frances said.

"Yes," Edward agreed. "Not immediately, but yes."

"Love," Bernie said. He glanced around the room.

Frances followed his gaze. "Most men want younger women," she said. "I think it's a biological set, something to do with the perpetuation of the species."

"Is that right, Doctor?" Bernie asked Edward. "Or is it just the firmer T and A?" He popped a shrimp into his mouth.

"Have you looked at your ass lately?" Frances said. It occurred to Edward, not for the first time, that something might have gone on once between Frances and Bernie.

"I don't want a younger woman," Edward said, and he had a flash of Laurel walking naked across his bedroom, as if to make a liar out of him.

"The thing is, you could probably get one," Frances said, without apparent rancor. "That's the way the world works."

" 'Then come kiss me, sweet and twenty!' " Bernie recited. " 'Youth's a stuff will not endure.' "

"How can you hold all that poetry inside your head and still be such a Neanderthal?" Frances said.

"'Poetry makes nothing happen,'" Edward said. Bee had once read that to him from something. "Who said that?"

"You just did," Frances said.

"Auden," Bernie said. "Good for you. And good for him."

"What?" Frances said. "You don't believe poetry changes people?"

Bernie tapped his chest. "Only in here," he said

"Didn't you ever want to get married?" Edward asked.

"No," Bernie said. "My parents saw to that."

"Were they divorced?"

"No, even worse; they stayed together out of spite."

"Edward, dear, really," Frances said, "don't give up. You need to be with someone."

"I was with someone," he said.

"Exactly," Frances said. "And now you have to start all over again."

"I don't think I have the energy."

"Yes, you do. Do you want to spend the rest of your Fridays in Bruno's bullshitting about what women want? Or do you want to find out for yourself, out in the field?"

"Or in a bed," Bernie said. "What you need, my friend, is to get laid." As usual, he had the last word.

18

Two Telephone Calls

The phone rang in the middle of the night. *Bad news,* Edward thought, thrust into wakefulness. This was how he'd learned about his father's death twelve years earlier—the shrill alarm of the phone and then his sobbing mother, who had found her darling Bud, lying still beside her and already cool to the touch. Like that woman, Claire, in the bereavement group, Evelyn Schuyler had sometimes checked her husband's vital signs as he slept. He had already survived two heart attacks.

"Daddy is gone!" she'd cried, as if Edward were a child rather than a fifty-year-old man. And in those first shocked moments, that was exactly how he'd felt. Then Bee was there with her arms flung around him, restoring him to his grown-up, newly sorrowful self.

This time a stranger's voice was on the line, a woman asking for Beatrice Schuyler. There was a clamor in the background—someone shouting, someone laughing—and Edward wondered if she was calling from a bar. "Who is this?" he demanded. The woman said that she was a nurse in the emergency room at Holy Name Medical Center in Teaneck, and she repeated her request to speak to Beatrice Schuyler.

"She's dead," Edward said. "She died more than a year ago." Their exchange struck him as bizarre, a crazy reversal of roles. But his confusion was dissolving as a feeling of dread developed. "Is this about her mother, Gladys Berman? This is her son-in-law. I'm the next of kin now; we never changed it on her papers." Next of kin—such an oddly ominous phrase, suggesting closeness and separation at the same time.

It *was* about Gladys, who still lived alone. "Ninety is the new seventy," she had gaily told Bee when she'd urged her to move into an assisted-living facility. "Yes, and death is the new ninety," Bee shot back. Gladys finally gave in to wearing a medical alert device on a chain around her neck. "My baby monitor," she'd said, mockingly, declaring it a waste of money and ugly besides. "It will probably strangle me in my sleep," she warned, but Bee had wheedled, and then insisted. "For *my* sake, Ma," she'd said, "for *my* peace of mind."

And just like the old woman in the television commercial, Gladys had fallen on her way to the bathroom and couldn't get up. When the police came, they'd found the extra key she had "hidden" in the soil of a small potted evergreen outside her door and let themselves in. She had broken her hip.

Edward got dressed and drove to the hospital. The emergency room was jumping with activity and brilliantly lit. It might have been a bar in purgatory. He was led to the curtained cubicle where Gladys lay, looking child-sized and cadaverously pale. A mummified child. She managed a faint smile for Edward before the tears fell. "Honey," she said. "Look where I am."

She had been given sedation for the pain, but as the resident informed him just outside the cubicle, Gladys would have to have surgery as soon as possible to repair her hip. If she didn't, pneumonia would undoubtedly set in. Her age, the resident explained, was a negative factor in either scenario.

Edward decided to call the children before the surgery, which was scheduled for 10 AM. He woke everyone, but at least it was already morning by then, and they seemed less dazed than he had been in the night. And it was Saturday, so no one had to think about going to work. They were grateful to have been summoned, to get to see their grandmother, who was still in the emergency room when they arrived.

Julie was especially upset, though. "Is she going to die?" she asked Edward, after visiting briefly with Gladys. "I don't know. She might, Jules," he said. "She's very old." When Julie's face crumpled, he added, "But they wouldn't operate if they didn't think she had a chance." And she hung on to that and to Edward's hand, twin lifelines.

By the time they came to wheel Gladys away, her speech was slurred from the drugs they'd given her. "Some country," she announced loudly to the room at large. "Assisted living, but no assisted dying." She sounded a little drunk. "Good luck, dearie!" a voice called from another cubicle. Someone else said, "Shut up, I'm trying to sleep." The wheels of her gurney shrieked, and Gladys murmured, "A little 3-in-One for that, honey," and closed her eyes.

Amanda brought coffee in a cardboard tray to the waiting area, where they sat huddled along with other families. Gladys's surgery would take about two hours, they'd been told. As he was making muted, distracted conversation with the children, Edward was suffused with shame about his first impression when he'd answered the phone, that it was some strange woman calling him from a bar. Who did he think he was—an irresistible Lothario? This dating business had severely distorted his perception if he believed he was being pursued even as he slept.

And although Bee had died at home, the hospital's anxious atmosphere had sent him reeling backward to that whole horrific time. Julie and Nick were probably having similar thoughts from which he could not defend them. He remembered blithely telling Roberta Costello that he had inherited Bee's children, and he looked at them now as rare treasure, a bequest that couldn't be stolen by any interloper, floozie or not.

Gladys didn't die during the surgery. After a few hours, they were each allowed a couple of minutes with her in the ICU. Edward went in last. She seemed deeply asleep and older than Methuselah now. All that paraphernalia. They had brought her back from the edge of somewhere she both wanted and didn't want to go. How extraordinary she was. His own mother had followed his father into death within a year, the way she used to nervously follow him around the house.

Once, after Bee's diagnosis, Gladys had said, "When she was a little girl and she got sick, you know, an earache or a fever, I would take care of her and she got better. But what can I do now—stroke her forehead, give her a little soup?" "Yes," Edward said, and she did.

He stood next to her bed in the ICU and said her name. She opened one eye and then the other, like a battered doll. "Is Beattie coming?" she said, and Edward pressed her hand, but couldn't speak.

He was beyond ordinary fatigue by the time he got home again. It was evening by then and starting to snow. He had taken the children out for a meal, something between lunch and supper. "Lupper," Julie called it, making everyone, including herself, smile. "No, slunch," Edward said, and they actually laughed. If Bee had been the glue that held them all together, then he was the Velcro. Not as secure, maybe, but there would be an awful tearing sound if he pulled away.

He must have fallen asleep on the sofa. The television was playing, some police procedural. A murder suspect was being given the third degree. It was a little past ten, according to the cable box. An empty brandy snifter was on the coffee table next to Edward's feet. The telephone was ringing again. It took him a moment to realize the sound wasn't coming from the television set. He stumbled into the kitchen and picked up the phone. "Hello?" he said, hoarsely and with trepidation.

A woman's voice again, but there weren't any noises in the background. "You're no gentleman," she said.

"Frances?" Edward asked. It didn't sound like her, but hadn't she recently said something about his being a gentleman? And then Bernie said that Edward needed to get laid.

"No, this is Sylvia," the woman on the phone said. When Edward was silent, groggily scrambling to come up with a face to match the name, she said, "Sylvia Smith, the date you stood up tonight."

19

Third Date, Postponed

Edward apologized and explained about Gladys's emergency. "In all the excitement," he said, "I simply forgot." He offered to set up another date with her later that week. "No," Sylvia said. "Let's wait until she's out of danger and you feel more relaxed. Why don't you call me when you're ready."

"Thanks," Edward said. "That's very kind of you." It *was* kind of her. They'd arranged to meet at a bistro she knew in Chelsea, close to where she lived, and he imagined her waiting for him—looking at her watch, sipping water or wine, becoming self-conscious and finally angry. He was relieved by her instant forgiveness, and he liked the sound of her voice with its trace of a southern accent.

"Not at all," she said. "And just think—we've had our first quarrel and we haven't even met."

Gladys's recovery was slow and bumpy. First she spiked a fever; it wasn't pneumonia, as everyone feared, but a urinary tract infection that was soon brought under control with antibiotics. Then there was a false alarm about a blood clot in her leg. And for the first time since Edward had known her, she had moments of confusion, especially in the evening. She called him "Doctor" once when he peeked into her room. What she said was, "Doctor, honey, please let me go home now."

"It's only Sundowner's syndrome," a nurse explained. "Lots of older folks get it. A strange environment, shift changes, the meds. Just try and keep her focused."

Edward and the children took turns being with Gladys, so that she had at least one visitor every day during her stay in the hospital. After that she was scheduled to be moved to a rehab center for physical therapy. They put the overhead light on as soon as the daylight dimmed, and read the newspaper to her, omitting the most aggravating items. They hung a large-print calendar on a wall near her bed and crossed off the days she'd spent in the hospital. "Just like in prison, Gladdy," Nick said.

"Only the food is worse," Gladys answered, rallying. So they brought her treats from outside, despite her flagging appetite, coaxing her with morsels of smoked salmon on toast points and spoonfuls of frozen yogurt.

Gladys had been a milliner and then the millinery buyer for Bamberger's many years before, and liked to say that women looked half naked without hats. She spoke with nostalgia about Jackie Kennedy's pillboxes, Hedda Hopper's flamboyant toppers, and a certain sequined beret she'd sported on her own honeymoon in Havana, which she still owned. In fact, she had a whole assortment of vintage hats, several of which she'd made herself. Gladys claimed that if you held on to something long enough, it always came back into style.

Nick picked up an assortment of silly hats, from a giant, striped stovepipe to a fur cloche with bunny ears, and shoved one of them onto his head each time he entered her room. He made her laugh and he encouraged her to get out of bed for excruciatingly slow walks in the hallway, using a special, padded walker.

The kids kept her up to date on their lives, in which she had a keen interest. Was Julie seeing somebody nice, for a change? Yes, she said, even though it was still only the odious Todd. And were Nicky and Amanda thinking about "you know what"? A baby was what she meant, which wasn't on their immediate agenda. But they told Gladys that they certainly thought about it.

She wasn't as invasive with Edward, asking mainly about his health and his work. He felt grateful and guilty at the same time. He'd sent flowers to Sylvia Smith and reread the letter she'd written in response to the ad. She seemed like the most promising candidate so far—a widowed social studies teacher in the city school system, who said she hoped his politics were liberal, and that she enjoyed the natural world.

Maybe he hadn't contacted her first because she seemed too good to be true, or because he wasn't prepared to meet someone that compatible. He might call her again that evening, just to say hello. Here he was, sitting with his ancient, feeble mother-in-law and chief co-mourner, daydreaming about a woman he'd never seen. He cleared his throat, as if that might also clear his mind. "Gladys," he said. "You're really doing well. They call you Wonder Woman out at the nurses' station."

"Pooh," she said, but she couldn't suppress a smile of pride. Then her brow furrowed. "Sometimes, lately, I get a little mixed up," she admitted.

"Me, too," Edward said, thinking about the date he'd forgotten. "Just today, I was teaching Mendel's laws of inheritance—"

"The peas," she said, "right?"

"Right. I must have given that lesson a few thousand times. Yet I said 'recessive' when I meant 'dominant' characteristics. A student corrected me."

"'And a little child shall lead them,'" Gladys said. "That's from Isaiah."

"See, you're still pretty sharp."

This time her smile flickered only briefly before it went out. "Honey," she said, "I'm so sad. I'm always going to be sad."

"I know," Edward said. "I am, too."

"Do you believe in God?" she asked.

"I don't know, I'm not sure. How about you?"

"Oh, I still believe in him. I just don't like him very much anymore."

Edward felt a pinch of envy; maybe even an unlikable, vengeful God was better than none. Darwin, he remembered, had started out as a cleric. And Mendel, the Augustinian monk, had managed to keep his faith and his scientific work separate and intact, a fact that both stymied and impressed Edward.

During the lesson that afternoon, one of the boys made the usual joke about Mendel peeing in his garden, to the raucous appreciation of his buddies. But they all looked at one another with fresh interest when Edward spoke about the genetic determination of eye color and height. Maya Lin, the Chinese girl adopted by Caucasian Americans, drew some curious, sympathetic glances from other girls. And Brandon, the only biracial boy in the class, received even more furtive and inquisitive notice.

Edward's thoughts wandered to his own blue-eyed parents. He remembered his mother telling him that the doctor who'd delivered him had shaken his finger at her playfully, warning that the baby, Edward, had better have blue eyes, too, unlike the milkman. He was the dead end of his particular genetic line, although his fair-haired, blue-eyed sister, Catherine, had passed on some of the familial traits—selected by dominance over rather than blending with those of her dark-eyed, dark-haired husband—to her children.

Edward had no biological connection to Nick and Julie, yet occasionally someone who didn't know their story remarked on Julie's resemblance to Edward. People who lived together, he knew, often began to resemble each other. Facial expressions and mannerisms are inadvertently copied—nurture transcending nature. Some people even grew to look like their pets.

When he mentioned that to his gifted seventh-graders, there was an eruption of laughter and barking that he waited out before he continued. He drew a generational diagram of Mendel's peas on the blackboard and began to explain the sequence of genetic inheritance, while he idly wondered what Sylvia Smith looked like. That's when he said "recessive" instead of "dominant," and the hands, even of the most inattentive students, flew up.

20

Third Date, Achieved

There was only one woman standing alone at the busy bar of the bistro, the same bistro where he'd failed to show up for his earlier date with Sylvia Smith. She turned and fluttered her fingers at him when he walked in, as if she'd always known him, although they hadn't even exchanged photos. She was slender, with long, wavy blond hair, and his first, surprised, impression was that she was much too young for him. Her whole manner, in her letter and on the telephone, had seemed so mature.

He went up to her and received his second surprise, a shock, really. She wasn't young at all. The lights in the bistro were low—to create a romantic atmosphere, probably, or to keep the noise level down. The woman at the bar had appeared to be in her twenties or thirties from the entranceway, but up close

Edward saw that it had only been an illusion. She was probably nearer to his own age, although that was still difficult to gauge.

Sylvia had undergone what Bee and her friends used to call "serious work" on her face. There were no apparent lines or wrinkles, no emotional history written there, and there was an unfortunate mask-like tightness to her skin, and even to the plumped-up line of her lips. Once, a few years ago, Bee had yanked up both sides of her face and said, through her stretched mouth, "How do I look?" and Edward said, "Scary. Please don't do that."

What he'd meant was that she didn't look like herself or like anyone capable of the vast variety of human expressions. He supposed that Sylvia was kind of attractive, especially from a distance, and even ageless in a way. But he wondered what she'd looked like before and why she'd chosen to expunge what must have been her recognizable self. A line from Yeats came into his head: *But one man loved the pilgrim soul in you, and loved the sorrows of your changing face.* Probably it was Bee who'd read that to him in the first place, or maybe it only reminded him of her, of the changes he would miss seeing. In any event, she seemed to be his invisible chaperone again.

When he and Sylvia were seated at a corner table, she said, "How is your mother-in-law?" Her interest seemed genuine, and Edward felt ashamed of his own concentration on her appearance; he might be the more superficial person on this date. "Better," he said. "Remarkable, actually. She's in rehab now, trying to get her strength and balance back."

"Good," Sylvia said. "You must really love her."

"I do," Edward said.

"Your wife was very lucky, then. On all counts."

"Thank you," he said. "I mean, I think that was a compliment."

"It was. You're a sweet fella."

Edward felt his face grow warm under her friendly, admiring gaze. And he noticed—how could he help it?—that the breasts rising from Sylvia's low-cut blouse were like snowy globes. Too globe-like, really, too buoyant, for the rest of her. Had they been altered, as well?

Bee used to say that plastic surgery was useless for older women unless they had their hands cut off. The hands were the giveaway, she'd claimed, and Sylvia's were graceful and beautifully manicured, but thin-skinned and threaded with veins. Did she regret what she'd done to the rest of her?

There was nothing artificial about her personality, though, and Edward was more comfortable in her company than he had been with anyone in a long time. The southern accent he'd detected in their phone calls—she'd grown up in Virginia—was melodic and seductive. They ordered two different dishes and shared them, as easily as they shared stories about their school lives. It was a little like being with Frances, toward whom he'd never felt more than brotherly, with the added frisson of sexual tension. There was no doubt about that, despite his critical appraisal of her physical self. Maybe the illusion of youth was a reasonable substitute for the real thing.

Even while they'd stood together at the bar, he had become aware of the faint, woodsy scent she was wearing, and at the table she leaned toward him whenever he spoke as if he were the most interesting man in the world. She may have just been a little hard of hearing, but he didn't really care by then. And soon after their dessert was served, when she said, "Will you walk me home? I'm practically around the corner," he signaled for the check without hesitation.

They held hands in the street and going past her inscrutable doorman and in the elevator of her high-rise building. She dropped his only long enough to unlock the door to her apartment. There was no conversational foreplay, no pretense about their intentions. They kissed inside the doorway and then she led him through the dimly lit foyer to her bedroom.

When Edward reached for the light switch, she said, "Don't," and pulled him toward the bed, where they fell together onto silken sheets and undressed each other. Well, he probably wouldn't benefit from illumination, either, with his thinning hair and the paunch he couldn't really suck in anymore. Her skin was soft, and that scent was in her hair and on her neck and between her breasts. She touched him as eagerly as he touched her and he felt himself rise under her hand.

He closed his eyes as he slipped into heedless pleasure, but an image of her pulled face rose immediately behind them. And the breasts he stroked and kissed so avidly were too firm, too resilient, even for someone young. He was slackening, deflating, and they both grew still, as if they were listening for the sounds of an intruder. The only intruder, though, was his own mind, with its relentless, imperishable thoughts and pictures. "Sylvia, I'm sorry," he said. "I really am."

He was apologizing to her again and his apologies were sincere, but he knew that would be small comfort now. "It's been a long time," he said. "I seem to have lost my concentration."

Sylvia moved away from him and reached for the switch on her bedside lamp. The bed was pooled in light, like a stage set. She drew the top sheet up and covered them both. "That's not what you've lost, darlin'," she said, but her tone was only slightly sarcastic and not unkind. Before he could respond, she said, "It's my age, isn't it?"

"No, no," Edward said, a slick, easy answer to a complicated question.

"How many responses did you get to your ad?" she asked in a seeming non sequitur.

"A few," he said.

"More than a few, I'd wager," she said. "Was anyone else as old as I am?"

Another tricky question, but one that demanded honesty. "I don't know how old you are."

"I'm seventy," Sylvia said defiantly. "Seventy-one, to be precise."

"I'd never—" he began, but she held up her hand. "Please don't," she said. And then, "I noticed that you never mentioned your own age in the ad."

"My children wrote that. I didn't know anything about it."

"That's beside the point, isn't it?" she said. "The thing is, it doesn't matter how old *you* are. You're a man, so your sex appeal, your attractiveness has a much later expiration date." Pretty much what Frances had said at Bruno's, only delivered with more bite. Maybe Frances hadn't given up on men, after all. Maybe they'd given up on her.

"I don't feel too attractive right now," Edward said, which was absolutely true. And this was the most awkward conversation he'd ever had with a woman he was lying next to.

Sylvia must have had a similar thought, because she slipped out of bed and wrapped herself in a kimono that had been draped across a chaise on the other side of the room. "Shall we have some coffee?" she said, and went through the doorway without waiting for his answer, giving him a chance to get dressed.

When they were sitting opposite each other in her dinette, she touched her face and said, "Maybe this turned you off." Her hand went to her breasts next. "Or was it these?"

"You're a lovely woman," he said, referring to her essence

now, so that he could remain honest without being hurtful. "And I'm out of practice."

"But there's no chemistry, right? You're the science teacher, you should know."

"I teach biology, not chemistry," he said, offering a weak smile.

"Well, even better."

"Actually, it's called Life Science now." She was silent. "I thought there was chemistry between us," Edward said. "And I *like* you."

"Thank you," she said. "But like doesn't lead easily to love with women my age. And you get desperate. I have a friend who reads the obituaries looking for fresh widowers before someone else gets to them. And all she requires is a penis and a pulse." Edward remembered those unsolicited phone calls so soon after Bee's death.

"If I put an ad in the personals that said 'Seventy-one-year-old woman longs for ardent lover,' how many replies do you think I'd get? Trust me, not many, except from some scoundrels or nut cases."

"I heard from my share of loonies," Edward said.

"So we get coy," Sylvia went on, "and we say 'seventy-one years *young*,' or lie about our ages. Or do this to ourselves."

"Men probably lie, too," he said.

"You bet they do. I've met a couple of eighty-somethings with contraptions like bicycle pumps to help them get it up. They'd advertised themselves as young studs. And a boy or two looking for financial support, like a sexual scholarship, or maybe just for their mothers. Who knows?"

"I'm sorry," Edward said again, feeling as if he were apologizing for all of crude, moronic mankind this time.

"Oh, drink your coffee," she said. "It's not your fault."

When he was leaving a little later, he thought, only briefly, of asking if they could be friends, which he wished was possible. He also wished that she would ask him to just hold her, the way women in the movies always did after a failed encounter in bed. In fact, he needed to be held, himself. So he put his arms around her and she returned his embrace. They stood that way, rocking a little, for several moments before they let each other go.

21

A Noble Experiment

Edward took the last two letters from the kitchen drawer and fed them into the shredder. He didn't even bother reading them again first, although he remembered that one had been a computer printout from a woman named Carole, and the other was written in a large, loopy scrawl and signed "Yours, Ann." *Well, not mine anymore*, he thought as the machine screeched and pulped her words, although he found bits of shredded paper stuck to his shoe, like confetti, hours later at school.

If any of his stepchildren brought up the ad—as they still occasionally did, fishing for news—he would say it had been a noble, if failed, experiment, and he'd try not to sound sardonic, or add *Like Prohibition.* And he'd put off Frances's subtle concern for his social well-being and Bernie's blatant questions about his sex life. He certainly wasn't "getting any," to use Bernie's vernacular, unless you counted pleasuring oneself, which in Edward's case seemed more of an appeasement than an actual pleasure. He would be sixty-four soon. In time, and without stimulation, even that need would go away.

On a bright Saturday morning in April, he drove to the Greenbrook Sanctuary, where the usual spring crowd of swallows and crows chirped and cawed and rustled in the trees, which were just beginning to bud. There were other birders ahead of him on the path, so he lingered in a copse of paper birch and was rewarded by the sighting of an airborne purple martin, a species that usually nested closer to human habitation. Edward had never seen one before in all the years he'd visited the Palisades. An adult male, he guessed, from the full iridescent plumage. He watched it soar and bank and dive—a daring solo aerialist—and finally fly off before he noted it in his journal.

That evening, he took his family out for dinner, to everyone's favorite Chinese restaurant. Edward picked up Gladys, who used a walker now and required a daytime aide. But she had thrown off the mental fuzziness of the hospital, and was dressed up for this outing in stylish layers of wool and silk. To top it all off, she wore a rakish green felt hat from the 1940s that made her look like an aged Robin Hood in drag.

On the phone, Amanda had said that she and Nick wanted to hold a sort of intervention at the restaurant for Julie, who was still seeing, and being emotionally mistreated by, her boyfriend, Todd. In fact, she was only available to join them on a Saturday night because Todd had bailed on her again, with some flimsy excuse this time about work he had to catch up on. Since he had an entry-level job at Chase, it was hard to think of anything besides a heist that would require him to put in overtime hours at the bank.

"It's just dinner," Edward told Amanda. "I don't think you want to corner Julie there."

"It will be informal and loving," Amanda assured him. "Totally constructive."

"Yeah," Nick agreed on the extension. "And that girl needs help."

Before they hung up, he told Edward that he had a little surprise for him, too.

What now? Edward wondered. He hoped they hadn't planted another personal ad on his behalf, or intended to place one for Julie in some younger, hipper version of the *NYR*. But he, too, wished she'd get out of that relationship, and maybe it would only happen if she met someone new.

They had a round table at Tung's, with a lazy Susan at its center, which they rotated slowly to pass the fragrant variety of dishes around. Julie had seemed in low spirits at the beginning of dinner, but she'd perked up by the time the fresh pineapple and fortune cookies were served. Maybe it was all that protein or just being with her family. She'd even tried on her grandmother's hat, to general acclaim. Gladys said, "You could have modeled at Bamberger's in my day!"

That's when Amanda cleared her throat in an attention-getting way. Next, she'd be tapping on her water glass with a knife. Edward tried to forestall her by opening his fortune cookie and reading it aloud, the sort of thing Amanda or Julie was far more likely to do. "Listen to this," he said. " 'Strike iron while hot.' " It made him remember ironing Bee's blouses, but all he said to the table at large was, "So what do you think this means?"

The kids looked at one another, surprised by the question. Then Nick said, "English as a second language?"

"It means you're still hot, of course," Julie said.

Edward glanced nervously at Gladys, who was sipping her tea and appeared to be deeply within her own thoughts.

"But maybe not forever," Nick warned.

Amanda cleared her throat again. "Speaking of hot," she said. Edward could see the determination in her eyes and the set of her jaw. She would have used anything anyone said to her advantage.

"He could still strike while warm," Julie said to Nick.

"Yeah, but not *luke*warm," Nick countered.

"I believe I was speaking," Amanda said. She hadn't raised her voice, but everyone grew quiet and turned to her. "Jules," she said, and Julie, who had just broken open another fortune cookie, let the pieces and her unread fortune drop to the table. "You know we all love you very, very much."

"Just like a sister," Nick said, and Amanda put a restraining hand on his arm.

"And we *value* you," she continued, "more than we think you value yourself."

"You're a doll," Gladys said. "Just look at that hat face." Obviously she hadn't been let in on Amanda and Nick's plan.

"Listen," Edward said, "there's a time and a place—"

"What *is* this?" Julie asked.

"You're much too good for that a-hole," Nick said. "Sorry, Gladdy."

"We want to support you in giving Todd up," Amanda said.

"God, is there a camera hidden somewhere?" Julie looked over at the next table, where the people sitting there looked back at her, their chopsticks poised.

Edward signaled the waiter for the check.

Later, he called Julie at home and tried to put a good spin on Amanda and Nick's attempt, without condoning it. "It was a little extreme," he said. "But they really do love you and want you to be happy." Another noble experiment.

"They want me to try *speed*-dating," she said.

"Well, I certainly don't think—" Edward began.

"And maybe I just will," Julie said.

After they hung up, Edward took out his birding book and reread his notes for that day. He'd recorded the brilliant weather, the greening of the trees, and the avian commoners he'd spotted. About the purple martin, he'd written "Adult male, on his own." Hah!

As for Nick's promised surprise, he'd tucked something into Edward's breast pocket when they were all saying good-bye in the parking lot at Tung's. "You've got mail, bro," was all Nick had said at the time.

And Edward forgot about it until he was on his way to bed that night. He went to the closet then and retrieved an envelope from his jacket pocket. It was addressed to Science Guy at the same PO box number as the letters he'd shredded a few days before. The loopy handwriting looked eerily familiar. When he pulled out the note inside, he saw that it was signed, "Yours, Ann."

22

Fourth Date: Another Chance

Of course it wasn't one of the letters he'd shredded, magically made whole again, but it was from the same Ann who'd signed the previous one. There was no salutation this time; he seemed to recall a simple "Hello" at the beginning of the other letter. Now she'd written, "I was disappointed not to hear from you. I suppose you were besieged by mail—as that rare thing, a single, viable man—but that's no excuse for overlooking a truly good prospect like me. Please tell me the dog ate my letter." Well, this one had no shortage of self-confidence. Maybe it was catching; his own ego could certainly use a boost. And she seemed to have a sense of humor.

She went on to say that if he decided to give her (and himself) another chance, they should forgo the usual drink/meal/coffee routine of blind dates and do something less predictable and more active. A walk in the park, perhaps, or a museum visit.

Had he seen the Abramović thing at MoMA? She was a native New Yorker who'd strayed from home for a long while, but had returned recently and wanted to catch up on everything. "Why don't you call me," she'd written him, an invitation and a command.

Edward had let his cultural life lapse since Bee's death. They'd had dual memberships at MoMA and the Museum of Natural History, and a subscription to the New Jersey Philharmonic, none of which he'd renewed when the time came. Once in a while, he bought a single ticket to a concert, or went to a movie by himself or with friends, but his mind always tended to stray.

He'd remember how Bee used to seize his hand during a moving passage of music or a suspenseful moment in a movie's plot. And he would miss her simply sitting beside him in the darkened auditorium. So he hadn't seen the "Abramović thing," although he'd read opposing reviews of it, and listened to Sybil and Henry argue at dinner one evening about the artistic value of performance art.

Henry was of the old school; he believed that classical materials like canvas and paint and marble couldn't be replaced by what he called the "whimsy" of using anything at hand, including urine or feces or blood and, now, naked bodies. He said this was madness, not art—just another case of the emperor's new clothes.

"Or *lack* of clothes," Sybil said. She agreed with Henry that exhibitionism and a touch of sadomasochism—those ladders of knives!—were at the heart of what Marina Abramović did, but she believed that artists had to find new ways of expressing themselves, even when that disturbed or perplexed their audience. "Think of Stravinsky," she told Henry.

"You always bring up Stravinsky," he said. "But at least his performers were dressed."

Edward called Ann Parrish and made plans to meet her in MoMA's lobby the following Saturday at noon. "I'll be nearer to the Fifty-third Street entrance, at the membership desk," he told her. "But it gets pretty crowded on the weekend. How will we know each other?"

"Well, I'm on the slim side, medium height, and I have darkish hair and a medically frowned-upon tan."

"And I'm tall," Edward said. "What's left of my hair is blond, or gray, according to the light. Shall I wear a carnation?"

"Don't worry, I'll find you," she said.

The museum lobby was especially crowded, even for a weekend day in the spring. There had been all that buzz about the Abramović exhibit, and a simultaneous show celebrating Tim Burton's career. So many of the women milling around and seated at the large circular ottoman across the room were dark-haired and slender. A surprising number of them appeared to be suntanned, too.

And how many tall, balding men were standing in Edward's general vicinity? Easily enough for a Rogaine commercial. It was folly to think they'd recognize each other with such minimal description, and he couldn't go around asking various women if they were named Ann, like some desperate old lecher. Probably several of them actually were.

They hadn't exchanged cell phone numbers, another mistake. You would think he'd have gotten the hang of this kind of meeting by now. It was twenty past twelve when someone tapped him on the shoulder. "Dr. Livingstone, I presume," she said.

"Ann?" he said. A woman near his own age, an animated

bronze statue. Brunette, as she'd described herself, and slightly weathered, but lovely—in a strange way—as if she'd willed herself to be.

She gazed back at him. "Well, if I'm not, I'm going to pretend I am."

"Shall we sit down somewhere, have coffee?" he asked.

"Later, maybe," she said. "Let's go look at the art first."

Edward had bought two tickets of admission as soon as he'd come in, and they went straight to the Marina Abramović exhibit, The Artist Is Present. As indeed she was, seated at a table, clothed, slightly hunched and staring ahead, but not directly at the woman sitting opposite her, a museum visitor who'd helped herself to the facing chair.

Edward could never have thrust himself into the spotlight that way. He would feel too shy, and he was already weary of the culture of instant fame. "Could you do that?" he asked Ann. "Just plunk yourself down opposite her?"

"Yes, of course," she said. "But I don't particularly want to."

In another room they were assaulted by the images and noise from several screens hanging from the ceiling and set into the walls. It was bedlam, like the dayroom in an asylum, like an orchestra tuning up, readying to play Stravinsky. "Enough," Ann said—his thought exactly—taking his hand and leading him into the next gallery.

That's where the nude couple, made famous by art critics and news writers, was standing in a narrow passageway, facing each other, less than a couple of feet apart. They were anatomically correct, but were somehow as neutered as store mannequins, as Barbie and Ken. It seemed that you were expected to sidle between them to continue on in the exhibition. Edward had read somewhere that there was another, conventional way into the adjacent room, and that the artist had objected in vain to this more conservative option.

According to an item in the *Times*, a man, a patron, had made his way between the naked pair, allegedly patting the male actor on the butt in the process, and had been summarily ejected by one or more of the guards. The accused had also been deprived of his long-standing membership in the museum. Henry said it was entrapment; Sybil called it rough justice.

Edward was looking around for the other way in when Ann dropped his hand and darted as quickly as a hummingbird between the nude sentries. She stood on the other side and said, "Come on, what are you waiting for?"

In a fairy tale, this would be the ultimate test, that defining moment when one could turn out to be the hero of the story or merely an ogreish chump. Wasn't he too old for this sort of challenge? Didn't those two nudists ever take a break for a smoke or the restrooms?

Out of nowhere, he thought of the whirling *hora* dancers the night he first met Bee, and how he'd stood on the sidelines, struck by longing, until he was pulled into the swiftly moving circle that became his life. He smiled at Ann, still hesitating, and she called, "Let's go, Edward. Lighten up!"

It was like a blow to the head of an amnesiac, similar to the one that took his memory, except that this one served to restore it. She was older by thirty-some-odd years and like a sepia negative of her former ethereal, silver-haired self. She bore a different name, for some reason, and the burnishing of age and sunlight, but, God, it was Laurel, it was her! He threw off his inhibitions, like cumbersome garments, and passed through the guarded doorway to the other side.

23

Payback

For the rest of his life, Edward would wonder why he hadn't just turned away from Laurel and left the museum. He would play that moment over and over in his head without ever coming to a definitive conclusion. When it happened, when she called to him and he followed her into the other gallery, he felt propelled by shock and rage, as well as by something else he couldn't name. "You!" he cried, when he reached her, that single word ablaze with recrimination. She didn't cower or even step back, but at least she'd stopped smiling.

Of course she had the advantage of having known who he was from the time he'd phoned and introduced himself. How many Edward Schuylers could there have been in her life? She hadn't given anything away then, though, except for saying, with such certainty, "Don't worry, I'll find you." And then there was the penetrating way she'd gazed at him in the museum's lobby.

But that was all hindsight. At the time, he didn't have a clue as to who she was—not with a new name, her once breathy voice coarsened by years of use out of his earshot, the whole physical transformation.

"Yes, it is," she said.

"*Why?*" he said, hating the plaintive sound of his own voice, and the way he was reduced to monosyllables, as if he couldn't force more than one sound at a time up through the clogged pipes of his throat. What was he really asking her? *Why did you go through with this, once you heard my name? Why did you pursue me after I destroyed your first letter?* Or, *Why did you leave me stranded like that more than thirty-five years ago?*

He wasn't sure what he meant and Laurel—Ann was her middle name, he suddenly remembered—wasn't going to help him figure that out. She said, "We have to talk, Edward." And whatever she saw in his face made her add, "Please."

"No," he said. "I think the statute of limitations has run out on that little talk." Well, at least his voice and vocabulary were restored. He sounded like a lawyer now, like the stuffed shirt she used to tease and seduce into abandonment.

"You have to give me a chance to explain," she said.

"I do? Really?" *Well, fuck you*, he thought, something he had never said aloud to anyone, but had to stop himself from saying now. As he turned to go, he saw a naked woman climbing a ladder against the far wall. Art or madness, Edward didn't know which and didn't care. He followed the exit signs, weaving between clusters of people until he came to the broad stairway that would take him down to the lobby. Without looking back, he ran down the center of the steps, almost tripping a couple of times.

She must have been close behind him. He heard his name called above the conversational din as he made his way across the lobby, cutting between people again. "Hey!" a man said as Edward brushed against him in passing, but he kept on going, through the revolving doors that spun him out onto the street. "Edward!" he heard. "Wait!" Bee's last words. He wanted to laugh, or cry.

He headed toward Fifth Avenue, out of breath and a little light-headed. His legs were much longer than hers and he'd hardly slackened his pace, but she caught up to him, anyway. "Come on," she said, "this is crazy."

"No, *you're* crazy, if you think I want to talk to you." He continued to walk, despite the feeling that he might pitch over onto the sidewalk any minute.

"I am crazy," she said. "Or I was crazy. Edward, I was *sick.*"

He stopped, with his fists on his hips, his heart struggling like a flooded engine. Sick! She looked extraordinarily healthy to him. Why wasn't she panting, too? He was reminded of the lame or exaggerated excuses students often gave when they'd been absent or hadn't turned in an assignment. "Do you have a note from your mother?" he said, his tone as coldly contemptuous as Maureen Wheeler's. *Are you sitting on your brain?*

But Laurel seemed to take the question seriously. "My mother is dead," she told him.

Mrs. Arquette in her lilac-colored dress, her drooping corsage. "Everyone's mother is dead," he said. Except for Bee's, except for poor Gladys.

"I'm sorry," she said, and for one incredulous moment he thought she was offering condolences about his mother. Then he realized that she was trying to apologize with those two easy words for the devastation she had once wreaked.

"Are you?"

"Yes. *Oui. Je suis très désolée,*" she said. It had always sounded so much more sincere in French—like utter desolation instead of mere regret. "Can we go somewhere?" she asked. "For that cup of coffee you offered before?"

"I offered that to Ann Parrish," he said. "This isn't a date anymore, in case you haven't noticed." His breath had returned and he started walking again, turning onto the avenue and heading north. He had no particular destination; he just had to keep going.

She walked alongside him. He tried to stay a few steps ahead of her, but she kept catching up. When they reached Central Park South, with the park on the other side, he headed toward it, stepping off the curb just as the lights changed. He had to hurry across the wide street as the traffic began moving, and he heard horns honking behind him, but he didn't turn around to see if she'd made it safely across, too. What a gentleman he used to be, what a sap.

When he entered the park, it was if he'd gone from the gritty black-and-white world of the city into the Technicolor palette of nature—Dorothy gone from Kansas to Oz. Everything that had happened seemed just as unreal. Yet all around him, Edward saw evidence of ordinary life: babies, dogs, bicyclists, trees. He made his way down a path to a lawn and sat under a red maple, leaning back against its trunk. There was no sign of Laurel. He might have invented or dreamed the entire episode, or simply willed her away. He closed his eyes, feeling the dappled sunlight strike his lids between the new leaves of the maple, like a blessing.

But he didn't feel relaxed. He was still simmering with anger and beset by an inexplicable melancholy. His own reaction surprised him; he'd put her out of his heart and head ages ago. And even when she'd still been on his mind, and he'd imagined running into her somewhere, he always saw himself as being civil, if not exactly cordial. Yet today's encounter had wrenched him backward to that church where he'd stood and waited, as if no time had passed at all. And walking out on her at the museum hardly seemed like adequate payback.

Payback! What was he thinking? Edward had never considered himself a vengeful person, someone who had to get even for being wronged. His parents' style had been conciliatory, and he'd been raised to turn the other cheek, or to at least be tolerant of other people's foibles and transgressions. "Forgive and forget" was his mother's motto, "Live and let live," his father's. "Kiss and make up," they'd chorused when he and Catherine had quarreled as children. Clichés by which they'd lived such honorable, orderly lives.

Maybe that's why he'd let Laurel get away with so much when they were together. That entrenched passivity, and his being so helplessly in love with her. Had they married, his patience would have worn away in time; he knew that now. They'd have made each other miserable and probably wouldn't have lasted. But the chronology of his life would have been altered, and maybe he'd never have met Bee and known genuine happiness.

The wonder of that, of such random, lucky cause and effect—like the high number he'd drawn in the draft lottery during the Vietnam War—gave him a feeling of peace that seemed to radiate from his chest to all of his limbs. The anger seeped away. He thought that he might even fall asleep in the shifting, glittering shadows of the tree. It wasn't as if he'd forgiven or forgotten Laurel, and they certainly would never kiss and make up. But when it came down to it, she had really done him a great favor.

24

DSM

For the first time, Nathaniel Worth went past Edward's lab in the company of someone who appeared to be—from the way they were shoving each other and laughing—his friend. Or maybe his clone, with that skinny frame and those standout ears. It was the final Friday of the school year, and for once Nathaniel wasn't going to need tutoring during the summer vacation. Not that he was excelling in any of his classes, but at least he had passing grades in all of them, including Bio/Life Science, which he had ended up having to repeat.

Edward had gotten him out of Maureen Wheeler's clutches, though, by asking the headmaster to transfer the kid to the class of another, more humane and laid-back colleague. Parents had no say in these matters at Fenton, but there was no rule against faculty interference. It was like a reprieve from the governor. Since then, Edward had heard, Nathaniel became more focused and had even lost the nickname "Worthless." Now he was known as "Worms," which, in the brutal and mysterious kingdom of childhood, was somehow considered cooler.

Bernie and Frances were sitting at their usual table at Bruno's when Edward walked in. "Hey," Bernie said, "if it isn't Casanova."

"I thought you were going straight home after you cleaned out your desk," Frances said.

"I decided to celebrate with you." Edward sat down as Bernie signaled their waiter for another glass.

How strange it was to feel celebratory, to actually welcome this time of year again. Edward felt as if he'd shed heavy armor or lost a few pounds. What he'd actually lost was the anchor of mourning that had weighed his heart down for the last two years. Amy Weitz had promised the bereavement group that this would happen in time, and she was right, at least about him. But it made him sad to think about it. And afraid it might return, like a post-traumatic stress flashback.

Frances clinked her glass against his and then against Bernie's. "No more lessons, no more books, no more students' dirty looks."

"Amen," Bernie said. "*L'chaim.*" To life. And he didn't feel the need to throw Edward an apologetic glance.

"When are you leaving?" Frances asked.

"The first of July," Edward said. "How about you?"

"Monday. I'm too old to delay gratification."

Frances was flying to the south of France with two women friends, and Edward was going back to the Vineyard for a month, although not to the rented house he'd shared with Bee. Bernie was staying in town. He was one of those people who claimed to love New York City in the summer, when everyone else deserted it.

But Edward hadn't come to Bruno's to discuss their vacation plans; he wanted to talk to Frances and Bernie about his encounter with Laurel. He needed to tell someone. Neither his family nor his Englewood friends knew anything about her, and he had no intention of enlightening them.

Bernie had been at Fenton when Edward was supposed to marry her. He'd been in attendance at the church that fateful day, too. And even if he hadn't been, it was the sort of scandalous event that stayed in the collective memory of an institution. Back then, students still passed scribbled notes and nobody had cell phones yet, but the news spread quickly, anyway. These days it would have been even worse, the story proliferating wildly via texting and Facebook, probably embellished, and maybe even illustrated with Photoshopped nude pictures.

The only other mercy was that Laurel had wanted a late-June wedding, so that Edward was able to escape from the physical place for the summer. By September, when school resumed, he'd already begun to restore his ego and his social life. Laurel was gone and there was new gossip to keep everyone occupied. Not that anyone really forgot about the jilting—it just wasn't current enough to be that interesting. Bernie's advice hadn't changed over the years. What Edward needed then, too, was to get laid, which he did, in the freewheeling 1970s, as often as he could.

Now he took a sip of beer and said, "You won't believe who I ran into last week. A ghost from my past: Laurel Arquette."

His audience was rapt. Frances, who knew all about Laurel's betrayal, even though she'd been hired at Fenton years later, hadn't ever brought her up with Edward. That was a kindness, he knew, a measure of their friendship. But he could see by her face that the story was alive in her mind. Bernie whistled softly. "You didn't recognize her? I thought she'd be tattooed on your brain."

"She's changed," Edward said, suddenly wondering why he hadn't known Laurel's eyes. People's eyes, those famous "windows to the soul," didn't change, did they? And hers had been large and an unusual light grayish green.

"Well, of course she's changed," Frances said. "How many years has it been?"

"No, it's not just that she's older, or even that she has a new name. She might as well have been wearing a disguise. Her hair is dark, her skin, too. Remember her hair, Bern?"

"Who could forget it? She was the White Goddess, the Snow Queen." He collected himself. "And a first-class bitch," he added.

"Seeing her again like that must have been awful," Frances said to Edward. "Are you okay?"

"Yeah, sure. I don't know. It was a shock. And I acted like an asshole."

"Why, did you kill her?" Bernie said. "Trust me, no jury would convict you."

"No, but I felt murderous. She ran after me for blocks."

Bernie laughed. "That's poetic justice, my friend. Revenge, in your case, is really 'a dish best served cold.' "

"Come on," Edward said. "Revenge? What am I, a Blood or a Crip?"

"What did she say?" Frances asked.

"She said that she used to be crazy, that she was sick when she walked out on me."

"Sounds about right to me," Bernie said.

Bee had come to the same conclusion years before. When she and Edward were falling in love, they began to talk intensely about their previous lives, but not just about former lovers as Laurel had insisted they do, swearing it would be cathartic rather than cruel.

He and Bee had exchanged episodes from childhood, tales of family and growing up. The time she'd forced a pussy willow bud up her nose and had to go to the emergency room to have it removed. Her impossible longing to look like Audrey Hepburn. The day that six-year-old Edward got lost at the beach in Far Rockaway, and believed he would have to get a job and live on his own.

They'd met so late, Bee said, they had to catch up with synopses of the past to truly know each other. Of course, that included the saga of Bee's first marriage and Edward's experience with Laurel. Recounting the latter was embarrassing—a loss of face while he was still romancing Bee—but it also felt strangely confessional, as if he'd somehow been the wrongdoer, or that she would perceive him that way. "So, what do you think?" he'd asked when he was done, trying to sound casual.

"That she's nuts," Bee said.

Absolution! He was washed with relief. "Is that your professional opinion?" he said.

"Well, I could look in the *DSM* and come up with an official diagnosis. Offhand, I'd say she had a borderline personality disorder, with narcissistic pathology." She looked at him in that unnerving, concentrated way of hers. "But she was just plain nuts to give you up."

In Bruno's, Bernie said, "It was a lousy coincidence that she found you again. What are the chances? But she's gone for good now. If you ask me, you got lucky. Twice."

Frances shredded a paper napkin and made a careful little pile of the pieces. "I'm not so sure," she said, finally.

"What do you mean?" Edward asked.

"I don't think she's finished with you."

Edward's scalp crept. Were women more prescient than men, as Bee used to claim, or just less willing to be falsely reassured?

"Now you're the one who's nuts," Bernie told Frances. "Or maybe you've just seen too many Michael Douglas movies."

"I didn't say she's going to boil his kid's rabbit," Frances said. She turned to Edward. "She sounds—I don't know, really *persistent*—running after you like that."

That was when he told them about the phone calls.

25

Unknown Caller

On Sunday, the day after Edward's contretemps with Laurel, he stayed at home to do some gardening, and to catch up on his reading. The telephone rang while he was outside pulling up weeds in Bee's perennials bed, and he decided to let it ring. He'd already spoken to Gladys and the children that morning. If anyone else really wanted to reach him, there'd be a message waiting when he went back inside. But when he put his tools in the shed and went into the house through the kitchen door, the message light on the phone wasn't blinking.

He took a shower and then lay down on the sofa with a Coke, *The New York Times*, and the pile of scientific journals he'd been meaning to get to. As soon as he was settled, the phone rang again. This time he answered it, but there didn't seem to be anyone on the line. What now?

There had been the usual rash of crank calls at the beginning of the school year. Most of the teachers had received them, so they'd likely come from students. It seemed to be an annual ritual that always lost its appeal as the term progressed. Not the stuff of Edward's boyhood, when he and his friends, posing as agents of the electric company, advised mostly bewildered old ladies to blow out their streetlights or catch their running refrigerators. These modern kids didn't say anything—they seemed to understand the greater psychological impact of silence—although occasional muffled giggling could be heard in the background.

And several months later, between two of Edward's failed blind dates, he'd had what seemed to be another silent caller. But it turned out to be only hesitation on the part of Lucy James, a member of the bereavement group he'd abandoned. It took her a moment to speak after he'd picked up, and a couple of moments for him to place her as the woman whose husband had died of a stroke. He remembered being wedged between her and another widow on the sofa. Lucy, he was pretty certain, was the one with blondish hair and that dispirited posture. She'd wrung her hands whenever she spoke, as if she was trying to warm them. He couldn't picture her face, though.

She said she just wanted to say hello and to see if he was all right—he'd never come back after the first meeting. The group missed him. Edward doubted that; he'd hardly contributed to the conversation that night. He had called Amy the next day to say that he was withdrawing, and even she hadn't really pressed him to return. "That's very kind," he told Lucy James. "But I just needed to be on my own."

"Well," she said.

There was another pause, this one agonizingly long. He had to say something. "Please give my regards to everyone" was what he came up with in the end. *Say hi to the gang for me.*

"Oh, I will," she said. "And if you ever, you know, want to come back, I'm sure the others would . . ." Her voice trailed off.

She was so bad at this that he felt a stab of sympathy. But not enough to prolong the awkwardness between them, or to lead her on. "I don't think so," he said, "but thanks very much for calling." And that was that.

Edward hoped this wasn't going to be another uncomfortable exchange. He was still wearing his reading glasses, so he looked at the caller I.D. UNKNOWN CALLER came up on the screen for each of the two previous calls, the way it did for the students' crank calls. The age of instant access and cunning secrecy.

The third time the phone rang, Laurel said, "Edward, don't hang up." She sounded breathless, as if she were still chasing after him in the street.

"What's the point of this?" he asked. The sense of calm he'd achieved under the maple tree the day before had stayed with him. He'd been able to think about her since then without malice and with moderate curiosity. Where had she been and what had she done during all those intervening years? And now he sounded reasonable; he could have been speaking to anyone about anything.

"I understand how you feel," she said, "and I don't blame you."

She didn't blame *him*! A spark of anger ignited and just as quickly died out. "It's all history now," he said, as much to himself as to her. He was aware that he hadn't yet spoken her name. "Let's just let it go."

She sighed. "I wish I could," she said. "But I can't seem to."

The night before, Edward had taken Bee's *DSM*—the bible of mental disorders—down off the shelf. He still hadn't gotten around to giving away her books. He'd looked up the on-the-spot diagnosis of Laurel she'd once made, and read about the prevalence of mood shifts, the intensity and instability of personal relationships. Fear of abandonment. Grandiosity and fragile self-esteem. Despondency.

"Laurel," he said into the phone, and she seemed to take this as a sign of reconciliation, or at least intimacy. "Please let me see you again," she said.

"That's not a good idea," he told her. "Listen, I've gotten past it and you should, too. It really is history—ancient history." *We're ancient, too, or almost so,* he might have added, although right then he was envisioning the silver-haired girl stretched out across his bed.

He expected her to argue or plead, to continue their volley of words—he was even trying to ready his own response. But she only said, "All right," in a weary, resigned voice, and then she hung up.

After Edward had related most of this to his friends at Bruno's, Frances said, "Oh, God, Edward. She really might boil your kid's rabbit."

He smiled. "No, I told you, she went quietly this time."

"A little too quietly for her, don't you think?" Frances said. After a beat, she added, "Had you given her your number?"

"I'm listed," he said. In the fall, a whole new generation of student crank callers would be easily able to reach him. Anybody would.

"Maybe you shouldn't be," Frances said

Bernie looked thoughtful, but he hadn't said anything at all yet. "What do you make of it?" Edward asked him.

"Have a great summer," he said. "Eat lots of lobster and spill your seed freely." He took a long swig of his beer. "But watch your back."

26

Reincarnation

Edward and Bingo took the car ferry from Woods Hole and arrived in Vineyard Haven in the early afternoon. It was a radiant summer day, with slow-moving cumulus clouds in a cerulean sky. Their old real estate agent had left the keys to the rented cottage under the mat inscribed WIPE! at the front door. It was a two-bedroom saltbox that had been advertised to "sleep six." Some of them would have to hang from the rafters in hammocks, Edward thought as he walked around, getting the feel of the place. But it would be big enough when Julie came to visit for a long weekend. And he liked the small, low-ceilinged rooms, despite the kitschy décor that made them seem even smaller. He wouldn't rattle around in here.

For the past few days, he'd had some misgivings about coming back to the Vineyard. What if his solo return triggered grief or anxiety rather than mere nostalgia? So far, though, even nostalgia was at bay. He couldn't imagine Bee in this cottage with its Alpine cuckoo clock, its busy wallpaper and glut of Hummel figurines. Hansel and Gretel's witch would have felt more at home. Edward opened all the windows, letting in a salty breeze that dispelled the scent of other people's lives and the competing perfume of potpourri.

That evening, he would have supper at Peggy and Ike Martin's house on the lake, next door to the rambling place he and Bee used to rent. No doubt another family was staying there now. Maybe they were invited to supper, too, or would be visible from the Martins' veranda, where they always dined in clement weather.

Edward hadn't seen Peggy and Ike since they'd driven down from Boston for Bee's funeral, almost two years before. They'd spoken on the phone and exchanged emails, mostly to keep in touch and share family news. There was a grandchild now, Edward remembered. Photos had been sent via the computer, but he wasn't sure now if they had been of a boy or girl baby, the sort of detail Bee would have known. Something bald and florid. Beloved, too, judging from the looming, gloating adult faces above the bassinet. He'd probably be clued in later, with a name or some other gender-defining fact.

The realtor had placed the usual welcoming gifts in the refrigerator: a halfway-decent bottle of Pinot Grigio, a wedge of Brie, and a carton of orange juice. Edward would pick up supplies before he drove to the Martins', to whom he'd bring the Pinot Grigio.

He found himself whistling as he went out through the kitchen door to the backyard, a commensurately tiny space with some metal furniture and a silly, electric-powered water fountain, all overprotected by a tall stockade fence. There was an awning that screamed like a seagull as he unfurled it. But it would provide shade and, with a throw pillow or two borrowed from the living room sofa, he could have breakfast or read out here. He didn't even regret leaving his laptop behind, a last-minute decision to be on vacation from everything, including the scientific research that helped fill some empty, late hours at home. *I'm okay*, Edward told himself, and realized that it was true.

The feeling lasted for the rest of the day. But when he pulled up at the Martins' and saw the yellow house next door, with the green wicker couches and two-seater swing on its wide porch, he had a bad moment. There were bicycles lying in the gravel driveway, a dilapidated doll—similar to one Julie once had—seated on the swing. This was what it would be like to come back from the dead, only to discover that you were replaceable, that the world continued without you. Something you always knew but didn't have to witness. Bee had never made peace with that idea, but having children helped, she said, and that it would be much, much worse if you believed in reincarnation. To be an ant at the picnic of life was the way she'd put it.

The Martins' door was open and Edward went inside, calling, "Hello! Hello!" Then he was in Peggy's ample arms before he was passed like a baton to Ike, who crushed him in a wrestler's hold. They'd always been bone-breaking huggers; he'd almost forgotten that. But for once their physicality didn't feel excessive or make him shy. He seemed to have come a greater distance than ever to get here, as if he'd traveled through time itself, and this was only a proper hero's greeting.

Peggy linked arms with him as she led him through the house to the screened-in veranda facing the lake. There were other people already standing there—Edward heard the murmur of voices as he and Peggy approached, and detected that sensory cocktail of sunblock and gin. Some were old acquaintances, others new. There were friendly handshakes and more modest embraces than Peggy's and Ike's, for which he was grateful. He was no sci-fi spaceman, after all; only another vacationer who'd gone by ferry over the sound from Woods Hole, along with his dog and his Honda Civic hatchback.

The new renters next door, Louise and Howard Glass, *had* been invited. They were somewhere between their mid-forties and early fifties; Edward always had trouble discerning anyone's age. They offered him a look around at the house later, if he'd like. For some reason, maybe the instant martini buzz, that struck him as an excellent idea. And when he became aware, after a while, of the one woman at the party who'd come there alone, on her bicycle, he didn't have paranoid thoughts of betrayal, of having being set up.

She was attractive, somewhere in the same broad age range as the Glasses, with sun-streaked hair; tanned, athletic legs; and the kind of bangles Bee used to wear, sliding musically up and down her arms. Her name was Ellen—he lost her surname in all the chatter around them—and she was separated from her husband and sold real estate in Connecticut. "Have you been up this way before?" she asked.

"For years," he said. "My wife and I rented the place next door." He glanced at the yellow house, where lights were on, as if someone was home. She waited, and he filled in the rest, about Bee dying and his reluctance to come back the previous summer.

"That was my first time here," she said, "so we missed each other." She said it matter-of-factly, without coyness. "But I intend to make this a habit." An ambiguous statement: did she mean the Vineyard or him? It didn't matter; he felt emboldened by her open, attentive face, and by the fact that she said, "Shall we sit here?" indicating a cushioned wicker love seat, after they'd filled their plates at the buffet table.

At the end of the evening, when Louise Glass asked Edward if he'd like to go next door, he invited Ellen to come along, too. He'd already offered her a lift home. The new hatchback, which Amanda had dismissed as "a date repellent" when he'd bought it, would make it easy to stow Ellen's bike.

They went in through the back of the house, the way he and Bee always used to after a party at Ike and Peggy's. The Glasses had left the door unlocked, too. There was the kitchen, unchanged as far as Edward could see. His family's favorite room, because it was so big and had that large, butcher-block table at its center—a gathering place. As Bee used to, Louise kept the blue striped bowl there filled with cherry tomatoes. What did Edward feel? That he had to ask himself this question was a good sign, or simply the grace of temporary emotional numbness.

He remembered the way the light crashed in through the picture window in this room every clear morning and the cool feel of the Spanish tiles under his bare feet. But he didn't expect to see Bee or one of the children appear in the doorway, or even sense a lingering specter, an after-image of their occupancy. It was an old house and a recurrent rental; people had come here before them, and still others would follow. All of them transients, really. This place, revisited by everyone at once, would be like heaven, if it existed—a mob scene of phantoms.

Maybe he was helped by having Ellen at his side, not picking at the scab of memory but asking questions about the architecture of the house, guessing correctly, with her realtor's eye, the decade it was built, and that the sunporch had been a later addition. "Lovely," she said, about the layout of the rooms, the uncluttered furnishings. They could have been a couple considering a rental themselves.

In the car, she said, "That was brave of you," and he said,

"Thank you for coming with me." Then he said, "I have to ask you something. That baby, the Martins' grandchild. Is it a boy or a girl?"

She laughed. "They're pretty androgynous with their diapers on at that age, aren't they?"

"I thought I'd get a clue, but the kid's name is Morgan, for God's sake. And all Peggy said was, 'What do you think of our Morgan?' She could have been talking about a horse."

"They don't have a horse," Ellen said. "And the baby's a girl."

"Well, then I guess it's a good thing I didn't ask if it's harness-trained yet."

They'd come to Ellen's rental, a medium-sized A-frame about a mile from Edward's. As he lifted her bicycle from the car, he decided to rent a bike himself, as he and Bee used to do every summer. He'd cycle to the wildlife sanctuary at Felix Neck again. Maybe he would ask Ellen to go with him. At her door, she took a pen from her purse and scribbled her phone number on the palm of his hand. Then she turned her face up and he kissed her lightly on the lips.

Back in the witch's cottage, he lay awake for a while, despite his drowsiness. He went backward through the events of the long day, from the kiss at Ellen's door to locking up the house in Englewood. Then his thoughts meandered, the way they do right before sleep. For some reason he remembered that Houdini had promised his wife to send her a sign from the hereafter, and that she'd never received one. "If I *could* come back," Bee once said in the last weeks of her life, "I would want another shot at being myself. But only with you."

27

Silver and Gold

Julie was among the first passengers off the ferry. When he saw her, Edward was reminded of picking her up at school once when Fenton was closed for one of its ersatz holidays: Founder's Day or Reading Day or something. He'd been waiting outside Grove Elementary in Englewood, along with other parents and nannies and siblings, when the doors burst open to release a mob of children, all of them rushing forward noisily, like a gaggle of geese. You'd think the building was on fire.

Julie was a second-grader and Edward fairly new to his stepfathering role. For a panicky moment, he wondered if they'd recognize each other. Then he spotted her—how small she looked, even among her peers—and he thought, with a startling rush: *Mine!* She'd seen him, too, and began waving and separating herself from the others to run toward him.

Now he heard her call "Poppy!" and had the same pleasantly

surprised, proprietary sensation. Bingo, who'd come along for the ride, barked at her until she threw her arms around him. In the car, she was as chatty as she'd been as a child. So much had happened in the short time Edward had been away. For one thing, Nick and Amanda were trying to become pregnant. Amanda had confided this to Julie under penalty of "death by torture" if she blabbed about it to anyone. "But I don't think she meant you," she told Edward.

Edward was still trying to absorb that news and its ramifications. He might become the grandfather, the step-grandfather, anyway, of a child Bee would never know, and he began to think of the time he and Bee had tried to have a baby—their initial excitement and the ultimate letdown—when Julie continued. She'd visited Gladdy, who looked, to Julie's distress, "about a hundred."

"She's not that far from it," he said.

"But I want her to be at my wedding," Julie said.

"Oh, are you getting married?" he asked.

"Well, not right away," she admitted. "Anyway, I've broken up with Todd."

Since this was a bulletin she'd delivered a couple of times before and then rescinded, he didn't become too hopeful. But then she said, "I've met someone new, though."

"Hmm," he said, knowing that he wouldn't have to probe to get a few salient details.

"His name is Andrew Gold. Silver and Gold, can you believe it? We could name our first kid Sterling. Sterling Silver-Gold!"

Their first kid. "How long have you known this metallurgic soul mate?" Edward said.

"Not that long, a few weeks, but we're really close. And you'll never guess how I met him. Speed-dating!"

"That doesn't mean you have to proceed to speed-loving," Edward said, pleased that she seemed so happy.

"Oh, you!" she said.

Julie liked the cottage. "It's really quaint," she said. "It suits you." Was that how she saw him—an old eccentric who belonged in this gingerbread house? Maybe others did, too.

At least Ellen had declared the rental a complete mismatch when she'd come for lunch a few days before. "I did ask for something very different from the yellow house," he told her as they sat at the metal table out back eating soft-shell crabs and drinking iced tea. The dog, easy with his affection, lay on his side at her feet.

"And you certainly got that," she said.

When he activated the fountain, they discovered that the water was illuminated by blinking red, white, and blue lights. The thing was musical, too, playing, of course, "Three Coins in the Fountain." Edward had trouble turning it off and they couldn't stop laughing.

After Julie had dropped her things in the second bedroom, she turned to him and said, "I almost forgot—somebody called the other day looking for you."

"Who?"

"Some woman. I think her name was Laura. Lauren? She said she was an old friend of yours."

Edward stood in the doorway, holding on to the frame. "What did she want?" he said, although he already knew the answer to that.

"She'd been trying to reach you, she said. I told her you were up here. That was all right, wasn't it? I mean, she sounded really nice."

"It's fine," he managed to say. How had Laurel located Julie?

And just how much information had Julie given her? He couldn't ask without sparking Julie's curiosity.

"Was she just a friend or an old girlfriend?" Julie asked, her curiosity already sparked without any prompting from him.

"You've got romance on your mind, Mrs. Silver-Gold," Edward said.

"That's because of this stupid TV show I've become addicted to. *First Love, Second Chance*? I'm sure *you've* never seen it. Do you still only watch those things where animals devour each other? Anyway, they reunite people who broke up when they were younger—"

"You're right on both counts, I've never seen it, and it does sound stupid."

"But that's the latest thing," she said. "And it's kind of fascinating—long-lost lovers finding each other again." Then, mercifully, her cell phone rang and he left the doorway to give her privacy. As he walked down the hall to his bedroom, he could hear her whispering and laughing.

Edward took Julie out for dinner that night. He'd thought of asking Ellen to join them, but decided that Julie would probably need his focused attention; she was going to be with him for only three days. And it might seem presumptuous to introduce Ellen to a member of his family, even under these casual circumstances. But he did tell her that Julie was visiting and that he'd call her in a few days. "If you don't, I'll call you," she said.

Their lunch in his backyard had followed a morning bike ride to Felix Neck. At the edge of one of the ponds, they saw a pair of green herons and a family of mute swans that Edward noted in his journal. "Fine weather, fine company," he added. And in the woods, Ellen pointed out an orchard oriole, a bird he had never seen there before.

The night before the visit to Felix Neck, they'd been invited to the same July 4 beach party. When Edward took her home that second time, the kiss at the door lasted longer and was more charged. "Wow, are you seeing fireworks, too?" he said, as the last of the skyrockets boomed in the distance and lit up the night. They kissed again, but when he asked if he could come inside, she said she'd rather take things slowly, if he didn't mind. Her separation was pretty recent and she was still adjusting to a whole new way of being.

Of course he minded. He was aroused by the kissing, and his celibacy was beginning to seem like a grotesque private joke. He hadn't been this sexually frustrated since adolescence. What if he forgot how? But maybe it was like riding a bicycle, something your body holds in memory for you. And he was a little wobbly at first on the rented bike the next day, after a two-year hiatus, but soon he was rolling along easily beside Ellen on the way to Felix Neck.

"So tell me about this Andrew Gold," he said to Julie at dinner.

"Well, he's an accountant—not the most glamorous job in the world." That distinction belonged to Todd, of course—a bank clerk who'd started moonlighting as a deejay at a club in Noho, one of several venues where he came on to other women.

"Steady, probably, though," Edward said, "and lucrative. Baby Sterling's gonna need new shoes."

"He's very funny," Julie said, "Not funny ha-ha, but in a wry way, like you." She took a deep breath. "And he thinks I'm beautiful," she added shyly.

"Then he has good taste," Edward said.

"Or he needs glasses. Actually, he *wears* glasses."

"Jules, you're an idiot," he said. "But a beautiful idiot."

Much later that night, Edward passed her bedroom on his way to the bathroom. There was no light visible under her door, and he assumed she was asleep. But then he heard her talking softly, probably into her cell phone again. Her voice sounded querulous this time, and then beseeching, and he guessed that she wasn't talking to the new guy, to the twenty-four-karat Andrew Gold.

Back in bed, he tried to remember exactly what Julie had said about Laurel's call. Julie was so trusting, she'd probably offered his phone number at the cottage, and with very little effort Laurel could find his cell phone number, too. But it had been days since her call to Julie, and he hadn't heard from her yet. Maybe she was just playing out some fantasy about contacting him again. Or she might have changed her mind. God knew she was unpredictable. *What if*—he wondered, and couldn't complete the thought. Maybe his brain had fried from all that conjecture. *Oh, just go to sleep,* he commanded himself, and before long he did.

28

An Unavailable Man

In the morning, Edward began thinking about asking Ellen to have dinner with them that evening. Julie had triggered the idea with her starry-eyed talk the day before about his having a "girlfriend." He decided that she'd enjoy meeting someone friendly and pretty who just might fit that title, and that Ellen probably wouldn't mind the invitation. He checked with Julie at breakfast, and she said, "That sounds great."

So he called Ellen's number, long transcribed from his palm to his cell phone speed dial, but her message said that she'd be off-island for a couple of days, and would return calls as soon as she was back. Edward was disappointed, and curious about where she'd gone. "Sorry I missed you. I miss you," he said. Did that sound weird? He was always unprepared for a taped message when he expected a live human voice.

That afternoon, he and Julie visited Peggy and Ike. "Now I feel as if I'm really here," Julie said after the hug fest was over, which gave Edward a jealous twinge. It was the place as well as the people, he reasoned. This was where Julie and Nick had often played with the Martins' three children, and where they'd hung out as teenagers.

But when they stepped out onto the veranda, and Julie looked across at the yellow house, she started to sob. "I'm fine, I'm fine," she wailed. At least nobody said that they knew how she felt. Edward put his arms around her, and Peggy went inside for some Kleenex. While Julie dried her eyes and blew her nose, Ike asked if she'd like to go out with him in his kayak.

Edward, watching them glide by on the lake like figures on a picture postcard, was relieved now that Ellen wasn't available for dinner. Despite Julie's playful hints about his love life, memories of their summers on the Vineyard as an intact family would have pervaded the evening, making it gloomy and uncomfortable. This wasn't the right time or place to introduce her to a new woman he was seeing. In some ways, he was still an unavailable man.

And he was right about Julie—she wanted to talk about her mother during dinner. That view of their old rental house had unleashed whatever she'd been suppressing. "Two years!" she said, as if Edward wasn't aware of the passage of time since Bee died, or that an eternity without her awaited them both. He didn't shy away from the subject—how could he?—but he tried to emphasize the happiness they'd all once known, and the astonishing privilege of it. "Mom used to say how lucky we were." He didn't add what Bee usually had, about enjoying their luck while they could, that someday they'd be coming up here with their attendants and walkers.

The thing was, they'd expected to grow old together, as if

that was their due, especially after their late start as a couple. "Do you remember the Wexlers?" Edward asked Julie.

Of course she did. Herb and Belle, the elderly pair down the street in Englewood, were the standard-bearers for the horrors of aging, with their diminished faculties and mobility, their loss of patience with each other. They fought over the wattage of lightbulbs and the expiration date on milk, about which one of them had left the water running or put the pot scrubber in the freezer. They always accused each other of deliberately mumbling. And all of their friends had predeceased them. The Wexlers split up and got back together again almost as often as Julie and Todd.

Except that neither of them had anywhere else to go besides separate corners of their house, where they fell into twin soliloquies of silence. Until one day Belle would say, out of forgetfulness or forgiveness, "Do you want me to reheat the chicken for dinner?" or Herb would offer to set the table, and that particular battle was over.

"We were terrified of becoming like them," Edward told Julie. He meant old beyond the possibility of pleasure, and frightened and angry. Sometimes, when Edward misplaced his glasses or keys, Bee would say, "Uh-oh, Herb." And if she yelled "What?" from another room, he'd yell back something about her needing Belle's ear trumpet. Someday, Bee predicted, Edward would refuse to throw the neighbors' kid's ball back over the fence. And she would serve shrunken, stale "old lady" ice cubes to guests, who would surreptitiously spit them back into their flat seltzer. "We'll be so decrepit by then," she said, "our deaths won't seem tragic to anyone but ourselves."

"You wouldn't have been like the Wexlers—you *loved* each other," Julie said.

"We did, very much. But maybe Herb and Belle were in love once, too, and all of their losses ground them down."

"So, are you saying it's better to die young?" Julie asked.

"No, no, of course not." Then what *was* he saying? "It's just that you should choose someone to spend your life with who's likely to wear well, someone kind and with a sense of humor." *The un-Todd*, he thought, but didn't say.

As soon as Julie left on the ferry the next day, Edward felt available again. He wondered once more when Ellen was returning to the Vineyard, and he anticipated her call. He even checked his phone once or twice to make sure it was working. In the afternoon, he bought a couple of lobsters and a bottle of Sancerre, and when he got back to the cottage he lay down on the couch and began to read the second novel in the Stieg Larsson trilogy. He and Ellen had talked about *The Girl with the Dragon Tattoo*—how intelligent the characters were, how sex seemed more of a natural aspect of life in Sweden than it did in the United States. That was before their second kiss and her gentle rejection—a postponement, really. And this was now.

He fell asleep wearing his glasses, and with the book open across his chest. When he woke, he was slightly surprised by his surroundings, and then by the way the light in the room had begun to fade. He looked at his watch and at the mute phone on the table next to him. Hours had gone by. The Sancerre was still cooling in the refrigerator next to the live, seaweed-wrapped lobsters. Like Herb and Belle, bound together until their demise. How long could you keep lobsters alive in there? If he'd brought his computer with him he could have Googled the answer or fired off some emails. Where the hell was Ellen?

Edward wasn't exactly hungry, but he stood in the light of the open fridge eating crackers and cheese, washing them down with orange juice right from the carton. Then he showered and shaved for the second time that day, grabbed his book, and went out to the patio. His backyard neighbors, unseen behind the stockade fence, were having a party. Music, voices, and outbursts of laughter kept interfering with the words on the page. Sweden and New Jersey seemed equally distant and foreign. It was like being on the other side of life itself.

He went back into the house. It was too late to make other plans for dinner and too early to go to bed. The nap had left him wide awake, yet unrefreshed. He opened the refrigerator again, browsing for food he didn't really want. This was how so many lonely people must become obese. It occurred to him to cook the lobsters while he still could, and make a salad out of them the next day, when Ellen would have surely returned.

He had set a big pot of water to boil when he heard a knock on the door. Can the heart actually lift? Of course not, but it can beat madly, like a bird's wings before flight. *Just in time*, he was going to say. *Welcome back, I hope you're hungry!* And—in a reprise of his clumsy phone message—*I missed you.* But when he threw off his apron and opened the door, Laurel was standing there.

29

Therapy

"What are you doing here?" Edward said. He was so stunned and let down at once that he might have added, *And what have you done with Ellen?*

"I came to talk to you. You wouldn't listen to me on the phone."

"God, Laurel, I told you there's nothing to talk about."

Her shoulders, all of her, seemed to droop. If she melted into a little puddle right there on the step, he wouldn't have been surprised. "Edward, I'm dying," she said.

"What!"

"I mean inside, I mean emotionally." He sighed in exasperation and she said, "Look, could I just come in?"

He saw then that there was a car parked behind his in the driveway—a dusty red Fiesta, too scruffy to be a rental. She must have taken the Woods Hole ferry. Well, she could turn right around and take the next one back.

"I have to use your bathroom, anyway," she said. "Please."

He hesitated and then stepped aside, letting her go past him into the house.

She glanced around. "What a dump," she said, Bette Davis–style.

He looked at her coldly. "The bathroom's down the hall on the right. Second door."

The water in the lobster pot was boiling, and he turned off the jet. The telephone rang and rang, but he didn't answer it. He could hear the toilet flushing, and then the water in the bathroom sink run, and screech as it was turned off. The plumbing in the cottage was particularly noisy, as exaggerated as the sound effects in a school play.

When Laurel came out of the bathroom, he was waiting by the front door, with Bingo beside him, to usher her out. The dog, almost completely deaf now, had been asleep in the kitchen when Laurel had knocked on the door and come into the house. But he'd probably been awakened by the raucous plumbing, and had loped in to see what was happening.

When Laurel saw him, she stepped back, and Edward remembered that she was afraid of dogs. She had been bitten by a stray when she was a little girl, or had claimed to have been, anyway. He held on to the dog's collar and said, loudly, "Bingo, stay."

Laurel, somewhat emboldened now, said, "Bingo? Edward, really!"

"My daughter named him," he said. "She was just a child." Why was he offering her an explanation? Why was he talking to her at all? "He won't hurt you," he said, in an affectless tone. "You can leave."

She still stood a few feet from him with her hands clasped at her waist, like a nervous student about to recite in class. "I know what I did," she said. "It was terrible, it was worse than terrible. It was criminal. Over the years, whenever I let myself think about it, I wanted to die."

"But you're still here, I see," he said.

"I'm a coward, too," she said, and attempted to smile.

"I told you that I'm over it. It was ages ago."

"After I left Joe, I actually got married."

"Congratulations."

"Edward, don't," she said. "It was spur-of-the-moment—a justice of the peace—or I wouldn't have gone through with it. Allen Parrish, a nice enough guy. I stayed for about a month."

"I don't want to hear the story of your life," he said. He looked at his watch. "And I'm expecting somebody."

"I did try to kill myself. But I screwed that up, too."

He was silent and she said, "I took pills and put a plastic bag over my head. The kind that's stamped THIS IS NOT A TOY? Maybe I didn't take enough pills, but I began to suffocate and I pulled the bag off." Her hand went to her throat. Despite all the lies she had told him, he knew she was telling the truth about this.

"I went into therapy with this shrink in Phoenix, Aaron Steinman. He wanted to put me into the hospital, but I promised I wouldn't do anything to myself and that I would show up every day. And I did—at seven AM, five days a week. Do you want to hear his diagnosis?"

Edward shook his head; he already knew that, or at least the gist of it. "How long did you see him?" he asked.

"For six years straight. And then on and off for booster sessions. I had a teaching job out there, decent health insurance. It strapped me anyway. But I finally found out why I was the way I was. Why I had to leave everybody before they left me. Starting with my parents, but they got the last word."

"They always do," he said.

"I've changed, Edward," she said. "And I don't just mean physically. I've finally grown up."

When he didn't answer, she took a deep, shuddering breath and swayed a little. "Do you think I could sit down?" she asked.

He ushered her into the living room, where she dropped into one of the two overstuffed chairs. He took the dog down the hallway to his bedroom and closed the door. Then he went into the kitchen and brought her a glass of water. Her hand shook a little when she took it from him. The cuckoo popped out and marked the hour, startling both of them. Seven o'clock. Edward sat down opposite her, on the other chair.

Laurel sipped the water and said, "I was going to write to you, but it seemed inadequate—pitiful, really. Hateful. I kept looking you up on those people-search sites, relieved that you were still alive, hoping that you were happy."

"I was," he said. "I am. I married a wonderful woman. I lost her, but I have children, a family."

"Edward, I'm glad! I mean about you being happy, about your family."

"You knew about them, though. I told you everything in that first phone call, when you were calling yourself Ann."

"I started using my middle name. I guess I didn't want to be Laurel anymore."

"But you didn't tell me who you really were."

"You'd never have agreed to see me if you'd known."

"You're damned right about that. But you couldn't drop it. Why couldn't you just drop it? You even called Julie, my stepdaughter."

"I did. I felt like some deranged stalker. And she was so sweet on the phone, as if she wanted to hook us up."

The phone rang again, and again he didn't answer it. "Laurel, do you want me to say that I forgive you?"

"Yes, but only if you really mean it."

Everything she'd ever consented to had been conditional. "All right," he said, "I forgive you. I was angry as hell, but I recovered. Okay?"

"You still sound a little angry."

He clutched his head. "Jesus, what do you want from me?" he said.

"I guess I want you to believe how truly grieved I am, and to know that I ruined my own life when I walked out on you."

For the first time he looked directly into her eyes. They were still that arresting gray-green color, her gaze as intense as he remembered. Why hadn't he recognized her at the museum? "You were sick," he said. "You don't need forgiveness for something you couldn't help. And I'm sorry you've had such a bad life."

"But I'm better now. I mean right now, being here with you and hearing you say that."

"Good," he said, "so that's settled," realizing that he meant it, and that he felt relaxed for the first time since her arrival. "What time is your reservation?"

"What reservation?" she said.

"For the ferry going back." That line from Edna St. Vincent Millay ran through his head: *We were very tired, we were very merry—We had gone back and forth all night on the ferry* . . . Bee and Julie sometimes recited, almost sang, it together as they sailed across the water to or from the Vineyard.

"I didn't make one, I kind of left it open-ended. I didn't know if you'd be home, if I'd have to wait for you . . ."

He knew it was hopeless, but he called, anyway, and of course the ferry was solidly booked. There was a cancellation for the noon trip the next day, though, and Edward took it in her name. "We'll have to find you a bed-and-breakfast for tonight," he said.

"All right," Laurel said. "But could I take you to dinner first? I'm pretty hungry—famished, actually. I feel as if I left the city in another lifetime. Or are you still expecting someone?"

"Not anymore," he said. She was always given to hyperbole—famished instead of hungry, freezing when she was merely chilled, half dead rather than tired. It used to amuse him.

"Do you still like lobster?" he asked.

30

The Dream

He didn't listen to his messages until Laurel was in the guest bedroom with the door closed. Only one of them was from Ellen. "Hi, Edward, I'm back," she said. "Can we get together? Call me." The other message was from Julie, thanking him for the "great" weekend. A word she used too easily, wantonly, about everything from junk food to clothes to movies. Even Todd was great when he wasn't being a total shit. "That sounds great" was what she'd said about Ellen joining them for dinner, not long before her meltdown at the sight of the yellow house. Well, maybe the weekend *had* been great for her, at least in terms of catharsis. And he hadn't lost touch with Ellen, after all.

It was bizarre having Laurel in the bedroom down the hallway, where Julie had slept so recently. As if he were running a shelter for troubled souls. It struck him that both women suffered from a fear of abandonment and that he'd turned out to be the steadfast figure in Julie's life and, finally, a source of atonement in Laurel's. Of course, Julie's problems and her self-destructive tendencies were kid stuff compared with Laurel's.

After Edward had found out that there were no vacancies for the night anywhere on the island—it was the heart of the season, and someone getting married had claimed multiple rooms for out-of-town guests—he'd briefly considered asking Ike and Peggy to put Laurel up. But he couldn't imagine explaining to them who she was and why she couldn't stay with him. It was easier to treat her like another stepdaughter, an old friend, anyone at all for whom there was room at the inn.

The lobsters were wonderful, briny and sweet. Laurel ate hers with the joyful zest he remembered from their happiest days, her chin and fingertips glistening with melted butter. How young she looked for her age, how unself-conscious she appeared to be. Between them, they finished off the bottle of wine. After dinner, while Edward loaded the dishwasher, she went out to her car and came back with a large tote bag that seemed to contain whatever she'd need overnight. Just as well. In his bachelor years, between Laurel and Bee, he'd kept a couple of new toothbrushes, some scented body lotion, and even an extra bathrobe in his apartment, just in case. Now he had the basic belongings of a monk.

Laurel showered first, the water shrieking through the pipes like someone being murdered. She was in there for a long time—what was she trying to wash away? When it was Edward's turn, there was hardly any hot water left in the inadequate tank. He was in and out in a couple of minutes, before brisk turned to icy, and he would have to put the dishes through in the morning.

The spare bedroom had bunk beds, contributing to the "sleeps six" claim of the realtor. Julie had chosen the top bunk, saying cheerfully as she bounced on the mattress that it was just like sleep-away camp. Edward hadn't reminded her that she'd hated camp, and had suffered so much from homesickness that he and Bee had to retrieve her in the middle of her stay. If asked now, she'd probably say that camp had been great, too. Everyone rewrites personal history to drum up a better self-image. Maybe he was glorifying himself as Julie's savior and Laurel's redeemer. And was his marriage as blissful as he remembered? Was Laurel really that terrible?

She'd chosen the bottom bunk. When he came in with the linens, she called him "Warden" and asked if she had a cellmate. A joke, of course, but there was some underlying seriousness to most humor. Bee used to say that.

But his own sober analysis of everything was starting to get on his nerves. "Good night, and don't let the bedbugs bite," he said to Laurel, which his mother had always said to Catherine and him when she'd tucked them in at night.

"Sweet dreams, Edward," Laurel said, and he left the room, shutting the door behind him. That was when he played his voice messages. It was almost eleven by then, too late to call Ellen back, and he wouldn't feel comfortable doing that, anyway, with Laurel in the house. As soon as she left for the ferry the next day, he would make plans to see Ellen that afternoon or evening.

Edward went to bed feeling drowsy and lighthearted. His muscles ached, but not unpleasantly, as if he'd earned a good night's rest through hard labor rather than psychological rumination. He tried to read, but the words blurred and wouldn't stay in his head, so he closed the book and let himself doze off. In that zone between wakefulness and sleep, he began floating away in a canoe from the shore of the lake behind the yellow house, where Bee and the children were waving and calling out to him. Their voices coming across the water warbled like birdsong.

Then he was in his old bed, their bed, on Larkspur Lane in the sultry darkness of another summer night. "What are you thinking?" one of them said, or thought. They'd often said that in the prelude to sleep. First he was spooning Bee, the warm curve of her spine against his belly, his face in the perfumed tangle of her hair. Then she was spooning him, her breasts pillowing his back, her mouth against his neck. "Edward. My Edward," she whispered, and he turned so that they were facing each other, much closer than that naked couple in the museum, so close that they became one being that began to move rhythmically to the refrain: *What are you thinking, what are you thinking, what are you thinking?*

And he came awake fucking Laurel, who'd entered his dream and his bed, probably at the same moment. When he moaned, in passion and in protest, she said his name again and again, in that breathless way, and he gave himself over to her, to the sweet, violent, arduous work of their joined bodies. Oh, God, it was good—great, even. He wanted to shriek like the plumbing, to stay inside her forever. What was he thinking? But he'd stopped thinking. His brain had detached itself from the rest of him that was rampant with wanting and pleasure.

He didn't last as long as he'd hoped to, not after all this time—that was probably why he didn't keel over from a heart attack. He lay there, holding her, winded and sated. "Again, please," Laurel said.

He laughed. "Hey, I'm sixty-four," he said. "Could you wait a couple of weeks?"

She laughed in response, and planted kisses along his collarbone, which was suddenly exquisitely sensitive, as if it shared nerve endings with his cock. He kissed her, too, on the eyelids, her forehead, her eager mouth. Then they separated and looked each other over, as people might examine their own cars after a fender bender. Her small breasts still had a poignant beauty, and her pubic hair was silver now, the way the hair on her head used to be. She told him that she'd dyed the latter brown when her face was no longer youthful. And he apologized for the damage gravity had done to his own body. But as he fell asleep again, he was suffused with memories of their younger selves, as he suspected she was. As if time had rewound itself and nothing bad had happened yet between them.

They didn't have to wait a couple of weeks. In the morning, he surprised her and himself with an erection without the inspiration of a dream sequence or any little blue pills. This time he woke her, and the lovemaking was slower and less turbulent, but just as satisfying. He hadn't forgotten what to do, after all, and Laurel was still the nimble, inventive cohort of memory.

Afterward, he made coffee and scrambled some eggs. Laurel came into the kitchen wearing one of his pajama tops. It was so big on her that she looked comical and sexy at once. Her toenails were painted bright blue. "My final crack at funkiness," she explained, curling her feet over the rung of a chair. She seemed to have overcome her fear of Bingo, who stretched out next to her and sighed. In fact, she had to have gone past him to enter Edward's bedroom during the night, an act of courage and determination.

Over their eggs, they talked about the coincidence of her having answered the ad his children had placed, and, in a general way, about the divergent paths their lives had taken during the years they'd been apart. Casual, social, morning-after chatter. She didn't cling to Edward or declare her love, as she used to, as he'd worried she might. And serving her breakfast was simply a civil act. He couldn't get beyond what they'd done in bed to any feelings other than gratitude and a sense of wonder, of having been slugged by fate. Maybe that was why he was so slow to get to his feet when someone knocked on the door. And although he said, "Laurel, don't!" she sprinted to the entrance and flung the door open before he could stop her. This time Ellen was waiting there, a day late, clutching a bunch of yellow flowers.

31

The Next Day

Laurel left for the noon ferry, as planned. She'd kissed Edward ardently in parting, although his own ardor was on hold. She was living in Chelsea now, and he took all the vital information and promised, without genuine conviction, to contact her soon. To his enormous relief, she hadn't questioned him about Ellen, as she'd surely have done in the past, when it would have been her right. Laurel seemed to accept that she was the interloper here, reappearing in the middle of his life without warning. That he *had* a life.

After Ellen said, "Sorry, I must have the wrong house," and hurried down the path to her bicycle and sped away, all that Laurel said to Edward was, "I hope that wasn't something awkward." She'd behaved reasonably, for her, another sign that she might have really changed.

But it couldn't have been more awkward: Laurel at the

door in his pajama top and with her blue toenails, him lurking in the background in his bathrobe. A few of the yellow flowers had been dropped in Ellen's rush to get away, on the front step and on the path, and after Laurel was gone Edward had walked around picking them up, as if he were removing evidence from a crime scene. But instead of tossing them into the trash, he plunked them into a glass of water, where they hung listlessly over the rim, like spent swimmers.

He didn't know what to do after that. Ellen wasn't going to be amenable to an explanation. And what could he say, anyway? The truth was so complicated he could hardly process it himself. He felt guilty and wrongly accused at the same time. He imagined her shutting the door in his face, or not opening it to him at all. A phone call, in which he'd likely suffer a hang-up, seemed cowardly and too impersonal for the situation.

So for several hours he did nothing at all. In the interim, Julie called him again. "Poppy, did you get my message?" Edward only half listened as she flitted from one subject to another. He stared at the drooping flowers and at regular intervals interjected sounds into the phone, like "hmm" and "ah," as if he'd lost language as well as heart. Julie didn't seem to notice.

The next call was from Peggy, inviting him to a cookout the following evening. He took comfort from the sound of her voice, but he wasn't in the mood for ordinary social communion. And what if Ellen turned up there, too? What if she didn't? He asked Peggy if he could get back to her, he was just on his way out. And then he got on his rented bicycle and rode to Ellen's place. Her car was in the driveway, her bike lying across the lawn, like a careless teenager's. A single yellow flower lay next to it and he bent down and picked it up.

She did open the door to him, but she stood squarely in the middle of the threshold and didn't invite him in. Her body language wasn't difficult to read: arms folded tightly across her chest; chin thrust out, but trembling slightly. Edward felt like a character in a sitcom, the husband caught with lipstick on his collar. *Just let me 'splain, Lucy.* The only thing missing was the canned laughter. He shredded the flower, which he'd briefly considered handing her as a peace offering.

"*Carpe diem*, right?" Ellen said. "Or maybe I should say seize the man. You're quite a fast worker, Schuyler."

"It's not like that," Edward said. In all those hours, he hadn't come up with anything more intelligent or persuasive to say. "It's a long story."

"I don't think I have time for that," she said.

"Then I'll make it short," he said. "She was my old girlfriend, my fiancée once, actually. She just showed up and needed a place to stay." The *Reader's Digest* version of his history with Laurel.

"I see," Ellen said, although that was highly improbable. "Edward, you really don't owe me anything. We barely know each other. And we had an embarrassing moment, but now it's over."

"May I come in?" he asked.

"I don't think so."

"May I call you, then?"

"Not right now," she said. "I have a lot of things to sort out. You probably do, too."

As he pedaled back to the cottage, he realized that he'd never asked her where she'd been for the last couple of days. How could he?—it would be like trying to make small talk in the middle of a disaster. But he wondered if whatever she had to "sort out" was related exclusively to him. He found himself pumping slowly, doggedly, like a cardiac patient on a stationary bike. God, he couldn't take all this drama. How he missed Bee right then, and not just her, but the safety net, the delightful, sane, predictable days of their marriage.

He decided to go to the cookout at Peggy and Ike's the next night. If Ellen showed up, he might have an opportunity to talk to her again, to ease the residual tension of their doorstep conversation. And if she wasn't there, he would just try to unwind in the calm, friendly atmosphere of a party. In the meantime, he tried to direct his attention away from himself. He started just after supper with a phone call to Julie, to make up for his earlier distraction.

But she wasn't home, and he was treated to a voice-mail message he'd never heard before, a few bars of a song by a male vocal group that seemed to go, "Whassup, my brother? Whassup, my sister?" followed abruptly by a beep. Maybe he'd dialed the wrong number. Edward cleared his throat and said, "Well, sorry I missed you. I'll try again later." If it was Julie's phone, she'd recognize his caller I.D., if not his strained voice. And if he'd reached a stranger, his message was suitably anonymous and innocuous.

He called Nick and Amanda next, and the phone rang several times before Nick picked up and said, "*What.*" Edward hadn't heard that belligerent tone in Nick's voice since he was a kid. And where was Amanda, who always picked up another extension simultaneously? He hoped he hadn't called them in the middle of a quarrel. And then he remembered Julie's news about them trying to have a baby, and realized that he'd probably interrupted them in bed.

Edward thought of all the times Nick or Julie had interrupted him and Bee in the early days of their marriage, how they'd freeze in an embrace behind their locked bedroom door at the sound of knocking, how the children seemed to have some special radar that picked up the first hint of sexual contact.

"What are you doing?" Julie might say, rattling the knob. "The door is stuck." Nick would want to know where his Walkman or his Pogo Ball was, as if they were hiding it under their mattress.

"It's Dad," Edward said into the telephone. Good old Dad, with his perfect timing. Maybe it ran in the family.

"Hey," Nick said. "We're just in the middle of . . . of a movie. Is everything okay up there? Can we get back to you later?"

Why did Edward persist in thinking they all needed him—that his absence, even for a month, left them disorganized and defenseless?

At least he could count on Gladys being home after dark and not too busy to talk to him, unless she was in an emergency room somewhere. There had been another scare, less than a month ago—a fainting spell—another little rehearsal for the real thing. How would it be to go around thinking of your life as a tentative, ironic gift? Why didn't everyone feel that way all the time? That was the miracle, really, that we live as if we were immortal, that we shout "Hello!" to each other when "Good-bye!" would be so much more appropriate.

But Gladys answered the phone in a robust voice, with other, even livelier voices in the background. "Do you have company?" Edward asked.

"Only Keith Olbermann and that darling Rachel," she said. "Hold on a minute."

After a while, the background voices were cut off and Gladys said, "Did you hear the news?"

"Has something happened?" he asked, suddenly filled with apprehension about the larger world he'd left behind.

"Yes!" she said. "Nicky is trying to become a father!"

Well, that certainly hadn't been on MSNBC. "Did he tell you that?"

"No, no," Gladys said. "Julie did. But don't tell anyone, okay? It's a secret."

Some secret. If it were up to Julie, it *would* be on the evening news.

Then Gladys said, "So, are you having a nice time, honey?" and he almost burst into tears, or into a babbling confession of his screwed-up love life. But of course he didn't. He was confident that in Gladys's mind he still belonged to Bee.

32

Real Life

Ellen didn't show up at the Martins' cookout. Edward mingled with the other guests, trying to be sociable and not seem preoccupied, but he was like Bingo two years earlier, wandering the rooms of the house on Larkspur Lane, looking for Bee. When he finally worked up the nerve to ask about Ellen, as offhandedly as he could, Peggy said, "Oh, she was going to come, but then she canceled last night. She said she was coming down with something, some bug she must have picked up in Connecticut."

So that's where she'd been, where she spent the rest of the year in what he now thought of as her real life, where she lived and worked. Edward imagined some real estate transaction, a closing or a mortgage issue, that had required her presence. But then Peggy said, "I think she and her ex had some matters to iron out." When she saw Edward's face, she hastily added, "But she's back now, and this is probably just some twenty-four-hour virus."

He immediately saw the double standard of his thinking, the sophistry of the jealous rumbling in his chest. Even if Ellen had unfinished business with her husband, even if sex was a part of it, who was he to complain? Laurel had been in his bed and was still, to his surprise, very much on his mind. In fact, he had decided to call her. Without an emotional investment, he had nothing to lose. Had he reverted to the player he'd been between Laurel and Bee? No, of course not; he was way past all that. And he'd known absolute love since then, which was as good as a conversion. He would always long for it again. This would just be an intermediate dalliance.

That night he did phone Laurel, and she said, "I was afraid you'd forgotten about me," but not accusingly, or even in a self-pitying tone.

"That would be pretty hard to do," he said.

Their conversation was friendly and flirtatious. "*Tu me manques*," she said. She missed him, in two languages, and she never asked about the woman with the flowers at the door. Edward was aroused by her voice, by images he'd held of her body, of what they'd done together, recently and long ago. But he would call the shots this time around, keeping it uncomplicated and light. They made a date in the city for the evening after he got back to Englewood.

Then, two days before he left the Vineyard, he ran into Ellen at the checkout counter in the market. His pulse accelerated at the sight of her. They had unfinished business between them, too, although its nature wasn't entirely clear. "Is the moratorium on phoning you over yet?" he asked.

After a beat, she said, "You're leaving soon, aren't you? I am, too. Maybe we can speak after we're both home. I'll give you my number there." She borrowed a pen from the grocery checker. He started to turn up his palm, but she'd pulled a receipt from a shopping bag and, leaning on the counter, scribbled on it. "Safe trip back," she said, handing him the receipt.

"You, too," he answered, and he could swear his palm tingled, as if it had been slapped.

Back in Englewood, in his own real life, there was garden work to do and email to read and answer. He'd had his bills forwarded to the Vineyard, and Mildred had come by to water the plants and check on the house, so things were pretty much in order. But there was a static feeling inside the rooms that couldn't be dispelled by simply opening the blinds and windows to let in sunlight and air. "Well, we're home," he said to Bingo. "What do you think of that?" Although he'd sworn he wouldn't become one of those geezers who held one-way conversations with their dogs.

Laurel's third-floor walkup in Chelsea, with its thrown-together, thrift-shop décor, seemed youthful and temporary. It reminded Edward of Julie's place in Hell's Kitchen, except Laurel didn't have a roommate, for which he was very grateful. Minutes after he arrived, still a little winded from the stairs, they were in each other's arms. Sex first, then a nap, and then a hand-in-hand stroll through the neighborhood, which was filled with a variety of restaurants, to find the perfect place for supper. Edward discovered that he had a great appetite for all of it.

If Ellen entered his thoughts once in a while, and Bee far more often, he kept it to himself and didn't really feel disloyal to anyone. This was life, with its proverbial, restorative way of going on. He didn't tell anybody about his reunion with Laurel, either, and didn't consider himself duplicitous. It was a private matter, the honeymoon he was denied decades ago, only without the wedding, and in Manhattan rather than abroad. You don't take anyone else along, even metaphorically, even on a metaphorical honeymoon.

But he didn't invite her to Englewood, and she didn't ask to go there. Everything fit neatly into its own compartment: his immutable connection to his family; his friendships in the city and those close to home; and this strange, pleasurable interlude with Laurel. That's what he told himself it was, because he didn't really expect it to last. He just wanted to relish it while he could. Despite all the evidence of her new stability and the remorse she'd expressed for the past, he was still being cautious, watching for signs of the old restless and capricious Laurel, the one capable of disappearing as abruptly as she'd reappeared.

One day he could arrive as arranged at her apartment—he had keys to both the outer and inner doors now (a mere convenience, as she'd said)—and find strangers living there. Was that uncertainty part of the thrill for him? If so, it was definitely out of character. He was famously steadfast, a man of habit who took satisfaction from the quotidian, from people he could count on and who could count on him. Or at least he used to be. Maybe he would pull the disappearing act this time.

He'd intended to call Ellen, playing it cool to match her detachment by waiting a few days after he was home. But when he looked for the receipt with her Darien, Connecticut, number on it, he couldn't find it. Lost in the laundry, maybe, or left in the Vineyard rental along with his blue swim trunks and an unopened bottle of Pinot Noir. He remembered the second letter from Laurel, when she'd signed herself "Ann" and asked if the dog had eaten her first letter. That's what he might have told Ellen about the receipt, after he got her number from information. But he found out that she was unlisted. He couldn't remember the name of the real estate firm she worked for, and the minimal detective work required to figure that out seemed formidable. Of course he could have simply asked the Martins for her number, but he thought that Peggy had sensed his rift with Ellen, and didn't want to arouse her curiosity. So he let it go for the time being.

On the few occasions he told Laurel he couldn't see her because of a family commitment or other plans, she didn't question him or sulk or even ask to be included. She seemed to understand the unwritten rules of their new relationship. So he saw the kids and Gladys whenever he felt like it, and went to Sybil and Henry's for dinner, unaccompanied and unafraid. There were inquiries about his social life. Julie asked if that "old friend" had gotten in touch with him again, and he blithely lied about it. Sybil wondered aloud if he'd met anyone while he was on vacation, and when he said, "No one special," she looked at him sharply, but he withstood her scrutiny for once and simply enjoyed his dinner.

But when he ran into Bernie one evening on the way to Laurel's, he felt compelled to talk about her, without being directly asked. How did the conversation start? Bernie said something crude and intrusive, like "Getting any?" and Edward had an unexpected, adolescent urge to share his new-found excitement.

No details, of course—they were light-years from adolescence—only the fact that he and Laurel were involved again. He was suddenly bursting with that revelation, the way Julie needed to betray Amanda's confidence about trying to become pregnant. Did Edward want approval or envy? Not exactly, although he remembered the dreamy look on Bernie's face when he'd mentioned the silver halo of hair Laurel once had. This time, though, Bernie just seemed incredulous. "You're kidding," he said. "How did *that* happen?"

"It happened," Edward said. "How doesn't really matter."

"Well, good luck," Bernie said, clapping him on the shoulder, a little too hard. He was about to say something else, but then he seemed to change his mind. "Good luck," he said again before going off down the street.

33

Separate Lives

One afternoon, at the Lincoln Plaza Cinema, Laurel leaned toward him just as the main feature was starting and said, "Is there someone else, Edward?"

They were holding hands, but he was settling deeply into his seat, ready to give himself over to the life and landscape of the movie, an Australian crime drama, and the question, her voice in the plush darkness, startled him. "What do you mean?" he whispered. A woman sitting behind them said, "Shhh!" and Laurel turned to glower at her before putting her free hand up to Edward's lips. "Later," she whispered back.

Going to the movies in the afternoon had always seemed like a guilty pleasure to Edward, an instant escape from the glare of daylight and the business of the outside world. Laurel had suggested this particular movie, and she was good at conjuring up other means of entertainment. Since Edward's return from the Vineyard, they'd taken the Staten Island Ferry, followed by a picnic in Clove Lake Park; gone to Chinatown, where they ate at a communal table with a large Chinese family, none of whom spoke English, isolating the two of them in a silly, yet romantic way; read the first pages of several books sitting on the floor in the aisles of the Chelsea Barnes & Noble; and lay, gently vibrating, in side-by-side massage chairs at Hammacher Schlemmer.

They'd done many similar things together when they were younger, and even if some of them seemed a bit juvenile to Edward now, he was moved by Laurel's delight in revisiting old habits and haunts. Then there was the lovely lovemaking, the culmination of most of their outings. It was like having two separate lives, both satisfying, that never had to merge or even collide. That, he found out soon after they'd left the theater, was what was bothering her and had provoked her question at the start of the movie.

"I dated a married man for a while in Arizona," she said, "and it was something like this."

He felt a small charge, as if he'd touched a frayed wire. In his head, he heard: *I almost got married once before, you know.* "You've never mentioned that, have you?"

"Don't change the subject," she said.

"Laurel," he said. "You know that I'm not married. And I don't have the energy or the impulse to be seeing another woman. You still wear me out, I'm happy to say." They were walking down Broadway and he reached for her hand again, but she pulled it away.

"But you're not always available," she said.

It was true; he wasn't always free to be with her. Her uncommon patience, her easy acceptance of this arrangement was always going to expire; he just hadn't thought it would happen this soon. And he'd seldom lapsed into talking about Bee to her, but Laurel had what appeared to be uncanny intuition about such matters, and a history of unfounded jealousy. Of course, she'd been the unfaithful one, but he didn't point that out, and he didn't say he'd assumed it was his turn to be selfish. If he wasn't able to let go of the past, they couldn't move on, even as a loosely attached couple. "Sometimes," he said, "I need to see old friends."

"You never invite me along, though, do you?"

"You're right, I don't," he said. "Maybe I just want to keep you all to myself." *On our protracted faux honeymoon.* He almost believed his own glib answer for a moment.

She rolled her eyes. Then she said, "Or maybe you're, I don't know, ashamed of me or something."

Was he? No, it was more complicated than that. He was still ashamed—even after all this time—of having been dumped at the altar, and of hiding that whole episode of his life as if it had never happened. What he didn't have the impulse or energy for was explaining Laurel to anyone, of revealing himself, in his youth, as an innocent dupe, or of trying to justify their reunion.

"Of course I'm not," he said. "You're wonderful." And she was, in her own innovative way.

"I've never been to your house," she said. "That rental in the Vineyard doesn't count, and I had to practically force my way in there. Even my married lover took me home once, when his wife and kids were out of town."

While Edward was trying to envision that scene, it was supplanted by an image of Laurel entering the house in Englewood, of her shadow crossing the threshold of his marriage. Now he really wanted to change the subject. "Listen," he said, "do you remember Bernie Roth?"

She looked at him blankly.

"Short guy? In the English Department at Fenton."

"Oh, yeah, the little bantam rooster," she said.

Accurate, he supposed. Bernie did strut and crow a lot back then. He still did, at times. "Well, there's a place on Columbus Avenue, Bruno's, that we go to sometimes after school, Bernie and Frances Hartman and me. She's in math, hired way after your time."

"Are they together?" she asked.

"No. They may have been once, but not now."

"How old is she?"

"I'm not sure—you know how bad I am about people's ages. Fifties?"

"I see," Laurel said. What did she see? "Do they know about me?" she asked.

"Yes. Bernie was there when we were together, remember?" *He was at the church. His wedding gift was one of a trio of chafing dishes I had to return.* "He still talks about your amazing hair. And I've told them both about running into you again."

She didn't question him about the content of that conversation. Instead she said, "How long have you been at Fenton, Edward? It must be a million years by now. Haven't you ever thought about retiring?"

Yes, he had thought about it, and so had Bee. They were going to retire together when she turned sixty, and he sixty-five. What did Gladys say? *Man plans, God laughs.* It sounded better, or worse—more dire, somehow—in Yiddish. Yet he and Bee had made elaborate plans to travel, especially to the Far East, where neither of them had ever been. For his sixtieth birthday, she had bought him a field guide to the birds of East Asia. Do some of them sing in Mandarin? she wondered. For her part, she'd already started to research the open markets and bazaars in New

Delhi and Katmandu. They were not going to turn into the Wexlers, who'd stayed in New Jersey, squabbling, and squandering their remaining days.

"Sure, I've considered it," he said, "and the school board has offered incentives to get us old-timers out. But I guess I'm just not ready yet." He didn't say that work had been his salvation after Bee died, or that he still got a kick out of teaching. Laurel had taken her pension in Phoenix several years before, bored to death by generations of children and their lousy accents. She'd worked at a few odd jobs for a while afterward—mostly to help pay for refresher visits to her therapist—as a freelance translator, selling art objects in a gallery, and as a receptionist in a doctor's office. Was that her married lover? Edward didn't ask, just as she'd never mentioned Ellen again. Quid pro quo.

"I'll be going back to the salt mines soon," he said. "Bernie and Frances and I will probably all meet up at Bruno's to commiserate beforehand and review the summer. Why don't you come, too?"

"Maybe," she said. But she let him take her hand.

34

Late

When Laurel was twenty minutes late, Edward tried not to look at his watch again too soon. Instead, he glanced across the table at Bernie's oversized Fossil chronograph, which seemed to be running about ten minutes fast. He wished he knew which one was accurate; half an hour seemed significantly later than twenty minutes. Frances's watch was one of those tiny things with little jeweled dots instead of numbers and such delicate hands they were hard to discern from even a foot or so away. And she kept moving her own hands around, fiddling with her purse and realigning the salt and pepper shakers. When had she become an obsessive-compulsive? Edward wanted to clamp his hands over hers to make her stop and then, when she was still, take a quick, close look at the face of her minuscule watch.

They'd ordered a pitcher about fifteen minutes into their

wait and, despite a dry mouth and throat, Edward was nursing his beer. Bernie seemed to be guzzling his, and he'd already reduced the bowl of pretzels to a pile of salt and dust. "Traffic," Edward said, as if it were merely an idle observation, and although Columbus Avenue appeared almost deserted on this Friday before Labor Day. Even Bruno's was pretty empty. He didn't check his watch again for what felt like ages, but only ten more minutes had gone by. Laurel was officially half an hour, or perhaps forty minutes, late by then.

Edward hadn't been this fixated on the passage of time since what he now thought of with irony as his first wedding. The church had been filled, yet he hardly knew anyone there, including the minister, who'd met with the bridal couple only once a couple of weeks earlier, to discuss the ceremony and give them some perfunctory marital counseling. His language was archaic, Edward remembered. He said things like "Cleave unto each other," and went on about the "sacrament of commitment." Edward and Laurel had trouble containing themselves. And what a sad joke that proved to be.

Standing in the vestry with Laurel's father, Edward heard the wheezing, meandering notes of the organ, like a medley of numbers played on a cocktail lounge piano. All the splendid music they'd chosen awaited a signal to the organist that everyone germane to the occasion had arrived. His parents sat expectantly in the first row of pews on the groom's side of the aisle, which also held the overflow from the bride's side.

On Laurel's instructions, the two mothers had worn lilac-colored dresses. Evelyn Schuyler's was made of lace, and had what she'd kept referring to, with obvious pleasure, as a "sweetheart neck." Why were details like that still fresh in his memory? When they'd all first assembled on the steps to the church, Bud Schuyler, in a morning coat and striped trousers, patted his pockets repeatedly, probably for the notes he'd prepared for his toast to the newlyweds.

At Edward's wedding to Bee, Bud had raised his champagne flute and spoken extemporaneously. "What a beautiful day this is," he said, although dark clouds hovered, menacing the garden reception. "It is!" he insisted, when there was laughter and some wag opened an umbrella. "And what a joy to welcome our new daughter, Beatrice, and her wonderful children into our family." Edward had repaid his parents for the aborted wedding by then, although they'd wanted to forgive the debt.

He had weddings on the brain, and a feeling of dread growing in his gut. What had Laurel's father said to him in the vestry? "She was often tardy to school, too. Her mother always had to write these notes for her. 'Indisposed,' she used to say. It covered everything." Edward had received similar missives from students' parents over the years, and a few forged by the latecomers and absentees themselves—every teacher did. He stared at the man, who smelled of mothballs and breath mints, and he knew that Laurel wasn't coming at all. In an unhinged moment, he imagined a note from her mother. *Please excuse Laurel's absence from her wedding to you. She was indisposed.*

At Bruno's, he remembered asking her sarcastically if she had such a note when she'd tried to explain that she'd been sick, and how bewildered she had been by his meanness. He wondered if she'd considered this date a kind of thrown bone, an easy way of appeasing her appetite for the parts of his life he didn't share with her. And maybe she'd be right about that.

He got up from the table and went to the men's room, where he called her cell phone. It must have been turned off because he was connected directly to her voice mail, with its generic message to leave a call-back number at the sound of the tone. "We're waiting for you, Laurel Leaf," he said. "Hope everything is okay.

Well, see you soon!" A toilet flushed in one of the stalls before he hung up, a perfect finale to his forced cheeriness. Without planning to, he'd used a term of endearment—Lorelei and Lulu were others—from their early courting days. Was it out of nostalgia or renewed affection? Or just some magical thinking, an abracadabra to draw her there?

If so, it didn't work, and now there was no way to avoid addressing her absence. It was more than an hour past the appointed time, by anyone's watch. "I just left her a message," he said, plunking his phone down on the table and taking a long swill of his beer. "She should be getting back to me." Frances murmured something agreeable, but Bernie said, "If she's standing you up again, man, I don't want to be a witness."

"Bernie!" Frances said, but Edward was glad that the elephant in the room, or *not* in the room, was finally being acknowledged. "At least I won't have to return a gang of gifts this time," he said.

"How did you ever manage to do that?" Frances asked.

Edward pretended she was only referring to the physical challenge. "We had an invitation list, with addresses, and Laurel had made a notation next to everyone's name—you know, Joe Blow: ugly chafing dish."

"That's what I gave you, wasn't it?" Bernie said.

"Well, yours wasn't ugly, but yes, you and a couple of other Joe Blows. I just had to rewrap each gift and return it to the sender. It was their job to get a refund."

"I think I still have mine somewhere," Bernie said, almost to himself.

"You might have to take a store credit," Edward said.

"That must have taken you ages, Edward," Frances said.

"My sister helped," Edward told her. He didn't mention his own catatonic state or Catherine's critical commentary about people's taste and generosity, especially among Laurel's guests. "Gee, do you think the five-and-dime would take this back?" she'd wondered aloud as she held up some object between two fingers before smothering it with tissue paper. "You would have had to bury this in the backyard," she said about an open-mouthed, fish-shaped cigarette dispenser, "and it would probably have worked its way out again." Some of it actually seemed funny today, but everything anyone said to him back then felt like a physical assault. And reliving it all in Bruno's more than a quarter of a century later still generated a surprising sting. Where the hell was she?

Those were the true magical words, as it turned out, even if he hadn't said them aloud. The door opened and Laurel walked in and scanned the room. Edward would not have been completely shocked to see a willowy, haloed bride waving her bouquet of exotic flowers at him, instead of a shapely older woman in red, with one hand poised above her eyes, as she tried to adjust to the relative darkness indoors. He had a chance to really look at her before she found him. Did she seem flustered and out of breath, like someone who'd kept people—one of them a complete stranger—waiting more than a comfortable length of time? Was she contrite?

He couldn't tell, and as she approached he didn't truly care, his sense of relief was so great. He stood with his right hand to his hectic heart, like a patriot in the presence of the flag. "This is Laurel," he said, but who else could it be? Bernie stood, too, slowly, obviously marveling at how she had changed and who she'd become.

"*Mon chou,*" she said to Edward, offering her pursed lips for a kiss. "You wouldn't believe the traffic," she continued, taking the empty chair. "Sorry I'm late."

"Do you have a note from your mother?" Bernie asked.

35

Home Cooking

Mildred Sykes, Edward discovered, was a very good cook. He'd come home one day after school to find half of a small roasted and stuffed chicken in the refrigerator, with a note propped against it. "Left over from a lady I clean and cook for. Hope you enjoy it."

The reheated chicken was excellent, moist and crisp at once, with a fragrant, crumbly herb filling. Edward had still not gotten into the habit of making anything resembling a regular meal when he ate at home by himself. Sometimes he scrambled some eggs with grated cheese, opened a can or two, or brought in a pizza that served as supper for a couple of nights. He'd been living like a kid, or a young bachelor. But the ceremony of food preparation was still joyless without a partner. And Laurel and he usually ate out; her kitchen was so tiny and ill equipped.

He had asked Gladys and the children to come for supper

the following Sunday and intended to offer them the usual ethnic takeout—Thai or Vietnamese, dished out directly from the cartons—before he'd encountered Mildred's surprise in his refrigerator. The next time he saw her, he asked if she would come in to cook something for his family and help to serve it and clean up afterward. They decided on a menu of lasagna and a spinach salad, with Moroccan spiced almonds and mushroom bruschetta as appetizers. She advised him to leave the choice of a dessert up to her.

For the first time in more than two years, the house was aromatic with home cooking, and Mildred had washed and laid out Bee's neglected best china and glassware, which Edward had been planning to hand over to Nick and Amanda one of these days. The dining room table was both formal and festive, with candles and blue linen napkins that Mildred had rolled into scrolls and tied with yellow satin ribbons.

Julie called about an hour before everyone was expected and asked if she could bring a friend, and Edward, distracted by all the activity in the kitchen, said yes without asking who the friend was. Not that he would have rejected anyone, but after he hung up he hoped it wouldn't be her allergic roommate, requiring Bingo's banishment, or Todd, whom she was still seeing when she wasn't seeing Andrew Gold. Like Edward, Julie was living a divided life, and so far they were both getting away with it.

Nick and Amanda picked Gladys up and arrived first. "Is this a special occasion?" Gladys asked when she saw the table. Edward could tell she was worried that she might have forgotten someone's birthday. But as a foil against memory loss, she kept a log of that sort of data, including lists of the gifts she'd given everyone for previous birthdays to avoid repetition.

The dog was stalking Mildred in the kitchen, as much out of a desire for scraps—she dropped bits of food with the *sang-froid* of Julia Child—as out of devotion to her. Even Julie couldn't get his full attention, but at least she had Andrew Gold's. The two of them had turned up soon after the others. He was tall and lanky, with dark curly hair and scholarly-looking rimless eyeglasses. His eyes sought Julie out in what Edward recognized as a love-sick gaze, but he noticed that she didn't cling to Andrew the way she did to Todd, which he took as a promising sign. She didn't seem to be afraid that this one might get away.

Edward ushered everyone, except for Bingo, out of Mildred's way and into the living room, where she'd laid out the appetizers. There was an unfamiliar reserve to the family gathering, marked by courteous outbursts, like "Have some nuts! They're delicious!" and protracted silences, broken only by the noisy crunching of the nuts. Was it the stranger in the kitchen or the one in the living room who made them all so self-conscious?

When Mildred appeared in the doorway to announce that dinner was ready, Edward looked at her as if she were the comic relief in a ponderous play. "Good!" he said too loudly, bounding up from his chair. "Let's eat!"

At the table, he scanned the faces of his children and Julie's date, trying to discern if any announcements were forthcoming—about a pregnancy, perhaps, or an engagement—that would turn this stiff little affair into a celebration. But no one seemed about to make any. And Gladys, on whom Edward could usually count for some lively comments, quietly attended to her food, which she then pronounced superb. That gave Edward his cue to summon Mildred from the kitchen. She'd declined to join them for dinner, but when he called, "Mildred, come out and take a bow," she came to the doorway and actually bowed deeply from the waist, while everyone clapped and Bingo barked.

As soon as she'd returned to the kitchen, the spell of constraint was broken and the conversation picked up. There were no earthshaking bulletins, but Andrew told Gladys that he loved her hat, a metallic turban that resembled a coiled cobra, and was impressed to learn that it was older than he was. Amanda said that she'd kill for the lasagna recipe. By the time Mildred came back with a trembling mound of zabaglione, they were all chattering away comfortably. Edward insisted that she sit down with them for dessert, and, still wearing her apron, she allowed him to pull up another chair for her between Amanda and Julie.

"Are you a Gemini?" Mildred asked Julie.

Julie put one hand to her throat. "How did you know?" she said.

"I sense a duality in you," Mildred said.

"You mean she's schizoid, right?" Nick said.

"Shut up, Nickhead," Julie told him, before turning back to Mildred. "Do you do horoscopes?"

" 'It is not in the stars to hold our destiny but in ourselves,' " Andrew quoted, and Edward looked at him with new interest, but Julie ignored him.

"Horoscopes, Tarot, palms, numerology," Mildred said.

"And a divine zabaglione," Edward added, in a pathetic attempt to redirect the conversation.

"This is just a sideline," Mildred said, with a dismissive gesture at the debris of dinner.

"I'd love a reading," Julie said. "I mean, for your usual fee, of course."

"My treat!" Gladys cried. Since when was she an advocate of the mystical?

"Do you happen to have your Tarot cards with you?" Julie asked Mildred.

Of course she did—she probably had a crystal ball in her oversized tote, too—and after Mildred had cleared the dessert dishes, with Julie's help, she went off to get the cards. "Wouldn't you rather play charades?" Edward said, an unlikely suggestion from him. He usually had to be dragged into party games.

"No!" Julie and Amanda cried in unison. Maybe Amanda was another two-faced Gemini.

As Mildred began to lay the cards out on the table, Edward went into the kitchen and began to rinse the plates and stack them in the dishwasher. After a couple of minutes, Nick and Andrew followed him. "What!" Edward said, in mock disbelief. "You guys aren't into that stuff?"

"I asked her if the Mets still have a shot at the playoffs and she gave me a dirty look," Nick said.

"Then she must know her baseball," Andrew said. Nick gave him a dirty look.

"Hey, I'm a fan," Andrew said. "But I'm also realistic."

Mildred had left the carafe of coffee on the warming cycle, and Edward poured some into three cups and put them on the counter. "We can wait this out," he said. "Have a seat."

They sat on bar stools around the counter and the two younger men compared the former and the new Beltran, talked about whether Minaya or Manuel should be fired, and why the Mets hadn't acquired any new power or relief pitching during the trades in August. Edward's interest in baseball was peripheral, although he'd loved the Yankees when he was a boy and had followed the games with Nick when he still lived at home.

And right then Edward's mind was in the dining room with the women, hoping that Mildred was predicting positive things for susceptible Julie and, no matter what was being foretold, that she and Amanda wouldn't take any of it too seriously. What would Bee have said to Julie—*believe in yourself*? No, that sounded both corny and meaningless. If only she'd left a manual of instructions.

When the men went back inside, with Edward in the lead,

bearing a tray of filled coffee cups, Mildred swept up her Tarot cards and put them into the pocket of her apron. She took the tray from Edward and returned seamlessly to the business of serving. "Sugar?" she asked. "Splenda? Cream?"

Read our minds, Edward thought.

Amanda said, "Did you enjoy your brandy and cigars, gentlemen?"

"Where did you go, honey?" Gladys said to Edward. "You missed *everything*."

Edward looked at Julie, whose face was flushed but unreadable. He sat down next to her, with his arm across the back of her chair. "Well?" he said, as soon as Mildred had gone back to the kitchen, "what's in the cards for you?"

She looked at him with glittering eyes. "Happiness," she said. "But it's up to me."

36

The Unicorn in Captivity

One Sunday afternoon, when they were young lovers, Edward and Laurel had visited the Cloisters up in Fort Tryon Park. Everywhere they went together back then seemed romantic, but that serene and beautiful site was especially so. He remembered embracing Laurel on a balcony overlooking the shimmering Hudson, feeling as if they were at the top of the entire world, not just Manhattan. A less inhibited man, or Fred Astaire, anyway, would have broken into song and dance.

In Edward's memory of that day, there were Gregorian chants being piped in behind them while, in the distance, traffic streamed steadily across the George Washington Bridge. They were not so much caught between centuries and civilizations as poised in some timeless place. Of course, youth alone can give one the illusion of trapped time. How slowly the days melted into one another, and how much the same he and Laurel remained and would remain.

It was Edward's suggestion that they go back to the Cloisters, and Laurel's eyes shone with delight when he proposed it. "Yes, Edward, yes!" she said, as if he'd just proposed marriage again. And he was happy to have elicited her happiness that easily. Ever since that evening at Bruno's, which had turned out astonishingly well, she'd become more endearing to him, and more agreeable about the time they still spent apart.

Bernie and Frances had recovered quickly from their annoyance with Laurel for being late. She was charming and funny, recalling things about Bernie—his passion for Yeats and Larkin; the way the kids at Fenton had called him Poetry Man, after that Phoebe Snow song—and flatteringly curious about Frances. How had she overcome the usual female math panic? Where had she gotten that stunning brooch? Later, Bernie told Edward that Laurel, so physically transformed, was still a dish. And Frances admitted that she hadn't expected someone quite so sympathetic and nice. "I guess people really can change," she said.

Once more, Laurel and Edward walked hand in hand through the cool, dimly lit rooms of the Cloisters, into history. Thirty-five years had wrought considerable alterations in both of them, but it was reassuring to see how well those medieval treasures—the tapestries and religious sculpture and the stained-glass windows—had endured. And in one of the sunny courtyard gardens, with its crab apple trees and fragrant herbs, nature, too, continued.

When they went back inside for another look at the Unicorn Tapestries, a group of tourists were taking photographs on their cell phones, and Laurel and Edward waited until the room was empty, except for another couple, before they approached.

Of the two most popular interpretations of the tapestries, they'd both opted long ago for the romantic over the religious. In mythology, the unicorn, which could only be captured by a virginal maiden, was more readily seen as a bridegroom succumbing willingly to love rather than Christ being hounded and killed, especially to a newly engaged, agnostic couple.

Now, as Edward was wondering if the Crucifixion theory might not be more accurate, after all—why were there precisely twelve hunters, if not to represent the twelve Disciples? And they weren't dressed for a hunt—Laurel said, "Look, all that blood without a single wound." She had turned from the first tapestries to the most famous, and final, one: *The Unicorn in Captivity.* The woman of the other couple turned around, too. "It might not be blood at all," she said, "but the juices of the pomegranates in that tree."

"Well, he doesn't seem hurt, in any event," Laurel said.

"No, he doesn't, does he?" the woman said. "And he seems to be enjoying his 'captivity.' That fence is so low, he could just bound right over it."

"But he's shackled," Edward pointed out.

"Not tightly," the woman's companion said.

"By a lover's knot, maybe," Laurel said, and Edward blushed, remembering silk ribbons, his hands loosely tied to bedposts.

They were all gathered in front of the tapestry now.

"This one might not be part of the series, you know," the woman said. "The unicorn is killed in the sixth tapestry, but here he is again, alive and sprightly."

"Christ, risen," her companion said in mock pious tones.

"We always have this argument," the woman said. "Love against death."

"Death *and* resurrection," the man amended.

The woman gestured. "See the orchids and thistles? They're symbols of fertility. This tapestry may have been woven separately, to celebrate a wedding."

Edward looked from one of them to the other. Had he seen them somewhere before? The man was bearded and a little portly, a professorial type rather than someone he actually knew. But the woman looked familiar. Small and slender. Eyeglasses. The mother of a student, perhaps. So many parent conferences, so many faces over the years. Had he once told her that her daughter had an aptitude for science, or that her son was an inattentive doofus? He couldn't place her, and she didn't seem to know him.

"No, truly," she said. "Whether or not this one is part of the series remains a mystery."

Laurel glanced around the room. "They're all gorgeous. Just look at those colors. How have they lasted this long?"

"With great curatorial care," the woman said. "The backs of the tapestries are covered with linen. They're mirror images of these, but the colors are far more brilliant because they haven't been exposed to the elements."

"You know a lot about them," Laurel said.

"It's my—our—field. The conservation and restoration of medieval tapestry. Pretty insular and obsessive, I'm afraid."

"*Chacun à son goût*," Laurel said. She held out her hand. "I'm Laurel Parrish. And this is my . . ." She considered Edward and their relationship. "This is my friend Edward Schuyler." She'd given up on using "Ann" after Edward had refused to call her that.

The woman squinted at him from behind her glasses. "Olga Nemerov," she said. "Lovely accent," she told Laurel. "Are you French, or is that *de votre goût*?"

"À mon goût, c'est vrai. Mais, merci, madame. Je suis flattée."

The man extended his hand to Laurel and then to Edward. "Elliot Willets," he said.

Edward shook it absentmindedly as he stared at the woman, Sybil Morganstern's cranky cousin, who seemed to have been humanized by art. Edward had recognized her the very moment before she'd given her name, which he'd lost, although he knew it was something Russian.

"So, are you still living in the wilds of New Jersey?" Olga asked Edward.

"You know each other?" Laurel said. It was her turn to squint at him.

"Not really," Olga said. "We met once."

"I have never been," Laurel said pointedly.

"To Jersey?" Olga gave a dismissive little wave. "I was born there. Believe me, you're not missing anything."

"You can't condemn an entire state for one misspent childhood," Edward said.

"I left before I was three," Olga said, and Edward pictured a bespectacled toddler, with a knapsack on a stick, thumbing a ride on the Garden State Parkway.

The church tower bell pealed out the hour: one o'clock.

"I'm hungry," Elliot Willets announced. "Would you care to join us at the café for some lunch?"

"His stomach is programmed by a clock," Olga said. It was the sort of thing one says with fond irritation about a spouse or, perhaps, a dear colleague.

In the Trie café, which was really just a few tables and chairs overlooking another garden, they ate their sandwiches and sipped bottled iced tea. Nervy sparrows hopped from the garden to the stone floor beneath the tables, looking for handouts. Olga crumbled a piece of crust from her tuna sandwich and sprinkled it in their path. “Litterbug,” Elliot said. He, too, sounded affectionate in his disapproval.

“How did you two meet?” Laurel asked.

“In graduate school,” Elliot answered, although the question wasn’t addressed to him, or even about him. “I used to dip her pigtails in my inkwell.”

Edward looked at Olga’s sunlit, spikily cropped auburn hair, like that of a nun who’d recently left a strict order and was letting it grow out.

She took off her glasses and gazed out at the garden. “This is how Giverny must have looked to Monet near the end,” she said. She wasn’t instantly converted into a glamour girl, like those secretaries in the movies who remove their spectacles and free the undulant waves of their pinned-up hair. Her hazel eyes simply seemed dreamy and unfocused, as if she’d had too much to drink, or had just been roused from anesthesia. *Where am I?* she might have been thinking.

Edward understood Laurel’s question. “Our, *my* friend Sybil—Olga’s cousin—tried to fix us up once,” he said.

“Really!” Laurel exclaimed.

“Really?” Elliot echoed.

“She’s insane,” Olga said.

While Edward was trying to decide if he was offended by that remark, Elliot said, “That’s where we’re going next Saturday, Ollie, right?”

“To Sybil and Henry’s?” Edward said. Why did he sound so amazed? They were blood relatives. At least Sybil and Olga were.

“I don’t know them, do I?” Laurel asked, clearly a rhetorical question that Edward didn’t feel obliged to answer.

“Family dues,” Olga said.

“They’re wonderful,” Edward surprised himself by saying,

surprised, too, by the swell of emotion in his chest. His wedding, the one that had actually taken place, had taken place in the Morgansterns' garden. *The canopy of wisteria under that threatening sky. His father's toast. Bee.*

"Are you invited, too?" Laurel asked him.

"What?" he said. "Oh, to Sybil and Henry's, you mean? No. No."

But the very next day he *was* invited. And so was Laurel.

37

Sleeping Arrangements

If he had been prepared for the purpose of Sybil's phone call the following afternoon, or simply a better liar, Edward might have gotten out of it. Theater tickets, dinner plans in the city—sorry, thanks anyway, some other time. But he was like a murderer with a sketchy time line and a bad memory. And Sybil would have grilled him with a homicide cop's tenacity. What play? But you hate musicals! Dinner with *whom*? *Where?*

Olga had told her all about their chance meeting at the Cloisters, and Sybil didn't let him sidetrack her with talk about the tapestries or the view of the Palisades. As usual, she went right to the crux of the matter. "Ollie said you were with a very attractive woman. Not someone we know, I imagine."

"Don't we know any attractive women?" he said, in a feeble

try at levity, a bid for time. And when Sybil didn't deign to answer, he sighed and went on. "Laurel's an old friend, from Fenton, another teacher. I ran into her at MoMA a while back." Remembering how he'd run *away* from her that day, he had to suppress a laugh.

"Well, bring her Saturday night. Ollie's bringing Elliot, of course, and it will be just the six of us—casual and cozy. Is there anything I should know about her?"

Plenty, he thought, before he said, warily, "What do you mean?"

"What do you think I mean? Is she a vegan? Is she lactose-intolerant, or allergic to shellfish?"

Two things came into Edward's mind at once: Laurel sucking the meat out of a lobster claw in the Vineyard, and a stray line from Sylvia Plath: *I eat men like air.* "No, she's easy to please."

"Ah," Sybil said, whatever *that* meant. "Good. Seven o'clock, then." And she hung up.

Easy to please seemed like an understatement once he'd told Laurel about the invitation. She practically whooped with joy. "What should I wear?" she asked. "Should I bring them something?"

"It's just a dinner party in the stultifying suburbs," he said. "Casual and cozy." But he was only playing dumb. The thing that thrilled her was the incursion into his other life. They had a brief back-and-forth about travel, in which he finally prevailed. He would stay at her place after school on Friday and drive her out to Englewood in time for dinner. Then they'd drive back to the city, where he'd stay until school on Monday morning. If she asked to stop off to see his house, he would think of something to deter her. The place was being painted; it was a mess; it was late; he didn't want to fall asleep at the wheel. Not tonight, dear, I have a heartache.

. . .

She got too dressed up; it made Edward sad and filled him with affection for her. He was carefully tactful. "Why don't you wear that blue sweater," he said. "I love it on you." Maybe the word *love*, which he hadn't uttered once since their reconciliation, not even in the final spasms of sex, moved her to change into a less formal outfit. Whenever she said, "*Je t'aime*," which she'd started to do again occasionally, he told himself it didn't count in French, as if it were merely one of those idiomatic expressions you can't really translate and that don't require a response. So far, she hadn't called him on it.

Olga and Elliot were already there when Edward and Laurel arrived. They were nibbling on olives and cheese and drinking a deeply hued red wine. Henry was something of an oenophile. "Just some tonic on the rocks for me," Edward said after the greetings and introductions. "We're going back to the city tonight."

"Too bad," Elliot said. "This is an excellent burgundy. Ollie and I are staying over," he added, and took a hearty swallow of his wine. For the first time, he seemed annoyingly smug.

"We could, too, couldn't we?" Laurel asked Edward. "At your house, I mean. It's not far, is it?"

There was an almost palpable charge in the room while everyone waited for his answer. It was like one of those long pauses in a drawing room comedy, with all its attendant sexual innuendo. Edward found himself speculating about Olga and Elliot's sleeping arrangements. "I hate Sunday traffic," he said finally, as if everyone else was fond of it. Who was writing his lines? "But you have some wine," he told Laurel. "I'm the designated driver."

Sybil smirked into her glass while Henry went to fetch the drinks, but Laurel didn't appear disconcerted. "What a pretty room this is," she said. She walked to the French doors and looked out at the backyard, where fairy lights were strung through the trees. "And no wonder they call this the Garden State." Did Olga snicker then or just cough?

The main course—a stew of beef and harvest vegetables, as if to herald the change of seasons—was delicious, and Edward relaxed into the conversation, which glided from Olga and Elliot's work to the midterm elections to recent medical discoveries. Edward was curious about the restoration of those ancient tapestries. Where did they find wool to match the original fibers? Was the repair done on looms? Elliot explained some of the process, and Olga said that Edward and Laurel were welcome to visit the museum lab one day, and see it for themselves.

Later, someone brought up a news item about tests to predict who might develop Alzheimer's disease in the future. With all of their faculties intact, they began to discuss the hazards and benefits of knowing such a thing. Not surprisingly, Henry's take was clinical: an early diagnosis made you an ideal candidate for any new therapy down the road.

"You mean an ideal guinea pig," Edward said. "First trials are just to find out how much it takes to poison, not cure you."

Henry grudgingly agreed. "So, I'd try to get into a later one," he said.

"How about trying to avoid the whole thing in the first place?" Laurel said. "You know, use it or lose it? Some people swear that if you do the crossword every day, if you keep engaging your brain . . ."

Edward thought of Gladys and her jigsaw puzzles, and then of Iris Murdoch, philosopher and writer, who suddenly became lost in her native London. "It may be inevitable," he said. "Written into your DNA."

"Then I wouldn't want to know," Laurel said. "I'd choose to be happy until the last possible moment." His little hedonist.

Elliot agreed, but Olga said, "You might want to make plans for the future that you'd be incapable of making later."

"Like what?" Laurel asked.

"Finances, caretaking, a living will, even suicide. It's a terminal disease, after all, but one that takes away freedom of choice."

Sybil darted a nervous glance at Edward, but he smiled at her. "Olga's right," he said. "There are things to decide. When Bee was dying . . . ," he began and then stopped to test his own ability to go on. "When Bee was dying, we—she had to decide about dubious experimental treatments, about when to tell people, about what to do with her last days." He made it sound like a calm, sane period, without storms of weeping and irrational wishes—the terrible struggle to decide anything at all.

The whole table had grown silent. Henry looked solemn, Sybil close to tears. Edward had ruined the mood of their party, but at least he'd brought Bee back—if only briefly—to this room where she, too, had once enjoyed delicious food and vigorous, theoretical arguments among friends. He felt strangely relieved, even celebratory. He would have loved a glass of that wine right then. "Well," he said to Sybil, "what's for dessert?"

"I'd like to see your house," Laurel said as soon as they were in the car again.

"It's out of the way and it's late. I want to get on the road."

"Oh, for Pete's sake," she said, her tone turning it into a variant of *Lighten up, Edward.* "Just a quick look inside, and then we'll go."

There was no reasonable argument against it. So he drove the half mile or so in the opposite direction of the bridge to 31

Larkspur Lane. He parked in the driveway, thinking for a moment of leaving the motor running. The motion sensor lights blinked on as they went past the garage and up onto the porch. Somebody else's vigilant dog barked in the distance, but Edward's own house was silent. Mildred was keeping Bingo at her apartment for the weekend.

He couldn't help it: he saw everything through Laurel's eyes. At home by himself, he was hardly aware of the furnishings, which were always dependably in place and comfortable. He could find his way around with his eyes shut. When Bee was still alive, she'd point out the need for new slipcovers every few years, or that a fraying lamp shade should be replaced, and he'd agree. They both treasured what was familiar, though, and never made any radical changes.

But as soon as Laurel walked ahead of him into the living room, he saw a clump of dog hairs on the throw rug, and the way the cushions on the couch sagged from want of fluffing, or perhaps some extra filling. The seascape hanging above it was crooked. He had to keep himself from crossing the room to adjust it. She wasn't a prospective buyer or renter. He didn't care what she thought. Laurel turned to him then and said, "It's really very nice, Edward. Homey. And now I can picture you here when I'm not with you. Is that your favorite chair?" She pointed to his deep, plush Morris chair that still faced Bee's chintz-covered affair in a conversational pose.

Before he could answer, there was the scraping of a key in the lock and a woman's singsong voice, calling "Hello?" Mildred. She must have forgotten the dog treats, or the drops for Bingo's infected ear. But Laurel seemed stricken at the sounds, and Edward thought of that moment in *Fiddler on the Roof* when the shade of a woman whose husband plans to remarry demands, "How can you allow it? Live in my house? Carry my keys?"

After the introductions were made, and the eardrops retrieved, Laurel yawned and stretched like Goldilocks in the bears' house, and Edward knew she was going to make another case for staying overnight as soon as Mildred and Bingo were gone. He could imagine some of her contentions: She was so sleepy, wasn't he? All that heavy food. There'd be hardly any trucks on Sunday. And it looked like rain. His defenses were down. Even without the numbing effects of wine, he couldn't think as fast as she did.

But then, Mildred, the psychic, said, "It was starting to drizzle when we were walking here. Would you mind giving us a ride home?"

Edward wanted to hug her. Instead, he said, "Sure. No problem. It's on our way to the bridge."

38

Lost and Found

On Monday, Laurel tried to coax Edward into staying on at her place for a few more days, but there were errands and chores he had to get to at home, like taking the dog to the vet to check out his ear, refilling the bird feeders, and catching up on the raking. During the remainder of the weekend at Laurel's, she'd mentioned his house a couple of times—how charming it was, how peaceful his street seemed compared with the chaos of the city. She was hinting at being invited back without asking directly. He was tempted; they'd had a good time together—she'd been especially sweet and sexy—and despite his fears, her brief visit to Larkspur Lane hadn't proved traumatic or even unpleasant. But he didn't take the bait; he really did have things to do on his own.

Dr. Sacco said that Bingo's infected ear was slowly healing, but that his heart had fallen into a serious arrhythmia. He let

Edward listen through his stethoscope to the erratic sounds, the booming drum and the flutter, and he prescribed medication that might help to control the condition without curing it. Surgery was available, too, but such an elderly dog probably wouldn't survive any extreme measures. "Sometimes," the vet said, "it's best to let nature take its course."

In the late afternoon, Edward put on a pair of old chinos to do the garden work. He found some twine in the crazy drawer to tie back a straggling viburnum. When he was putting it into his pocket, he felt something there—a piece of paper, crinkled and stiff. He often forgot to empty his pockets before doing the laundry. Once, a single Kleenex had caused a snowfall of lint he had to pick off his dark socks for days. Another time, he'd found a twenty-dollar bill that had survived the washer and dryer in a worn, but still spendable state.

Now he withdrew the crumpled paper and saw that it was a grocery receipt. He put it on the counter and smoothed it with his hand. The few items listed were faded but still legible: milk, peaches, Pond's cold cream. He put his hand to his chest, found his own rapid, steady heartbeat. Bee had used that stuff, the Pond's. He remembered the green-lidded white jar on her dressing table, the smell of roses on her gleaming face and throat. How old *was* this receipt? The date wasn't readable, but the name of the store in the Vineyard was. Then he flipped the thing over and saw the telephone number scrawled there. It was only slightly blurry. That must have been a permanent marker rather than a pen that Ellen had borrowed from the checker.

Julie would say that this was a sign, and Mildred would probably back her up. Edward remained a pragmatist, though, even after finding what he had no longer been seeking, as if it had been seeking him. Serendipity brought about by mere random chance. Yet he remembered Laurel leaning toward him at the movie theater, asking if there was someone else, and he felt spooked by the notion of female intuition.

Bingo shuffled into the kitchen, and Edward reached down to stroke his head, careful not to touch the bad ear. "So, should I call her?" he said. He still hadn't resorted to conversing with animals; he was really only talking to himself, although he didn't appear to be any better than Bingo at coming up with an answer. So much time had gone by since he'd last seen Ellen. Maybe he'd missed his chance with her. He put the receipt back into his pocket and went out into the yard to work.

Crouching to lift and bag a pile of leaves, he remembered that when he was a boy and spent his allowance too quickly or foolishly, his father would say, "That money was burning a hole in your pocket." That was how Edward felt about the grocery receipt with Ellen's telephone number on it. It generated heat against his thigh, demanding his attention.

Still, he hesitated, remembering her cool demeanor at the market that July day, and holding Laurel in his arms this very morning. He had been careful not to commit himself to her, but that was mostly out of fear of being left again. Then why was he still thinking about Ellen? Maybe it *was* his turn to be selfish, even devious, but it didn't come naturally to him. And there was no one he could comfortably confide in and ask for advice.

Perversely, he believed that only Bee could have helped him straighten out his complicated feelings, and she had never been as absent as she was right then. Amy Weitz had said that the dead seem to hang around for a while, as if to guide and comfort us, and then slowly disappear into an unapproachable distance. How did we let them go?

Edward had only visited Bee's grave a few times since her death, and then it was to escort Julie, who'd asked him to go with her. He had held her while she bawled, and they'd weeded the ivied plot together, and laid a few small stones on the monument, like primitive visitor's cards, in the Jewish tradition. Edward had brought a handful of them from his own backyard. But he didn't really sense Bee there, in the cemetery, despite her name and dates etched into the polished granite, the terrible memory of the coffin being lowered into the freshly turned earth. She was elsewhere, she was nowhere.

He went back into the house and returned the remainder of the twine to the crazy drawer, but left the grocery receipt on the counter. Then he took Bingo out for a walk. The dog was going to die before long. All the panting he'd been doing lately wasn't due to the thermostat being set too high, as Edward had reasoned in his denial. And the uneven clatter of his ancient heart meant that it would probably suddenly stop. Still, he plodded from tree to bush to tree in his usual circuitous path, calmly attentive to business, and not for the first time, Edward felt as if he were the one being walked. He was already heavyhearted—he would miss Bingo's company, his unconditional canine devotion. Another living presence in the house. But the vet's words had gone right over that furry head. What separated man most notably from beast were language, the opposable thumb, and a knowledge of death. Oh, lucky dog!

He would have to prepare Mildred, though; it might happen on her watch. When he called to tell her, she said, "Yeah, I know." But she was referring to her observation of Bingo, not her psychic abilities. "He's been going downhill for a while," she said, "and they don't get much older than he is." She agreed with Sacco's advice to just let him be, as long as he wasn't uncomfortable.

For a crazy moment, Edward considered talking over his love life with Mildred—a neutral party, widowed herself, as he'd learned the day they'd had tea together. Someone basically practical, despite her paranormal dabbling, and trustworthy. But she was liable to break out her Tarot cards, or look for answers in the lines on his palm, and fortunately the moment passed. Like Julie, he was responsible for his own happiness.

As soon as he hung up, Edward glanced down at the receipt on the counter, and reached for the phone again. It rang before he could pick it up, startling him. He expected it would be Laurel, stopping him from his intention, instinctively or accidentally. They often spoke at about this time, when most couples he knew—as he and Bee had always done—convened to prepare supper, to have a drink together, and to review their respective days. The lonely hour, as he thought of it now, and he regretted not asking Laurel to come home with him.

But when he answered the phone, Sybil was on the other end. In typical Sybil fashion, she eschewed the formalities and got right to the point. Did he have paper and a pencil handy? Her cousin had asked her to give Edward her work number, so he and Laurel could arrange that visit to the conservation lab at the Met. He took a pencil from the mug on the counter, and after looking around in vain for something else to write on, he ended up reversing the receipt to its faintly printed side. "Shoot," he said, imagining himself framed in the sight of an executioner's gun.

Afterward, he poured himself some dry sherry and turned the receipt over and over in his hand until he chose a side and slapped it down on the counter. Then he picked up the phone again and punched in Ellen's number. A man answered and he hung up.

39

The Way We Live Now

During sixth period on Thursday, Edward was drawing a cross section of an animal cell on the blackboard: membrane, cytoplasm, nucleus, when the fire bell went off. It was cold and rainy, but they all had to leave the building immediately, without retrieving their jackets or slickers from lockers and closets. The headmaster's sonorous voice over the PA system reminded them of the protocol. Out on the street, the students shivered and rejoiced in the fate that had freed them temporarily from the tedium of academe.

As usual, there was no fire, but this wasn't just another drill, as Edward discovered in a quick conference with an eighth-grade dean. Someone had phoned in a bomb threat to the school, the third one since 9/11. They'd never found out who had called in the other two, although there was speculation: a student aspiring to new levels in telephone pranks, a disgruntled fired teacher, a crazy parent—it could have been anyone, really. And there were real bombs exploding somewhere every day. *The way we live now*, Edward thought as he herded his chattering, rain-soaked students in disorderly lines two blocks away from the police action. One girl held a page of notes over her head, its penned words dissolving into a blue blur.

It was another false alarm, they concluded, after the bomb squad had scoured the building. But by then the school day had ended, and the students were allowed to retrieve their belongings before being sent home. Edward erased the cell he'd been drawing on the blackboard, grabbed his briefcase, and headed for Englewood.

There was a message from Nick on the phone, asking Edward to stop by after dinner; he and Amanda had something to show him. There had been similar messages in the past, once to unveil a new car, he remembered, and once to surprise Bee and Edward with champagne and cake on their anniversary. He imagined he was going to be shown a sonogram picture this time, a swirly little black-and-white Rorschach in which one might discern a blip of new life, or pretend to, and he felt a buzz of anticipation, edged with sadness and something else he couldn't identify. Envy? Fear?

He did a quick calculation—the baby he and Bee hadn't been able to produce would be in college now. It wasn't like Edward to think this way, to sentimentalize something—somebody—that had never materialized. Even Bee hadn't done that. Despite her disappointment, she'd finally said, "But we have a lovely life just as we are, don't we?" She was thirty-eight by then, and her pregnancy with Julie had been difficult and tenuous. They decided not to seek medical intervention.

It wasn't the nonexistent child he mourned now, but those

months of hopeful lovemaking, their blinkered gaze fixed on the infinite, lucky future. And he wasn't afraid of moving up into the next generation, of making that leap toward the precipice. He was already almost there, even without a replacement in the wings. When his sister Catherine was pregnant with her first, their father had joked, "I don't mind becoming a grandfather, but I'm not crazy about sleeping with a grandmother." Well, that wouldn't be Edward's problem, or his pleasure.

But he envisioned telling people—Sybil and Henry, his friends at school and from the Vineyard—and the air of celebration. When had he last had any good news to share with anyone? What would Laurel think, or say? He stopped at a liquor store on his way to the kids' house and bought a bottle of chilled Taittinger, but he left it in the car, just in case the news didn't turn out to be what he'd expected. Maybe they were only going to show him a garden catalog and ask his advice about plantings, or roll out plans for finishing their basement, which Nick had been talking about for a while.

But there was Julie, peeking through the front window and waving at Edward, and when he went inside, Gladys was in the living room, too. The whole family hadn't been assembled to consult on some home improvement. "Close your eyes, everyone," Amanda ordered before she and Nick left the room. They all laughed, looking at each other like disobedient, scheming children. "I think I'm going to be an aunt," Julie whispered. Gladys took Edward's hand and squeezed it. "Be ready to call 911, honey," she said. "Surprises are dangerous at my age." Her bony hand was cold, but her grip was fierce.

Then Amanda and Nick came back in, and he was carrying a carton. "You can open your eyes now," Amanda said, although they were all staring at her and at the carton, which appeared to be shifting on its own in Nick's arms. "Voilà!" Amanda cried, and drew a white puppy from it, like a rabbit from a magician's hat. Gladys dropped Edward's hand and put it to her breast.

"This is Chanel, everybody," Amanda said. "Say hello, sweetie." The puppy was yipping and wriggling convulsively by then and Amanda dropped her into Julie's lap. The letdown Julie must have been experiencing seemed to be immediately replaced by her enchantment with the fluffy little dog. "Oh, look at you! Aren't you the *cutest*," she crooned, and Chanel reciprocated by lavishly licking Julie's face and neck.

"*Mazel tov*," Gladys said weakly.

Edward was glad he'd left the bottle in the car. He'd be damned if he'd break out good champagne for a French poodle.

"She's a bichon frise," Amanda said, as if she'd been reading his mind. "What do you think of her, Dad?"

Edward couldn't help himself. "I thought you weren't ready for a dog, for the responsibility," he said. He sounded as peeved as he felt. "That's why you couldn't take Bingo."

"That was such a long time ago," she said. "But we're ready now, right, Nick?"

Nick didn't look directly at her or at Edward. "Right," he said.

"And we thought we could ask what's-her-name, Mildred, to do some dog walking for us, too."

"Bingo and Chanel will be like cousins," Julie said, and Edward wondered if there was something wrong with her, if she was even more immature than he'd thought. He had planned on telling them all about Bingo's heart and his prognosis, but now the timing didn't seem right. Julie might even suggest that he get a puppy, too.

Amanda said, "Well, enjoy yourselves, we'll get some coffee," and she and Nick and the carton disappeared from view.

"A *dog*," Gladys said, the moment they were gone. "I was hoping . . . I thought we'd have someone to name for Mommy." Edward reached over and patted her arm.

"Poppy. Gladys," Julie said sternly, "we have to look happy for them."

"What are you talking about?" Edward asked her.

She shook her head at him and sighed, a teacher striving for patience with a slow pupil. "They probably can't get pregnant, and Chanel is just a consolation prize they've given themselves." She was cradling the puppy as if it were a baby, a role it seemed to enjoy.

"Oh," Edward said, chastened, and suddenly deeply admiring of Julie. She must have inherited some of her mother's natural instincts about human behavior. But he had a queer, pervasive sense of loss, too. Only hours ago, he'd stood in the rain near the school, contemplating children calling in bomb threats, and others carrying out actual bombings elsewhere. The animal cell erased from the blackboard, the words running from that girl's notepaper in the rain—an unlearning, the way we live now. It would be wanton to bring another hostage to fortune into this ephemeral, stupid world. So why did he feel so crestfallen?

Amanda and Nick came back inside. He set down a tray and went to Gladys and knelt before her. "I almost forgot," he said. "We have something else to show you." And he took a black-and-white picture from his shirt pocket and put it into her waiting hand.

40

The *Missing* Piece

Gladys didn't work on jigsaw puzzles to fuel her aging brain. She'd begun doing them as a young housewife—a break from marriage and mothering that required her concentration, but not her heart—and there was always one in progress on the bridge table in her living room. Bee had learned her colors and flower names from a botanical gardens puzzle, and there was a half-finished replica of the Rockefeller Center ice rink on the table when Edward came to tell Gladys about Bee's illness. Before he could speak, his glance fell on a twirling skater in a fur-trimmed red skirt, a dizzying image that stayed in his head for a long time afterward. He never saw that particular puzzle again, though, or any other at Gladys's apartment until Nick and Amanda brought her a new one as a ninety-first birthday gift, and sat down with her to get it started.

They'd all gotten into the habit when they visited of working a bit on whatever puzzle was under way. If the frame wasn't finished, they could look for a straight-edged piece or two to add—easy gratification—or try to join some of the scattered center pieces to one another and then look for a home for them. Julie had the least patience and perhaps the worst eye for the parts that might mesh. When she was little, she tried to force incompatible pieces together, bending them out of shape, and when they still wouldn't fit she insisted the puzzle was "broken."

Gladys told Edward that you could tell a lot about people by the way they approached the challenge of a dismantled picture. Bee had a wonderful sense of order, even at an early age. The frame had to be complete before she'd attempt to go any further. Nicky was good at seeing the whole in the parts, but he was careless in his execution and pieces went missing whenever he was around, to be found later under a sofa cushion or in the vacuum cleaner bag, or never seen again.

"What about me?" Edward asked Gladys as they sat side by side, trying to fill in the middle section of a safari puzzle. He was grateful for nature's patterns—zebra stripes and leopard spots—camouflage in the jungle, and clues for the would-be puzzle solver.

"You," she said, "are a good partner." She went on to say that he didn't grab all the easy fill-ins, or act too cocky about solving a difficult space.

But he believed that she was referring to him as a husband, as her lost daughter's partner, and he savored the balm of her approval. He had been considering telling her something about his dating, about Laurel, a low-key version of the truth to ease her into the idea of his wanting to be part of a couple again. Instead he said, "That's such good news about the baby, isn't it?"

"Yes! But between you and me, I couldn't make out a thing on that picture, even with my magnifying glass. And Amanda kept saying, 'See, there's the head, there's the foot!' I had to fake it. I hope they didn't catch on."

Edward found a place for the puzzle piece in his hand, completing a monkey almost hidden in a tree. "You're an excellent faker," he said. "And sonograms are hard to read, especially so early, when you're really just looking at a cluster of cells."

"They didn't have such things when I was carrying Beattie. And in those days, women weren't taught how to breathe—we just screamed, until they gave you something. Off to dreamland! Then I woke up and someone, a nurse, said, 'Hello, Mother.' "

Edward smiled. "Were you hoping for a girl?" he asked.

"I didn't care, so long as it was healthy. You didn't know until the baby came out what it was, which I forgot to ask—can you believe it? I heard that little cry, like a chicken, and I said, 'Does it have everything?' And the doctor—Weisman was his name, a regular wise guy—said, " 'Everything but a handle, it's a girl!' "

"You must have been very happy," Edward said.

"Oh, honey, it was the best day of my life."

"She was beautiful?"

"Well, not exactly. She took her time coming out, so her head was kind of peanut-shaped at first. I thought: *Lucky I can make hats*. And she had this hair on her shoulders, like a little fur cape!" She raised the magnifying glass to the puzzle. "Like that monkey. But thank God it fell out! And then she was beautiful."

They sat in silence for a few minutes, until Gladys said, "So, what's new with you, besides becoming a grandfather?"

"Me?" Edward said. She'd given him a perfect cue, but his courage flagged. Gladys couldn't imagine him outside the family frame into which she and Julie had pulled him that fateful day. "Surprises are dangerous at my age," she'd warned at Nick and Amanda's. She was only being playful then, but now she looked especially frail. "Not much," he said. "You know, gardening, school—that same old gang: Mendel, Burbank, Linnaeus . . . My birds."

Although he hadn't been back to Greenbrook since he'd returned from the Vineyard. And when he'd finally gotten around to refilling his own bird feeders, the neglected birds swooped down from everywhere—the trees, the rooftops, the sky. Like the women coming out of the woodwork after Bee died.

"And you have lots of friends," Gladys said, as if she were encouraging a shy child.

"I do," he said, "and they're all happy about my news."

After he'd called Catherine, who wept with joy about Amanda's pregnancy, he called Peggy and Ike Martin in Boston, remembering to ask after their little granddaughter, the one whose gender Ellen had identified for him. In what he tried to pass off as an afterthought, he inquired about Ellen, too, and was told that she and her husband had reconciled.

Of course that was what he'd assumed, while holding out some dim hope that it was her grown son or some other relative or friend who'd answered the phone the evening that Edward called and hung right up. Ellen had described her situation as a trial separation, so maybe this was only a trial reconciliation he could wait out. Who did he think he was he kidding? Seize the woman was what he should have done. But how many women did he need?

Only one, if the one he had wasn't so weirdly possessive and elusive at once, if he could trust that she would stay, and that he wanted her to. He was in the ridiculous bind of avoiding complete closeness with Laurel at least partly out of fear of being deserted by her again. But would she leave precisely because he was so wary of commitment? He was too old—almost a grandfather!—for the games of courtship, especially when he wasn't certain of the rules, or even if there were any.

When Edward had told Frances and Bernie about Amanda, they'd congratulated and teased him, but they both seemed more interested in Laurel. So was Sybil, despite her pretended indifference. In a follow-up phone call to the one giving Edward Olga's phone number, she asked if he and his "friend" had set up an appointment yet to visit Ollie at the Met. Sybil, who had an opinion about everyone and everything, didn't say another word about Laurel—a pointed omission. And when he announced Amanda and Nick's news, she said, "That's lovely, Edward. Bee would have been so thrilled."

But Laurel's reaction was the one he had wondered about the most, and all she'd said was, "I'm very glad for you." Like a detective, or a paranoid lover, he'd tried to decode some hidden message in that simple and apparently sincere phrase, and didn't find any. She really wished him well. But when he asked her about going to the Met with him, she said, "That sounds like more than we need to know, doesn't it? I mean, the glory is in the tapestries themselves."

"Is this part of the trees or the underbrush?" Gladys asked, startling him out of his reverie. He took the puzzle piece she'd proffered and tried to lay it here and there until it finally slipped neatly into place.

41

Glory

Laurel was right—the glory was in the tapestries—but Edward, who'd always been interested in process, was still curious about how they'd been restored to that glory. So one Friday afternoon after school, he went across town to see Olga and Elliot in their lab at the museum. Elliot met him in the lobby and escorted him to the private work area upstairs. Edward felt privileged, the way he had as a small child when his father had taken him behind the scenes at the post office, where the enormous stacks of mail being sorted and sent out gave him his first sense of the vast, populated world beyond their Queens neighborhood. That room, in his memory, was as large and imposing and well lit as the textile conservation lab at the Met.

There was less activity here, though. Two men sat at a table sorting through skeins of yarn from the palest pink to a deep plum, and a few women stood before a horizontal frame, examining the religious tapestry, a nativity scene, laid across it. "This one had bad repair work done somewhere else, long ago," Elliot said. He had Edward look through a standing magnifier, while he pointed to a section of the Virgin's hair that seemed to have resulted from a botched salon dye job. "We'll have to undo that first."

Next, they went past a large shallow tank where a tapestry lay under water being cleansed. It reminded Edward of the pre-digital days when student photographers' work would come into focus in developing fluid in Fenton's darkroom. Then Elliot said, "There's our Penelope," and Olga waved to them from her station at another, smaller frame on the other side of the room, where she resumed moving a long needle threaded in green wool in and out of what appeared to be a heavily worn tapestry.

As they came closer, Edward saw that it had a heraldic motif, and was missing most of its central area. That was where Olga, in a white lab coat, was plying her needle. After they'd greeted each other, he watched her work for a while, which she seemed to be doing from memory, or inspiration. When she looked up again, he asked, "How can you reconstruct what's lost without a blueprint?"

"It's something like a jigsaw puzzle, without the picture on the box to guide you."

The ice skater in the fur-trimmed red skirt twirled by behind Edward's eyes. "Then how do you know what's missing?" he said.

Elliot answered. "We look at other tapestries that may have been part of the same series or came from the same studio, and at paintings from the period," he said.

"There are repeated themes, objects, colors," Olga added. "Some of it's fairly easy, some just educated guessing."

"Easy for you, Leonardo," Edward said, earning a smile

from her. She told him that large, important tapestries, like the Burgos at the Cloisters, could take decades to restore, and that when it was finally hung there, members of the restoration team applauded and some even wept. Edward was moved, imagining the scene. The long patience, he thought, in art as in science.

When some of the other lab workers started to leave for the day, he asked if he could take Elliot and Olga out for an early dinner. But Elliot had paperwork to attend to and begged off. "Another time," he said to Edward before heading to an office down the hall.

Olga and Edward had a brief discussion about where to go. "There are a few places right in the building," she said. "Even the cafeteria food is pretty good, and I have my employee's discount." Good food or not, Edward didn't want an assembly-line meal. And he'd already staked out a few small, appealing restaurants on and off Madison Avenue. "It's my treat," he reminded her, "and don't you want to get out of here?"

They stepped out of the museum into a stunning spring afternoon, a blend of intense sunlight and temperate, dry air that you had to comment on, not just enjoy, even if that comment, on Olga's part, was only a deep breath, almost a gasp of pleasure. The steps of the museum were littered with people relishing the weather or simply felled by the beauty of it. "Let's stay here for a little while," Olga said, "okay? Let's join the tourists."

She found a place for them on a middle tier, away from the handrails, where museum visitors streamed up and down, and Edward sat down next to her. "I haven't done this in years," he said, leaning back on his elbows and turning his face upward.

"Sometimes we have lunch out here. Greasy, garlicky vendor hot dogs, ice-cold Orange Crush, dining alfresco. Heaven."

He looked at her, shading his eyes. She'd left her lab coat upstairs and was wearing what appeared to be a vintage silk dress, with a low waistline and a pattern of cherries. Gladys, Edward imagined, would say she had "style." Yet her eyeglasses were smudged, and there was a piece of green lint in her short russet hair. He stopped himself from reaching to pluck it out. "Do you and Elliot live nearby?"

She seemed amused. "Well, I live on the Upper West Side, near Amsterdam. Elliot is up in the Bronx."

"Oh," Edward said.

"Did Sybil give you the impression that we were a couple?"

"Actually, yes."

Olga sighed. "She never gives up, does she?"

"Pardon?" Edward said.

"She was trying to make you jealous. At our age! And then you and Laurel foiled her plans."

"So, Elliot and you . . . ?"

"Old friends, colleagues. We met in grad school, I think we told you that. But no sparks, ever, except in my cousin's fertile imagination. Elliot's divorced, and I'm a fifty-eight-year-old spinster lady."

They sat in silence for a few minutes and then Olga said, "You and I started off on the wrong foot because of her, didn't we? Hate at first sight."

"I wouldn't say that," Edward said.

She laughed. "Wouldn't you?"

"Well, not hate, exactly. More like . . . cautious animosity."

"You looked as miserable as I felt."

"My wife had died earlier that year. She was Sybil's best friend—it seemed like a betrayal."

"No wonder. What was she thinking? And I was just out of a bad situation—not feeling that crazy about men in general. Sybil's timing is lousy, and she's shameless in her scheming, but she truly believes in her mission. She can't stand for anyone to be lonely."

"Are you? Lonely, I mean. Wait, I take that back, it was an intrusive question."

"It was, but I'll tell you, anyway. I am, sometimes, but not always. There are advantages to living alone. You can sing loudly and, in my case, off key. You can hog the bed. I wear a ratty old nightgown that I still love. And, besides, hell really often *is* other people."

Edward glanced at the strangers scattered around them, with their street maps and bottled water. They all seemed completely benign—art lovers, sun worshipers, like Olga, like himself. Then he thought back to some of the dates he'd had since Bee's death. "Yeah, hell just about sums it up." Of course, that pretty well summed up loneliness, too.

"How long have you and Laurel been together?" Olga asked.

"About a million years, on and off," he said. Then, "I'm getting hungry, aren't you? Would you like to go someplace else?"

"Sure. My rear end is starting to get numb, anyway."

They ended up at one of the bistros Edward had checked out earlier, taking the last empty table. After their drinks came, he said, "So why do you despise the Garden State?"

"I don't despise it," she said. "It's just that I love the city, city life."

"Don't you miss nature?"

"What's wrong with Central Park?" She sounded a little testy, the way she had the first time they met. "I walk through it to work on nice days, on days like this. I get my fill of greenness."

"Hey, I like the park, too. And I used to live in the city, in Hell's Kitchen, a long time ago."

"How about Laurel?"

"She's in Chelsea now." He believed she was asking him something else, though. "We lived together for a while when we were much younger," he said.

She sipped her drink and waited, as if he'd only paused in the middle of a long story, which he had.

"We were going to get married then. But she left me stranded."

Olga didn't say anything, and Edward just sat there, taken aback by his own candor—he hardly knew this woman—and that he didn't feel the usual discomfort attached to that ancient event. That was the thing—it *was* ancient history, just as he'd once reminded Laurel. Then why had he held on to it this long, using it as a shield against her? "Sybil and Henry don't know about any of that," he said.

"Don't worry, I won't tell them. I never give Sybil any ammunition."

"What do you mean?"

"That she hasn't given up on *us* as a possibility, that imbecile. That she'd consider your history with Laurel as a strike against her, compared with my immaculate past."

"Is your past immaculate?" he asked.

"Only in Sybil's eyes. Of course, I don't tell her lots of things."

Now it was Edward's turn to wait, and it didn't take long. "Well, for one thing, I dated a married man," Olga said.

His heart spiked and fell. He remembered Laurel's blunt statements about her married lover, how she'd gone to his house when his wife was away. "Was that your bad situation, just before we met?" he said.

"Oh, God, no. It was back in graduate school, in Philadelphia, and he was a visiting professor, from the Midwest. He went home for holiday breaks and on occasional weekends, ostensibly to see his ailing mother. I was so dumb, I didn't realize for almost a year that he was married."

"And then you broke it off?"

"Yes."

Their food was served and Edward looked down at his plate, as if he'd forgotten what he'd ordered.

"I thought you were hungry," Olga said.

"I was. I *am.*" He picked up his fork and poked at his pasta. "This looks delicious," he said. But he was picturing Olga, lying in the middle of her bed in a tattered nightgown, singing at the top of her lungs.

42

Lying in Bed

Edward spent the weekend in Englewood, this time because Laurel had plans of her own in the city, with a friend visiting from Phoenix. He kept himself busy, puttering around the house and the garden, and even spent a couple of hours down in the basement, examining various fibers under the microscope. A bit of wool pulled from an old sweater appeared crimped and covered with overlapping scales, like a fish. The crimping, he knew, was what caused woolen fabrics to retain air and heat. Olga had said that those ancient tapestries were practical as well as decorative, that they'd also served as insulation against the cold. The sweater felt warm in Edward's hands.

Lying in bed alongside Laurel on Monday night, while she flipped through the channels on the muted TV, he told her about his visit to the museum, without mentioning his dinner afterward with Olga. It was beside the point, really, an omission rather than a lie. He expected her to be curious about what he'd seen and learned at the conservation lab, despite her reluctance to go there with him, but her interest lay elsewhere. "Were they both there?" she asked, without glancing away from the flickering screen.

"Elliot and Olga?" he said. "Yes, of course. They gave me the grand tour. It's pretty amazing, really painstaking work. Like adding another layer to history, one stitch at a time."

"They seem like a pretty tight couple, don't they?" Laurel said.

His own assumption about them, fostered by Sybil's carefully fabricated hints. This time he did lie. "I don't know," he said. "We concentrated on the tapestries, not on their personal lives."

He asked about Laurel's weekend with her friend. "We hit the usual hot spots," she said. "The Empire State Building, Chinatown, Bloomingdale's."

"Did you buy anything?" Sometimes she gave him a private, provocative little fashion show of new clothing that usually ended up with her purchases, tags still attached, in a pile on the floor, and Laurel naked beside him in bed.

She sighed. "Everything was too expensive," she said, "and designed for twelve-year-olds."

"Let me buy you something tomorrow," he said, "as an advance on your birthday present. I'll help you pick it out."

Laurel looked at him. Her birthday was months away, and he hated shopping almost as much as she enjoyed it.

His offer surprised him, too, for the very same reasons, but suddenly he'd been infused with feeling for her. He wanted to please and protect her the way he had when they were young and she'd been unhappy about one thing or another. "You can try it on for me later, and then you can take it off for me," he said. He took the remote from her hand and shut off the TV. Then he kissed her, and after a beat or two, she began to kiss him back.

He was aroused, as he always was with her, but for the first time in their long history he was unable to do much about it. "I'm sorry, Lulu," he said, and heard an echo in his head of his apology to Sylvia Smith on their one misbegotten date. He'd been metaphorical about it then, in his embarrassment, claiming to have lost his "concentration." And in her disappointment she was both caustic and kind.

Now he said, "Maybe I had too much wine with dinner," although they'd each had only a single glassful at a local Chinese restaurant. And then, "Do they use MSG in that place?" When she didn't respond, he added, "Or else old age is catching up with me."

"My old age, or yours?" she said.

"You're gorgeous, you know that. I love your body." A passionate truth, and one she liked to hear. He knew that this was the moment to say something else, something larger and more encompassing, like *I love you,* but he held back. It was too easy and too difficult at once. Instead, he said, "May I have a rain check?" And he tried to kiss her again, but she reached across him to the night table on his side of the bed for the remote and turned the TV back on, without the mute this time.

In the morning, he made up for his failure the night before. He was almost late for work because she held on to him for such a long time afterward. When he was getting dressed, she was still in bed, tangled in the sheets, observing him. "Were you thinking about her?" she asked.

Edward stood still, his hand poised at a button on his shirt. His heart banged against it. "About who?" he said.

"Your wife, of course. Who else?"

"Do you mean when I was making love to you?"

"Yes. And when you couldn't."

He hadn't brought Bee into Laurel's bed, which would have dishonored both of them. He sat down next to her and took her hand. "No, never," he said. "I'm with you now."

"When I was in your house," Laurel said, "I could feel her presence."

"Well, that's only natural. She lived there, it was her home. But there's nobody here but us chickens."

She reached up and pulled him down to her. He pressed his mouth to her neck; her skin was warm, almost feverish, and she smelled of sleep and sex. "Play hooky today, *mon cher*," she whispered. "Stay here with me."

"You know I can't," he said. "I have a roomful of kids dying to hear about the anatomy of the frog. But I'll see you later, okay?"

That afternoon, he met her at one of the designer shops in Saks, where a couple of other men of a certain age sat on strategically placed upholstered chairs, waiting for their female companions to emerge from the dressing rooms. One old guy, with several shopping bags at his feet, drooped in his seat, snoring softly. Bee had spared Edward this sort of expedition, knowing that it bored him and made him feel self-conscious. And aside from her flea market treasure hunts, she wasn't that enamored of shopping, either.

After Laurel disappeared with a salesclerk, he plunked himself down in an available chair with his briefcase and watched women rifling through the clothing racks as if they were searching for something they'd misplaced. The snoozing man across from him had slumped even lower, and Edward, who was growing drowsy, himself, in this carpeted, windowless environment, idly wondered if anybody ever died in one of these places, and if the body was carted discreetly away.

Then his mind drifted to the classroom, to the charts he had pulled down that day of the frog's highly developed nervous system, so similar to a human's, and of its digestive and reproductive organs. He'd explained that the male frog has vocal cords enabling him to croak, a noise that attracts the female during the rainy breeding season. "Ribbit, ribbit," one of the boys had intoned, while a couple of girls snickered and tossed their long hair. Edward's rambling train of thought struck him as mildly funny in his sluggish state—old men croaking in department stores as they waited for their women to reappear, and frogs croaking in the rain for the attentions of the opposite sex. Boys and girls . . . Of course he was soon asleep, too.

Laurel tapped him on the shoulder. "*Chéri,*" she said. "What do you think of this one?"

Edward opened his eyes. She was wearing a simple shimmery black dress, and she walked slowly up and down before him, like a model on a runway. How pretty she was! "It's perfect," he said. "Let's get it."

She stepped closer to him, while the saleswoman stood at a tactful distance, and wiggled the price tag near his face. "*Soldes,*" Laurel whispered, which meant that the thing was on sale, but still sounded like a foregone conclusion, an auctioneer's final word. Edward patted his pockets for his reading glasses, but remembered they were in his crowded briefcase, and he didn't want to fumble through it while Laurel and the saleswoman watched and waited. As he pulled out his credit card and hoped for the best, he noticed that the sleeping old man across from him was gone.

43

Urgent Personal Business

Bingo died in his sleep at home—what most people would consider a "good death," if there actually was such a thing. But even modest canine pleasures, like meals and walks and rolling around in a pile of dry leaves, seemed significant to Edward in their termination. And he felt worse than he'd expected. That terrible sensation of loss after Bee's death, from which he'd so slowly recovered, was revisited. Not in the same way, of course; the ache was more diffuse and not constant, but it also evoked a second round of grief for her. Without casseroles this time, or a bereavement group, and only a modicum of sympathy from friends. Bingo was just an animal, after all, and he was very old. Nature had taken its course.

It happened on a Wednesday night, and Edward took the rest of the week off from school, citing urgent personal business.

Then he canceled the plans for Thursday and Friday that he'd made with Laurel. "Poor Edward," she said, when he called with the news.

"Poor Bingo, actually," he replied, remembering her uneasiness around the dog.

"Why don't I come out to see you?" she said.

"I'm not great company right now," he told her. "And there are things I have to take care of."

"But don't you want someone to cheer you up?"

"You're sweet," he said, "but, no, really, I'm fine."

He had the body cremated and let the vet dispose of the ashes. Nick and Amanda commiserated with Edward together on the phone, while their dog yipped frantically in the background. Only Mildred and Julie paid condolence calls that evening. Mildred pulled out the vacuum cleaner in the middle of her visit and cleared the rugs and furniture of dog hair. When she left, she took the few battered rubber toys and the food and water bowls with her.

By the time Julie arrived, only the leash and collar were left, enough to set off an anguished moan from her. Edward supposed she was lamenting the puppy she'd once considered her own, or feeling guilty about so carelessly abandoning him later. Maybe Bingo's death was a reminder of her own mortality. *Margaret, are you grieving . . .*, he thought. But her sorrow wasn't just for herself. "Poppy, now you're all alone!" she cried.

He could have assured her that he wasn't, really, but he didn't think this was the right time to tell her about Laurel, although if she were there, as she'd wanted to be, no explanations would have been necessary. He maneuvered the conversation to Julie's life—her job, her boyfriends. She was thinking of applying to law school, something Bee had encouraged her to do. And money her mother had left her would help make that possible.

"That sounds good," Edward said, with cautious optimism; Julie had considered law school in the past.

She was still seeing both Andrew and Todd, and she'd gone on a blind date the week before. No one had asked her to be exclusive, she said, and she didn't want to limit her options right now. Edward tried not to appear as impatient and judgmental as he felt. Anything he said might tip her in the wrong direction.

After she was gone, he checked his email, and beneath the ads from Sears and Staples and Amazon, there was a letter from Olga. "Edward," she'd written, "Sybil told me about your dog, and then cleverly offered your email address, but believe me I'm not doing her bidding. I intended to write, anyway, to say how sorry I am. It's what you bargain for when you get a dog, I guess, but some of us never learn. Thanks again for that fine dinner last week. My best to you and Laurel. Olga"

Before he went to bed that night, he wrote back to say that he'd enjoyed having dinner with her, too. He thanked her for allowing him that special visit to the conservation lab, and for her kind note about Bingo. Did she still have a dog?

A question begs an answer, and early the following morning there was one. She had a seven-year-old pug, a heavy breather named Josie, for the Empress Josephine, whose own pug was said to have carried secret messages to Napoleon in prison. What breed had Bingo been?

Just a mutt, he wrote back, or a composite, to quote Mark Twain. And that was that.

Edward checked the computer for new messages a couple of times before he had coffee. He deleted a fresh round of ads and took a shower. He began to regret not having gone in to work now that his "urgent personal business" was finished. His students would be tormenting some pitiful substitute teacher by now.

And it was another dazzling spring day, too good to waste moping around indoors. He put his birding journal and binoculars in his backpack and started to drive to Greenbrook. But as soon as he got onto the parkway, the traffic slowed, and then kept stopping and starting; there seemed to be an accident ahead. Edward remembered what Olga had said about Central Park, about getting her fill of greenness there. It was an excellent birding site, too. He got off at the next exit and headed south, toward the bridge.

He found a garage on 84th Street between Park and Lexington and started walking in the direction of the park. As he was approaching Fifth Avenue, he thought of calling Laurel—how surprised and pleased she'd be—to ask her to meet him. That evening, he imagined, she would wear the terrific little black dress he'd bought for her at Saks, at what had turned out to be an astonishingly high reduced price. He'd even taken his phone from his pocket, but then he saw the museum, with its brilliant banners and populated steps, and he put the phone away and changed course.

Edward chose a place for himself close to where he'd sat with Olga. The steps were sun-warmed as they'd been the previous Friday, and the only birds in sight were the freeloading pigeons, pecking and cooing around his feet. Again he closed his eyes and turned his face upward. He could hear people nearby speaking in German or Dutch, laughing, and he remembered lying in bed as a boy, listening to his parents talking in the next room, in what had seemed like a foreign language when he was on the verge of sleep. He didn't know how long he'd been sitting there when he felt himself cast in shadow. "Hey, what are you doing here?" someone said. When he opened his eyes, Elliot Willets was standing above him.

This time Elliot asked Edward to join him for a meal, for

lunch, right there on the steps. He said that Ollie would be down in a few minutes, too. By the time the two men had climbed back up the steps with hot dogs and soft drinks, Olga was sitting and waiting for them in what she'd described the week before as heaven. She didn't seem as startled as Elliot had been to see Edward. "Hello," she said. "Do you have a reservation?"

44

My Old Flame

After lunch, they strolled into the park, where pedestrians, bicyclists, and skateboarders went by in a constant stream, as if everyone in the world was a truant from obligation. "Green enough for you?" Olga asked Edward, her tone like a poke in his ribs. The lawns and the foliage were intensely green—the word *verdant* came to mind.

"Milady considers this her own private garden," Elliot said, "but she deigns to let the peasants in."

"Gee, thanks, Ollie," Edward said. Her nickname had just slipped out. "Nice place you have here. Who's your landscaper?"

"Oh, Cézanne, most of the time. Sometimes Sisley."

Elliot and Olga couldn't venture too far or stay very long; they had to return to work, and Edward was torn between walking back with them to the Met to look at some actual Cézannes and Sisleys, and going farther into the park. Finally, nature won out over renderings of nature, and he shook hands with the other two and followed the path he was on for a while, then veered off to the left and kept on going.

He used to know Central Park pretty well when he lived in the city. He and Laurel had picnicked in the Sheep Meadow, and attended concerts and performances of Joe Papp's Shakespeare in the Park. *Twelfth Night* under the stars! And they'd cheered together for the Fenton soccer team on one of the playing fields.

Now Edward wandered around and found Cleopatra's Needle again, and gazed up at that imposing statue of the king of Poland on his horse. Then he went looking and listening for the birds. There were many to be found that afternoon: a magnolia warbler singing in couplets, a couple of rose-breasted grosbeaks, thrushes and wrens—and whole families of Canada geese and mallards floating on Turtle Pond, where dragonflies and damselflies darted and hung suspended in air. All of those creatures, even the common house sparrows and rock pigeons, gave Edward a sense of peace and pleasure. He sat under a tree on the low stone wall near the pond and entered them in his journal, adding a few notes about the park itself.

Then he took out his cell phone. There were two missed calls, both of them from Laurel, but she hadn't left any messages. The phone had vibrated in his pocket a couple of times while he was sitting on the museum steps having lunch, and he'd chosen to ignore it. Now he dialed Laurel's number. "Edward," she said, "I've been trying to reach you. Where have you been?"

"You didn't leave a message," he said.

"Of course I did, two of them, in fact."

"You mean at home?"

"Well, that's where I *thought* you were, where you *said* you'd be."

"I know," he said. "But I changed my mind; I'm in the city, actually."

"Oh? Did you decide to go to work?"

"No, I came in to do some birding, to take my mind off things."

"But when did you get in, and where are you?"

"I'm in Central Park." But as he said it, he didn't picture any of the good times they'd had there when they were young. He just saw himself being chased by her that day at MoMA, and ending up under a similar tree in similar flickering sunlight. "I'm feeling better," he said, although she hadn't asked. He might have been referring to that other time, to his gradual recovery from overwhelming rage and misery. "And I want to see you," he added.

There was a brief dead silence, and he wondered if the connection had been lost. "Laurel?" he said.

"I'm still here," she said, seeming to convey a lifetime of waiting.

"Shall I come downtown?" he asked.

Another silence before she said, "I made other plans, but I suppose I could change them."

Edward had a rush of remorse. He'd been selfish, unfair, keeping her at the end of a string he could pull or loosen at will. And she'd been pretty patient with him, for Laurel. Was he still just being cautious, or was he punishing her for past sins without admitting it, even to himself? "I don't want to mess up your plans," he said.

"It's all right, I guess," she said. "Why don't you come by about seven?"

Edward looked at his watch. It was just past three thirty. He'd hoped to ransom his car from the garage and drive downtown, where he might have been lucky enough to find a parking spot on the street. His back was beginning to ache and he felt tired. He wanted to take a hot shower and lie on Laurel's bed with her. They could have napped together afterward before going out to dinner. That morning he'd imagined her in the little black dress, but he was wearing chinos and a faded old T-shirt. He looked down at his clunky, scuffed hiking boots. And he'd neglected to shave for the last couple of days. He hadn't really thought any of it through, and then he'd made that detour to the museum.

Now he had to kill over three hours. He considered finding a movie in the neighborhood to fill the time, or checking to see if Frances or Bernie was at Bruno's. The Met was still open, so he could have gone back there, but none of those options really appealed to him. When he'd finished talking to Laurel, he called Julie at her midtown office and asked if she could take a long coffee break in half an hour or so. She was as surprised as Laurel had been to discover that he was in the city, but she sounded much happier to hear from him. "Sure," she said. "It's Friday, so my boss is long gone. I'll meet you at the Starbucks on the corner."

He had to put his car in another garage a few blocks from the Starbucks, and he was dragging his feet by the time he got there. She was waiting for him, sipping from some elaborate frozen concoction at a table against the wall. "Poppy!" she called. When he approached, she rose and kissed his cheek with cold, foamy lips. "Ouch, you need a shave," she said. "And you look like a mountain man."

"The birds didn't mind," he said. He ordered coffee for himself and a pastry they could share and sat across from her.

Before she could begin their usual chitchat, or a litany of the highlights and low moments of her life, he said, "Jules, I want to tell you something."

She put her hand to her breast. "You're not sick or anything, are you?" she said. Her face paled, the way it had in those moments right before he'd told her about Bee.

"No, no. I'm as healthy as a horse." What a stupid expression. And why was he reduced to clichés? He merely wanted to open up a little, to stop treating her like the needy child she no longer was. "It's good news, really. I've started dating again."

"You have?" she said. "Well, that *is* good news. Anybody I know?" Now she clapped her forehead. "That was dumb. I don't know anybody you could date, do I?" Before he could answer, she said, "So, are you exclusive?"

Another stupid expression. Edward thought of a realtor's FOR SALE sign on a lawn in his Englewood neighborhood, offering the property as a "co-exclusive." He didn't know how to respond. He hadn't been seeing anyone besides Laurel, but they'd never discussed an official arrangement. Maybe it was about time. Yet shouldn't he talk to Laurel about it first?

"Not really, not yet," he said. "But the woman I'm seeing later is someone . . . well, not someone you know, exactly, but you spoke to her once on the phone."

Julie looked blankly at him for an instant and then she cried, "Your old flame, Laura!"

A riff of that wonderful standard came into his head: *My old flame, I can't even think of her name* . . . He didn't bother correcting Julie; she'd get it right eventually. "That was a very long time ago," he said, implying that the flame wasn't eternal, that it may have burned itself out. "But yeah."

Julie wasn't deterred by his reticence. "Still . . . ," she said. Then, "Hey, we could double-date sometime!"

He almost burst into laughter, but she was serious. So he smiled and said, “Maybe, we’ll see,” that old tactic he and Bee always used with Julie whenever she’d wanted something—a pony, her own telephone line, a nose ring—they weren’t inclined to let her have. It seemed to still work; she allowed him to change the subject.

45

Eden

Laurel was wearing a terry-cloth robe when Edward arrived, with nothing on underneath. And when he kissed her, she seemed to like the rasp of his unshaven face; at least she stroked his jaw before she ordered him to make himself presentable. The bathroom was still steamy and fragrant from her shower, and he whistled and sang as he shed his clothes, as he let the water pummel the stiffness from his shoulders and back. He sang something in French that she'd once taught him, a children's song about rain and frogs and snails. Then he burst into "The Marseillaise" and finished with a medley of old ballads, including "My Old Flame" and "The Very Thought of You."

Sometimes, when he shaved, she sat on the edge of the tub or the closed toilet seat to keep him company. Now, when he lathered up and called, "Lulu, come in here, I miss you!" there was no answer. Maybe she was on the phone or in the bedroom with the door closed. Maybe she'd dozed off in there waiting for him. But when he came out of the bathroom with a towel wrapped around his middle, she was standing in the living room, dressed in jeans and a shirt. She was even wearing shoes. "Did I take too long?" he asked. A hopeless, pointless question, he knew, as soon as he saw her face, its bloodless pallor, the hard set of her mouth. "What's wrong?" he said. "Laurel?"

She didn't answer. That's when he noticed his backpack on the floor at her feet, with everything spilled out of it—the binoculars, his thermos and keys. He was sure he had left it on the bed. The birding journal was in her hand. "Hey," he said. "What's going on?"

"When were you planning to tell me?" she said. She spoke through gritted teeth, as if she were trying to throw her voice.

"What? Tell you what?"

She thrust the journal at him, and it fell with a little thud between them. When he bent to pick it up, his towel fell off. He had never felt so naked in his life. He clutched the towel against himself as he reached again for the journal. Several pages were curled and creased; a couple of them were ripped. "Hey," he said again, as much in bewilderment as in protest. "Wait," he told her. "Just wait a second, okay?" Then he went back to the bathroom and got dressed as quickly as he could.

When he came out, she was still standing in the same place, in the same position, but quivering now, like a taut, plucked wire. He wouldn't have been surprised if her body began to hum. His first impulse was to reach for her, but she jerked away from him. "Don't touch me!" she cried, as if he'd approached her with a blowtorch.

He held the journal, flipping through the damaged pages, looking for a clue to her fury. The names of birds flashed by like birds themselves—*thrushes, warblers, waxwings, flickers.* References to trees and to the weather, to drizzle and snow and sunlight. A page came completely away from the binding as he turned it. He stared at it and then at Laurel.

"Her private *garden*, Edward?" she said. "That's quite a euphemism."

"What?" he said. But he knew what she was alluding to. It was the last thing he'd written as he sat on the wall at Turtle Pond, in that euphoric moment just before he checked his cell phone for messages. "Ollie's private garden is beautiful, Eden, really. So glad she let me in."

He said, "That's not what that means." He tried to sound calm, reasonable, even amused. A silly misunderstanding! But his heart clamored and the hand holding the loose page trembled. He probably would have failed a lie detector test on the subject. "I was writing about Central Park," he added faintly.

Laurel snorted. "You must think I'm an idiot, Edward. How long has it been going on?"

"Nothing's going on. I swear it."

"You saw her today, didn't you?"

He might have lied about that, but he didn't. "Yes," he said. "We ran into each other, accidentally. Elliot was there, too. We all had lunch on the steps of the museum. Hot dogs." As if that homely detail bore out his story.

"Lunch! Ha-ha. You are such a fucking liar," she said. "You and your fucking whore! That's why you needed a shower in such a hurry. Is what's-his-name her cover? He's gay, isn't he, with his precious weavings and his unicorns. Tell me, is your dog actually dead?"

"Christ! Stop it! You're hysterical. You don't even know what you're saying."

"You waited a very long time to get even with me, didn't

you? You have the patience of a saint. That's how everyone thinks of you, I'll bet. Saint Edward, who got left in the lurch by his bitchy bride. That poor, holier-than-thou victim."

"Laurel, come on, this is madness." It was; he was certain of that. All the evidence was before him, and he couldn't look away: the things she'd done and said, the diagnosis spelled out in Bee's mental handbook, the warnings from his friends before she'd won them over.

Yet there was something that ate at his conviction, something inside himself. Laurel was correct in her condemnation; he wasn't saintly. He'd hated her on their wrecked wedding day, as he did that afternoon at MoMA, and he had held part of himself back from her ever since they'd reconnected. Self-protection was how he'd thought of it. But his motives didn't matter, did they? The unconscious doesn't lie; Freud said that. Or Bee said that Freud said that.

He'd held back, and now he wanted another woman, just as Laurel had declared he did. The very woman she'd accused him of wanting. The one with hair like a spiky crown of autumn leaves and a smile he strived to elicit, like a prize; the one who'd chosen loneliness over being with the wrong person. He only lusted in his heart, like Jimmy Carter, or in some hidden recess of his brain, but lusted, anyway, longed for her. Not in vengeance, though, only out of simple need. But he'd deceived Laurel, just as he had deceived himself. She was crazy, but she was also right.

"Get out of here," she said in a weary monotone. She might have been dismissing an unruly class.

Edward gathered his belongings, and she watched him with gleaming eyes. Tears, or only the shine of sick, sad triumph, he couldn't tell. He wanted to console her, he really did, but he didn't know how or if it was even possible. He could feign outrage about her snooping in his journal, and insist that nothing had happened, at least not yet—a technical, lawyerly truth—but the assurance she craved would have to be false. The thing was, he couldn't love her, though he'd been on the verge of saying that he did, telling himself that it was about time. How had that almost happened?

"Laurel, I'm very sorry," he said, the only honest thing he could think to say.

She turned her back to him. "Get out," she said again, and this time he did.

46

Aftermath

Edward lay low over the weekend, monitoring the caller I.D. on his phone, hoping and dreading that he'd hear from Laurel, while letting calls from Julie, Nick, and Sybil go right to voice mail. He wanted to know that Laurel was safe, without subjecting himself to another tirade—or worse, a cajoling recital of regret like the one that had put her back into his life up at the Cape. And he wasn't in the mood to talk to anyone else. The messages the kids left were casually chatty—he could wait to call them back, and Sybil offered a last-minute invitation on Sunday for lunch, concluding, as if she were mumbling to herself, that he was probably staying in the city with his girlfriend. It was easier to let her think that he was.

The only call he took was from Gladys, who just wanted to say hello. Mildred had been coming to her place a couple of afternoons and evenings a week to spell her regular home attendant, and to generally "help out," which included cooking and light housekeeping. According to Gladys, they also had some good talks and worked on puzzles together. Good talks about what, Edward wondered. The milliner and the psychic, almost a generation apart, didn't seem to have much in common. That evening Mildred was staying on to share the sole amandine she was preparing. Why didn't Edward join them? Another time, he promised; he was working on his lesson plans for the week.

He had been doing just that, sporadically, all day, having progressed from the biology and behavior of the frog and other amphibians, to reptiles. Snakes and lizards slithered and crawled behind his eyes while he also contemplated getting in touch with Olga and telling her of his feelings for her. What if they weren't reciprocated? And why did his pursuit of her seem premature? God, he was in his mid-sixties, almost three years widowed, and still dithering like a teenager. He had broken irrevocably with Laurel, yet he needed to establish her well-being before he could move on. Saint Edward.

Well, hardly. It was for himself, for achieving the serenity that comes with real freedom. He wanted Laurel to let him off the hook; the trick was in getting that done without having any contact with her. He thought back to her lengthy guest list for their wedding, all those friends she'd never mentioned again. Now he couldn't recall a single name, anyone he could simply call and ask to check up on her, to see if she was all right. It was emotional blackmail, he knew that, but it was self-imposed. He had gotten into this mess with some naïve idea that people can change, can even go from pathology to sanity. Laurel was a pretty good actress, but he'd been a willing audience, despite all his initial resistance. She'd insisted her craziness was a thing of the past, and he had conspired by believing her.

Edward's books and papers for school were spread out across

the kitchen counter. There were about twenty-seven hundred species of snakes in the world. He could cover only a few of them, their anatomy along with their social habits—they were largely solitary creatures—and evolutionary changes, the loss of limbs and outer ears, the opaque eyelid replaced by the transparent brill.

Earlier in the term, Edward had covered his students' favorite subject: human evolution, with its own list of vanished characteristics—the tail, the opposable big toe, a pelt-like coat of body hair, even certain molecules. He always avoided mentioning the coccyx, that vestige of their missing tails—the word was too uproarious to seventh-graders, although they'd find it less so if they ever fell on it without the cushioning of a furry stump.

In the unit on humans, Edward stressed the wonderful advantages of walking upright, of adaptive genetic changes, like the Tibetans' ability to breathe the thinnest air and the improved circulation that protected Arctic natives from frostbite. And he talked about the ongoing universal need to cohabit, to be part of a couple, a family, a tribe, a nation, that unshakable impulse against loneliness. In almost every class someone curious and brave, or simply provocative, asked why men still had nipples. Others wanted to know the purpose of wisdom teeth or the appendix, questioning the concept of intelligent design. Any discussion of their bodies thrilled and freaked them out at the same time.

Edward had had his appendix removed when he was in high school, his infection-attracting tonsils and adenoids years before then. His own evolved and lived-in body, like everyone's eventually did, showed gravity's pull and the disrepair of aging: less hair (where it was desirable, anyway); diminished sexual prowess; the sudden elusiveness of certain familiar words. It all starts going downhill earlier than we expect, not long after acne finally clears up. What was he waiting for?

He scribbled in his plan book while he ate a turkey sandwich for supper. The phone rang a couple more times, and, glancing at the caller I.D., Edward saved himself from listening to the pitches of some telemarketers. Later, when he was getting ready for bed, the phone rang again—it was after eleven, when only urgent news usually came—and without hesitating he picked it up. His heart bumped and Bernie Roth said, "I didn't wake you, did I?"

"No, no," Edward said. He had to sit down on the side of the bed. "What's up?"

"Well, I got a really strange phone call a little while ago."

"Who from?" he asked, although he was sure he already knew the answer.

"From your . . . from Laurel."

Edward had imagined getting a call from her in which she would threaten suicide. He'd told himself that it would be pure histrionics, readying his defenses before the fact. Yet now an image of her gasping inside that plastic bag filled his head. His own breath became short and ragged. When he could speak again, he said, "How bad did she sound?"

But Bernie answered his question with a question. "What the hell's going on between you two?"

"Nothing, it's over," Edward said, wondering if it ever would be.

"Yeah, that's what she told me. But I couldn't believe she'd do it to you again."

Edward ignored that last. "What did she say?" he asked, picturing Laurel shouting into her cell phone from a windswept bridge, slurring from the depths of an overdose. But why would she call Bernie?

"Here's the kicker, man. She wanted to have dinner."

"What?" Edward said.

"That's what the lady said. Did I want to meet her for dinner tomorrow night."

Edward flopped backward onto the bed, felled by relief and confusion. "So, what did you say?"

"Are you kidding?" Bernie said. "First of all, I don't mess with anyone else's woman, ex or otherwise. Even I have some standards. And dinner with Laurel—well, somebody's gonna be devoured, right? And I have a pretty good idea who it would be."

"But how did she sound?" Edward said.

"I don't know. Fine, I guess. Flirty, a little funny. Like herself."

"And after you turned her down?"

"She didn't stay on too long after that. But she seemed cool with it. Like, whatever, as our most eloquent students would say." Edward was silent. "You still there?" Bernie asked. "Maybe I shouldn't have even told you about this."

"No, it's okay, really, I'm glad you did." And he was.

This was the word he'd been waiting for all day, that Laurel had calmed down, that she wasn't suicidal, after all, that she was following her old pattern of looking for a new man to replace the one she'd lost, or felt in danger of losing. She was still attractive, and beguiling, in her way. Bernie wasn't going to take her on, but sooner or later someone else probably would. Edward was free.

47

Fifth Date

He felt the same unsettling mix of anticipation and dread he'd had before those blind dates resulting from the ad in *The New York Review*. But so much more was at stake here, and of course he already knew Olga—by heart, he thought, although they had met only a few times. The anticipation came from his desire to see her again and to declare himself, the dread from his fear of being rejected.

The phone call had been awkward enough. Whatever he had intended to say flew out of his head at the sound of her voice. "Ollie, I want to see you," he'd blurted, and then filled the ticking silence that followed by saying, "I need your advice about something." Where had that brainstorm come from? But she agreed to have dinner with him that evening, at an Italian restaurant on Columbus Avenue.

They came from opposite directions in the midst of a cloudburst, and almost collided in a sudden gust of wind at the restaurant's entrance. Her umbrella blew inside out, and Edward fumbled to right it. He wanted to embrace, to enfold, her then, but settled for a wet handclasp—with the umbrella between them, dripping on their shoes—before they went inside. The room was brightly lit and noisy—not the most romantic of settings. But she had chosen it after he'd said, "Pick someplace you like in your neighborhood," and this was clearly a neighborhood favorite.

After they'd been seated and ordered wine and listened to the specials, she said, "I suppose you're not in the market for a medieval tapestry, and I don't know much about investments or used cars. So, are you after some advice to the lovelorn?"

Exactly, he thought, but only said, "In a way." She waited and he continued. "Laurel and I have broken things off."

"Ah," she said. A noncommittal response in which he heard nothing he could interpret as surprise or pleasure or regret or sympathy.

"And I find I have feelings for you," he said. The racket in the background seemed to soften and recede as she looked back at him from behind her glasses with all of her attention. "I'm as surprised as you must be," he said. Why didn't she say something—anything? No, not anything; just the words he wanted to hear. But she didn't speak and he was forced to go on. "I think of you all the time." This was a truth he hadn't quite known until he said it.

"I think of you, too," she said. He waited for her to add *but just as a friend*, or *only not in that way.* She didn't, though, and the table between them became a snowy expanse he could have sprung across. Instead, he reached for her hand and looked at it as carefully as a fortune-teller, or a doctor about to remove a splinter. Her nails were short and unpolished. There were little nicks in her fingers that he imagined came from the needle he'd watched her ply at the museum. He gazed down at her palm with its crisscrossed lines of life and fate and pressed his lips against it.

"Oh," she said, that single word floating from her mouth like a perfect smoke ring.

The waiter brought the wine, and a busboy came with a basket of bread and a dish of olives. Edward and Olga glanced at each other through the blur of activity between them. No one who happened to observe them at that moment would have thought they were new lovers, or about to be. They would more easily be taken for an older married couple, out celebrating an anniversary or a birthday, or even some good news about a biopsy. But Edward *felt* new—younger, and flooded with expectation.

Over dinner, he told her something about his history with Laurel, calling it a *folie à deux*, revisited, with a slight pang about the use of that French expression. Then he spoke about Bee: the way they'd met, their marriage, her mother and the children, her illness and death. It sounded to his own ears like a crude abridgement of a long, complex novel. But Olga seemed to intuit whatever he'd omitted. "Bee sounds wonderful," she said. And, "You've been in deep mourning, and everyone expected you to just snap out of it."

"Yes," he said. "I hoped, I really *tried*, to snap out of it, myself, but it doesn't work that way."

"And you still love her."

"I do, in remembrance. But this—you—it's like the beginning of a new lifetime. Mildred, the woman who used to walk my dog, doubles as a psychic—a sort of suburban mystic. She believes in literal past lives. Who knows, maybe I've loved many women over the centuries."

Olga smiled. "Now you're making me jealous," she said.

She told him that she'd never come close to what he'd had with Bee, although there'd been affairs that had seemed loaded with promise before they fizzled. "I don't know why, exactly. Bad choices, bad timing, bad vibes—or maybe it was bad karma, as your friend Mildred might say. Sometimes, I think that I've missed out on everything. Other times, I just think of it as my life."

"Your past life," he amended.

"Yes."

They kissed as soon as they were back out on the street, briefly, as if they were sealing a contract. A moment with more tenderness than heat. Then they walked the few blocks in the rain to the brownstone where she lived on the second floor. He'd forgotten that she had a dog, but recognized the scratching and whimpering, that renewable excitement, behind the door to her apartment when she put her key into the lock.

"Don't worry, she's friendly," Olga said as the door opened and the pug leapt from one of them to the other, snorting and wheezing and bestowing affection, her curled tail quivering with happiness.

"There's an understatement," Edward said. He missed Bingo right then, but what a sweet dog Josie was, so instantly trusting. Maybe he'd been Napoleon in one of his former lives.

Olga set out the dog's dinner, and then she led Edward into her bedroom. She removed her eyeglasses and placed them on one of the nightstands before she turned to him. How undefended her naked face seemed. This time their kiss sent a shock directly to his groin.

He'd had some quick impressions of the room when they first came in, that it was smallish and uncluttered, with a faint scent of cedar in the air. Later, he would remember the glow of the bedside lamps, like moonlight; the thick, silky quilt; and the welcoming give of her bed when they lay down together. Edward had thought, had fantasized, about making love to her. Somehow he'd expected it to be good, but not sizzling—more like the modest charge of a small domestic appliance. She wasn't his type, because he no longer had a type. But her body was marvelous in its urgency against his, and his own surge of passion took him by surprise.

Afterward, still entwined, they shared a few moments of stunned, happy silence. Then he said, "You don't really hog the bed, you know." He marveled at how little space she seemed to take up.

"Just you wait," she said, but it was more of a promise than a threat.

"So, here we are," he said. "How did this happen?"

"I'm not sure. Do you think we've been possessed?"

"I have, anyway," he said. "When I remember you at Sybil and Henry's that first time—"

"Don't." She held one finger to his mouth. "I was such a bitch."

"Yes, you were. And I was an insufferable prick."

"That's true. But now we've both been transformed."

"Restored to our better selves," Edward said, and he realized that this was what he had missed more than anything, this easy, intimate talk before sleep that seemed to send you gently drifting off, away from the shore of the day.

When he was almost there, Olga stirred in his arms. She reached from under the quilt and groped for her glasses. Then she put them on and turned to him again, propping herself up on one elbow

"What are you doing?" he asked drowsily.

"I'm looking at you," she said.

"Not too closely, I hope."

"Why not?" she said. "You have a very good face."

"And you . . . you are entirely beautiful."

"Oh, Edward, that's just post-coital dementia."

"No," he said. "It's love."

48

The Seal of Approval

Chanel appeared as delighted to see Edward as Olga's pug had been a few weeks before. But in the puppy's wild excitement, she tugged his shoelaces open, nipped at the hems of his trousers, and peed a little on his shoes. "You bad girl," Amanda said, making it sound as warmly indulgent as praise. She even slipped Chanel a treat, while handing Edward a Kleenex for his shoes and inviting him to feel her belly, which had grown astoundingly since he'd last seen her. It felt like a basketball, freshly pumped with air and bounce.

Then she and Nick gave Edward a tour of the nursery, which he dutifully admired, although he was taken aback by the black-and-white color scheme. Amanda, who'd been researching prenatal development, explained that stark contrasts would help the baby's eyes to focus. She was already enhancing the fetus's brain by reading children's books aloud, listening to classical music, and eating foods high in choline and omega-3. They'd decided not to learn the baby's sex in advance, so they could greet it without what Amanda called "gender-ghettoizing preconceptions."

"Very nice," Edward said about everything, although the mobile suspended over the crib had the dizzying effect of an Escher maze.

When they were sitting in the living room, drinking coffee, Nick said, "So, what are you up to, Professor? You haven't been around for a while."

Edward couldn't have asked for a better opening, and he grabbed it. "I've been seeing someone," he said. What people usually said about casual dating, he realized, or about consulting a psychotherapist.

They both stared at him for a moment before Amanda punched Nick's arm and said, "I told you that ad would work!"

"Ow," Nick said. "You mean seeing, like in going out with?" he asked Edward.

"Well, more than that," Edward said, embarrassed by his own sudden shyness.

"You're in love!" Amanda shrieked. Even the baby must have taken that in.

"Yes," he admitted gladly, "I'm in love."

"Is she the one who sent her picture?" He looked at her blankly and she said, "*You* know. That pharmacist's widow in Hoboken, the perfumed letter?"

Dating after death. "Oh, no," he said. "No. She's not one of the women I met through the ad."

Amanda sank back a little against the sofa cushions.

"But the ad got me out there again, back into the social whirl," Edward told her, remembering how it had almost turned him into a hermit, but she seemed appeased.

"Well, this is *thrilling*," she said. "Tell us all about her. How did you meet? What does she look like? What does she do? What's her name?"

"Manda, you sound like the police," Nick said. "Give him a chance to answer."

"Her name is Ollie, Olga, actually. Olga Nemerov. I met her . . ."

Here Edward faltered. Did their first meeting at the Morgansterns' count? It was so long ago, preceding the ad by months, and such a disaster. "We met at the Cloisters," he said, picturing *The Unicorn in Captivity*, prancing and so lightly tethered. And he remembered Ollie feeding crumbs from her sandwich to the birds, taking off her glasses to look at the garden. It sounded like the absolute truth.

"God, that's such a romantic place. We should go there," Amanda said to Nick, who put one arm around her, his other hand splayed across her belly, as if he were about to dribble it across the court and shoot for a basket.

Edward described Ollie to them—her reddish spiked hair, her small frame and articulate, unadorned hands—what he'd come to think of as her accidental beauty. He talked about her ironic charm, and tried to explain her work and how honored she felt to have those precious relics in her care. Edward thought of all that he'd left out. Laurel, especially. But he hadn't intended to tell them the whole complicated story, just to announce his new status as part of a couple. He'd come alone to do it, just as he'd come alone to tell them about Bee's illness, the beginning of his uncoupling.

Back then, he'd given them the bad news and tried to deflect and absorb some of their grief. This time he sought their approval, their acceptance of his newfound happiness. And how easily that was obtained. Maybe it was because their own happiness was so fulfilling and preoccupying: their love for each other and for their baby, with its developing brain and limbs and personality; the house they were avidly decorating; their life together stretched out before them like a gloriously lush field.

If Nick had any sense of disloyalty to his mother, he kept it to himself. But Edward felt bound to bring Bee up. How could he not? He had been her husband and these were her children. "This doesn't undo my love for Mom," he said. "I'm not replacing her. She's irreplaceable. I'm just starting out again." And he thought of that novel, *Starting Out in the Evening*, that Bee had kept reading to him.

"We know that," Nick said. Tears stood in his eyes. He jumped up from his seat beside Amanda and threw his arms around Edward. "This is such great news, man," he said, his voice thick with emotion. "We wish you the best."

"The best," Amanda echoed. "And I'll hug you, too, Dad, as soon as somebody gives me a hand up."

Julie would be even easier. Edward had already told her something about Laurel, after being forced into it by her phone call to Julie, which Julie had blown up into some grand, reality-show-based fairy tale. Later, when he said that he'd been seeing Laurel more frequently, she'd seemed pleased, and eager to meet her. She had even suggested they double-date! Maybe she'd be disappointed to discover his new love was someone else entirely, but it was the matter of his loneliness that had mostly concerned her. What had she said, so dolefully, after Bingo died? *Poppy, now you're all alone.*

And he believed that she would like Ollie, that she would find her as witty and smart as he did. And, in due course, as dear, too. It was Gladys he didn't want to think about. He shrank from sharing his news with her almost as much as he'd resisted telling her about her only child's fatal illness. Maybe Julie, who was so close to her grandmother, would advise him on how to approach her.

But he was going to take it one step at a time. After he left Nick and Amanda's, he drove into the city to meet Julie for supper. This was the first Saturday in more than a month that he hadn't spent with Olga, but he would see her later, stay over at her apartment that night. He had told her that he was informing his stepchildren that he'd fallen in love. "That sounds a little tricky," she said.

"Not really," he'd assured her. "They tried to fix me up way before I was ready. They're really great kids."

"Yes," she said, "but they still might think of me as an interloper. You've been a family for such a long time."

"You'll fit right in, trust me," he said, thinking: *You are my family now, too.*

"Maybe they'll worry about their inheritance. Can you assure them that I'm not a gold digger?"

Edward laughed. "There's not a hell of a lot of gold to dig," he said.

"That's not the point. Just let them know I'm not after you for your money."

"What other reason could you possibly have?"

"Stop fishing," she said. "And tell them they never have to meet me if they don't want to."

"They'll have to and they'll want to," he said. "I'll make you sound irresistible, which won't be very hard."

"Poor Edward. You are so easy."

Julie was a little late. Edward had finished a glass of water and one of the rolls in the basket before she came in. He kept clearing his throat, as if he were about to go onstage with none of his lines memorized. Then she was there, making her way between the tables, mouthing, "Sorry, sorry," to him. She held one hand near her ear to indicate she'd been stuck on the phone.

He kissed her and pulled out her chair. "There's nothing to be sorry about," he said. "The important thing is that you're here. Are you hungry? I am."

They ordered and he waited until their food came before he said, "Jules, dear, I have an announcement to make." That was more formal than he'd meant to be. She had just speared some lettuce leaves with her fork, which she lowered to her plate.

"What?" she said. She looked primed for bad news, and he wished for her sake that her feelings weren't so close to the surface, that her face didn't always give her away. Punks like Todd probably used her transparency to their own advantage.

He smiled at her. "It's something good." He had an uneasy sense of déjà vu. This was similar to the conversation he'd had with Julie about Laurel. Would she think he'd become an over-the-hill playboy?

"Did you win the lottery?" she asked. She picked up her fork again.

"No, but this is even better. I've met someone special."

"Oh? You mean what's-her-face, that person you used to date a long time ago?"

"No, that didn't pan out," he said.

"Bummer," she said, munching her salad.

"Yes, in some ways. But then I met Olga."

"*Olga!* Is she foreign?"

"No. But her parents were into Russian literature." He'd just made that up. She'd been named for a beloved aunt.

"So, do you see her often?" Julie said.

Why was she being so dense, and why had she turned so ashen? "As often as I can. Jules, I'm very much in love with her."

The fork clanked to her plate. "What do you mean?"

"I mean that I've fallen in love with a woman named Olga Nemerov—Ollie—and, well, she seems to love me back."

"I see," Julie said. "So, are you getting married?"

"We haven't talked about that. We haven't even moved in together yet." That was only a half-truth, because, except for work, they were hardly ever apart or out of each other's thoughts. "Right now, we're just enjoying being together."

"How long have you known her?" Julie said.

"Not very long. A few months. It was sort of like a lightning strike."

"That seems pretty fast, the sort of thing you always advised *me* against."

She was referring to the way Edward and Bee tried to protect her from sudden crushes in high school on boys who were unlikely to even notice her. "I'm older than you, I'm an old guy," he said. "At my age, you can't afford to waste time." He sounded like George Burns in his nineties, explaining why he didn't buy green bananas anymore. "And this is the real thing," he added. "I know you're going to like her."

Tears welled in Julie's eyes, just as they had in Nick's. But these weren't tears of joy. "What about Mom?" she cried. "I thought *she* was the love of your life."

"She was, you know that. But I've been on my own for a long while now. My happiness with your mother is what made me want to be with someone again."

"Don't blame her!" Julie said. She was trembling with rage and sorrow.

Edward looked at her in dismay. His poor girl; she had genuinely wanted him to be happy, but not *completely* happy, because that might erase Bee forever. He longed to comfort her, to touch her arm or her head, but he didn't dare. "I'm not," he said. "I'm grateful to her, for so many reasons, including you." He touched his chest. "She's still in here, Jules. I'll never, ever forget her."

Julie appeared unconvinced. "Do you intend to tell Gladdy about this, about . . . *Olga*?"

"I'm not looking forward to it, but I think she'd want me to be honest with her. In fact, I was hoping you would—"

"You'll kill her," Julie said.

49

The Future

Gladys went to bed early—"Like a little child again," she'd told Edward—so he arrived at her place just after six o'clock, his stomach growling with hunger and nerves. Mildred let him in, wearing an apron, and then went back to the kitchen, where she'd been doing the dishes from the supper she'd cooked and the two women had shared. Gladys was in the living room, moving her magnifying glass over a newly started jigsaw puzzle.

"Long time no see," she said, like a B-movie femme fatale, when Edward came into the room, and he felt himself flush. With his ardent concentration on Ollie, he had neglected almost everyone else in his life. But he had deliberately avoided visiting Gladys, putting off the delivery of what he considered a terrible, yet inevitable, blow. She looked even more fragile than he remembered, but maybe his own guilty fear affected his view of her.

"Come sit next to me, honey," she said after he'd kissed her shirred cheek. "I need help."

So do I, Edward thought, but he sat down beside her and picked up a straight-edged puzzle piece from a pile of similar pieces she had set aside.

"Here's the picture," she said, holding up the cover of the puzzle box. "Julie bought it for me." Edward had a further failure of heart at the mention of Julie's name; the last thing she'd said to him and her look of betrayal were still in his head. At least he was certain she hadn't mentioned anything to her grandmother about Ollie. He was the designated hit man.

The puzzle was a pastoral scene, black-and-white cows grazing in a vast meadow. The green parts would be the trickiest. "Why are there always meadows or jungles or snow in these things?" he said. He sounded like a whiny kid, like Julie when she couldn't force a puzzle piece into the wrong space.

"To keep us on our toes, honey. Here," Gladys said, taking the straight-edged piece from his hand and fitting it into its proper place on the frame. She seemed to be the calm center of the room, the only person Edward could turn to for advice on what he was about to say to her. Maybe he should have enlisted Mildred's help. He probably still could, under the pretext of going into the kitchen for a glass of water. He could hear her puttering around in there, the clink and clank of dishes and pots such stabilizing domestic sounds. And didn't they always send two cops, at least on TV, to break bad news to someone, usually a woman? One to tell her and one to catch her. He remembered Gladys collapsing against him when he'd told her about Bee.

But it would be cowardly to involve Mildred in what he'd

now begun to think of as his crime. Could love be a crime? Well, maybe Julie and Laurel and Mia Farrow would think so, but he'd never intended to hurt anyone. What all criminals probably said.

Gladys turned to him, holding the magnifying glass to her eye, which in its enlargement seemed inescapable and all-seeing. "You look pale," she declared. "Are you hungry? There's plenty of chicken left."

The hunger he had felt when he'd gotten there was gone, although his stomach still bubbled and murmured. He hoped Gladys couldn't hear it, or read his mind. "No, thanks," he said. "I'm just a little tired."

"You work too hard. Maybe it's time to think about retiring."

He and Ollie had talked about that very thing the night before, making plans for the future the way he'd done with Bee. *Man plans, God laughs.*

"I am," he said. "I'm thinking about it."

"Well, good," she said. She put the magnifying glass down but didn't take her gaze from his face. "What's the matter?" she said, and he was startled by her insight—or did he just look as miserable as he felt?

"The thing of it is," he began—a phrase his father had used when he'd been stalled, trying to explain something difficult or complicated to his children. "Gladys," he said, "I've met a woman."

There. The gun had gone off in his hand, but she didn't fall over. She just sat upright in her chair, breathing, looking at him, waiting. The dishes were still clattering in the background. Were they left over from a banquet? Was Mildred throwing them at the walls?

"You're only human," Gladys said, at last.

"But it isn't just a fling, it's serious." When she didn't say anything, he said, "I didn't expect this to happen."

"Whyever not?" she asked.

"Because . . . because I loved Bee so much."

"I know you did."

"But I became very lonely," Edward said, his chest filling alarmingly with the very sensation he was describing. He was terrified that he was going to cry. He didn't, though, and neither did Gladys.

"So, this woman," she said. "Does she have a name?"

Edward thought about the way Julie had said "*Olga!*" as if she were spitting out something that tasted terrible, a foreign, alien food.

"Olga Nemerov," he said. "Ollie."

"Ollie," Gladys repeated, closing her eyes. She might have been trying to remember if she knew this person. Or maybe she simply couldn't bear looking at him.

"Forgive me," he said.

"For what?"

"For loving someone else. For hurting you like this."

"Oh, my honey boy," she said. "Dear Edward." Her eyes were shimmering now. "My hurt has nothing to do with you. And you made Beattie so happy; you *deserve* to be happy again yourself."

He wanted to lay his head in her lap in gratitude and exhaustion. Instead he took both of her hands in his, surprised by how much warmer hers were. "You loved Jake, too," he said, "but you didn't have anyone after he died, did you?"

She shrugged. "I was an old lady already. Past eighty. You're still a young man."

"That's relative, I suppose. Though sometimes I think of myself that way."

"Since Ollie," she said.

"Yes."

"Tell me about her."

"Well, she's Jewish. My weakness, it seems." She smiled at him. "She works at the Metropolitan Museum, restoring old tapestries. And she's Sybil Morganstern's cousin."

"My," Gladys said.

"Listen," Edward said, "I've told the children about all this. Nick and Amanda were fine with it, wonderful, really. But Julie is very unhappy, very angry with me."

"Oh, Julie," Gladys said dismissively. "It's her father she's really angry with. Don't worry, I'll talk to her. She'll come around."

Edward stared at her, this amazing, enduring woman. He had planned on enlisting Julie's aid in soothing her, and now she was the one who would soothe Julie, and him, as well. He knew that she was keeping much of what she was feeling to herself, for his sake, what mothers did.

The noises from the kitchen had stopped, and Mildred appeared in the doorway. "I'm finished now, Glad," she said, "so if you're ready, I'll help you to bed and then I'll get going."

"Wait, Mildred," Gladys said. "Edward needs to have his fortune told."

"Oh, you know he's not into that," Mildred said, and the two women exchanged a conspiratorial glance.

The connection between them had seemed so unlikely until that moment, when Edward understood that they were simply friends, with, at least, widowhood and an impulse for caretaking in common. "Well, maybe this once," he said. He would have done anything for either of them right then.

"Really?" Mildred gave him a skeptical glance. "What'll it

be, then? Tarot? Numerology? Psychometry? Name your poison."

She might have been reciting the specials at an exotic ethnic restaurant. "You choose," he said.

She moved closer to where he and Gladys were sitting. "Let me feel the energy around your hands," she said. "Put them on the table, palms up."

He did as he was told, suddenly submissive and vulnerable, as if he were begging for alms, or for his future.

Mildred pulled up another chair so that she was facing him, only a foot or so away.

"Shall I close my eyes?" he asked.

"No," she said. "I want you here, fully present." Then she raised her own hands, palms down, a few inches above his, moving them around a little before letting them just hover. Gladys leaned forward, watching, listening, while Mildred stared off into the distance above Edward's head, as if at someone else across the room.

Edward felt amused, a little giddy, and strangely hopeful and moved.

Hours seemed to pass, but surely it was only a matter of minutes before Mildred looked directly at him and said, "The universe is offering you a gift. Claim it."

50

Coda

Was there a happy ending? Edward wouldn't call it that, because it wasn't over yet. Not just his own story, but the story of the evolving, persistent world. And that was a continuum, with or without him. Richard Dawkins said that nature isn't cruel, only indifferent, and Edward agreed. He believed that people invented and then acted out their extravagant emotional dramas to give their lives shape and meaning. But he had experienced episodes of such uncommon bliss, they seemed ordained rather than random, and periods of darkness and sorrow that held their own mysteries. Bee was truly gone, having moved farther and farther from the center, and then the periphery, of Edward's life into pure memory, just as Amy Weitz had predicted she would.

Ollie was the one he would spend the rest of his days and nights with. They continued to desire and cherish each other, which didn't cease to astound them. "Let's never tell Sybil," she said one day. "I can't stand to give her the satisfaction." But love wants a witness, and their own satisfaction was even greater than Sybil's.

Soon they began spending the working week in the city and weekends in Englewood. Josie the pug preferred suburban New Jersey, with all that delightful greenery to kill. But Edward and Ollie were pleased to be anywhere together. He found himself wishing, with a lover's generosity, that Sylvia Smith and Ellen, and even Laurel—if that were possible—would know similar contentment and joy.

The first time he brought Ollie to his house, she paused in the doorway for several moments. She seemed to be waiting for permission to enter. Finally, he grabbed her hand and pulled her inside. "So this is where you've been all this time," she said, as if he'd been hiding out there, which in a sense he had been.

He showed her the kitchen, where they would have breakfast the next morning, and the bedroom, where they would lie down together, and even his makeshift basement lab—feeling a little like a real estate agent, pushing to make a sale. But she was already sold on the entire package.

They made defiant short- and long-term plans. They would build a gazebo in the garden, they would travel. Olga was eager to show him the tapestries in museums in Belgium and northern France. Edward wanted to visit a bird sanctuary in Cesena and Monet's garden in Giverny. They'd both put in for retirement at the end of the school year, and the Met had offered to retain Ollie's services as a consultant. Edward would miss teaching, but he was suddenly greedy for leisure, for the luxury of all those additional domestic hours. He wouldn't ever take them for granted again.

Although he kept expecting a phone call or a letter from

Laurel, Edward didn't hear from her, not even indirectly. Bernie asked about her a couple of times, and then she seemed to have slipped his mind as easily as she'd eluded Edward's grasp. Once in a while, in the beginning, he would see a slender woman with dark or silvery hair walk by him in the city, and feel a glancing rush of apprehension, but it was never Laurel, in any of her incarnations.

As Gladys had promised, she'd spoken to Julie, and Julie had come around, grudgingly at first, and out of her own need as much as his, but that didn't matter; Edward could still look after her, the only thing left that he could do for Bee. His influence was limited, though, as Mildred could have told him. She was one of those psychics, like the omnipotent, omniscient biblical God, who still allowed for free will. The universe had been holding out a gift to Edward, but he was required to accept it. Happiness was in store for Julie, but it was also up to her.

And she broke things off with Mr. Right, as Edward and Ollie and the rest of the family considered Andrew; there would be no Silver and Gold wedding, no baby Sterling. Instead she chose Todd, the archetypical Mr. Wrong, who dumped her the following week. Amanda was considering posting a personal ad for Julie on some new dating website called doyoucomehere often.com.

Two days before she was officially due to be born, Annabelle Beatrice Silver repositioned herself, feetfirst—as if she were late for an appointment, as if she intended to hit the world running—and had to be delivered by Caesarian section. She was bald and mottled and appeared to need ironing. Nick reported her Apgar score with the kind of pride usually reserved for college boards. Everyone insisted that she looked like Edward.

About a year later, Gladys died shortly after Mildred had

settled her into bed for the night. Her final words were, "What a long day this was." The jigsaw puzzle on the bridge table in her living room, a reproduction of the tapestry *The Unicorn Leaps Out of the Stream*—a gift from Ollie—was still a work in progress.

Acknowledgments

Several people shared their expert knowledge of various matters touched on in this novel. Any errors are my own.

I'm very grateful for the generous assistance of Steve Allen, Marilyn Beaven, Suzan Bellincampi, Sandra Bonardi, George Cooper, Dr. Eugene Decker, Luke Dempsey, Keith Glutting, Marge Goldwater, David Jácome, Françoise Joyes, Lorrie Kazan, Deirdre Larkin, Nuala Oates, Elizabeth Pastan, Nancy Slowik, Dr. Julia Smith, and Dr. Richard Soffer.

Many thanks to my good friends at Ballantine Books, especially Jen Smith, my wonderfully astute and patient editor.

An Available Man

HILMA WOLITZER

A Reader's Guide

A Conversation with Hilma Wolitzer

Helen Schulman is the author of the novels *This Beautiful Life* (a *New York Times* Bestseller), *A Day At The Beach*, *P.S.*, *The Revisionist*, and *Out Of Time*, and the short story collection *Not A Free Show*. *P.S.* was also made into a feature film starring Laura Linney and was written by Helen Schulman and Dylan Kidd. She co-edited, along with Jill Bialosky, the anthology *Wanting A Child*. Her fiction and nonfiction have appeared in such places as *Vanity Fair*, *Time*, *Vogue*, *GQ*, *The New York Times Book Review*, and *The Paris Review*. She is presently the fiction coordinator at The Writing Program at The New School, where she is a tenured associate professor.

Helen Schulman: In *An Available Man*, the newly widowed Edward Schuyler has a quiet hunger for the pleasures of life. The book, with its realistic grip on loss, also becomes in your able hands a social comedy. How do you manage to balance your humorous take on post–mid-life dating and the pain of losing the love of one's life?

Hilma Wolitzer: I grew up during the Great Depression and although my family struggled like so many others, I remember a great deal of laughter in our household. Since humor has always been such an intrinsic part of my own life, it seems only natural to find it in the lives of my fictional characters. Not that they (and I!) don't experience and recognize the dark side of things; it's just often leavened by a hopeful measure of lightness. As heartsick as Edward is over the loss of his beloved wife, Bee, he can't help being amused by the awkward dance of late-life dating, or as one personal-ad correspondent puts it—"dating after death."

HS: Somehow you were able to keep the departed Bee thoroughly alive in these pages. She is present in Edward's present action as a character of weight, someone we come to love and enjoy almost as much as he does. It's as if she's entered his bones. How did you arrive at this tact?

HW: Helen, you put that so well when you said "as if she's entered his bones." I believe you do incorporate the spirit of people you deeply love so that they're never fully lost to you—a sort of emotional cannibalism. Bee always seemed like a vibrant character to me as I was writing the novel. It would have been difficult to convey Edward's sense of loss without knowing who she was and what they had shared. So she lived in my head as much as she did in Edward's, even after her death. Of course, Bee's presence in Edward's thoughts both informs and hinders his efforts to be with someone new. And when he's finally ready to let go of the past and venture into the future, she retreats into what he thinks of as pure memory.

HS: I've always turned to your books for their wisdom and compassion, but also because they are so damned funny! When Edward reads the personal ads in *The New York Review of Books*, he remembers how he and Bee used to poke fun at them: "Sensual, smart, stunning, sensitive. Oh, why do they always resort to alliteration. . . . This one's a music lover! Well, who doesn't like music, besides the Taliban?" How do you come up with lines like that?

HW: Some of those lines seem to come directly from the characters, who tend to be rather cynical and irreverent—my favorite kind of people, in life and in books!—and some from my own sense of how ludicrous many things in this world are. What's so funny? Well, almost everything. And again, much of the comedic content of my work harks back to my childhood household and all of that laughing in the dark.

HS: I am interested in Laurel, the ex-fiancée who left him at the altar and then blows back into his life thirty-five years later. It seems to me that later in life, the people I know who find themselves alone often do return to the one-who-got-away or try to. Is that how this complex character entered your story?

HW: A few of my widowed friends reunited happily with early loves, so I was aware of that "second chance" phenomenon among older people. But the circumstances of Edward's first breakup were unique, and none of my real-life models were anything like Laurel, the hardest character to pin down. The challenge was to make her both believably appalling and appealing to Edward and to the reader. The passages about Laurel required more rewrites than any other part of the book. I had to show her seductiveness and Edward's sexual need and vulnerability, so that his forgiveness seemed possible, if foolhardy. To do that I tried to balance her lunacy with a modicum of sympathy.

Finally, though, everything isn't fully explainable, in life or in novels, especially human behavior.

HS: Julie, Edward's stepdaughter, is a fragile and sweet girl, trying with not much success to circumnavigate the rocky shoals of dating life, just as Edward is having his own comedic and frustrating forays. Did you pair them this way to illustrate that our desires for sex and love don't really change over time?

HW: I don't think I had any conscious plans to contrast Edward and Julie or to make a point about the ways in which we change or stay the same as we age. Like most of my characters, Edward and Julie just kept evolving (or not, in Julie's case) as the story went along. And the more they related to each other, the clearer they became to me. But it's true that our desire for love and sex and acceptance don't ever really go away. Often the elderly (and sometimes the young) merely subdue or accommodate those feelings.

HS: Off of that last question, I loved how frank this book, and all your work is really, about sexual need and desire. You give all your characters the dignity of their own humanity, no matter their ages. Is this something you think about consciously, a writerly agenda for lack of a better term, when picking out your subject matter? What really drew you to this specific story, if not the celebration of the corporeal?

HW: I never have an agenda when I'm writing a book, other than to tell a character-driven story I'd like to read. This one began with a few women friends who found themselves single again, through divorce or widowhood after long marriages. I'd listened to some horrific tales of online dating and fix-ups. Sexual frustration was certainly part of their collective complaint, but so was aloneness in a society of couples. At first I was going to create an older female protagonist because I was more familiar with women's situations. But then I began to wonder about men in similar circumstances and what they might experience. It seemed to me that loneliness was not a gender-specific condition. And then Edward Schuyler appeared, whole, in my imagination, a newly widowed, so-called "available man," ironing a shirt in his living room. Gradually, the rest of the novel fell into place.

HS: Finally, as much as this is a book about romance and connection, of being lost and being found, it also has a youthful energy and esprit. In some ways it feels like a young person's book—did you feel that when you were writing it?

HW: When I'm in the midst of a writing project, I usually stumble directly from my bed to my desk each morning (what Amy Tan aptly describes as "going from dream to dream"). After working for a while I'll get up and encounter my reflection somewhere on the way to the kitchen or the bathroom and be surprised by how old I am. As if I'd aged in just those few hours! The thing is, the young person I once was—her energy and outlook—is trapped in this old woman's body. All the stages of my life are still intact inside me and can be drawn on for my fiction.

Questions and Topics for Discussion

1. There are so many themes in this novel (romantic love, family relationships, loneliness, bereavement, and forgiveness). Which one resonated with you the most?

2. Why do you think there's such a dearth of "available men" above a certain age? Are society's expectations of aging women different from those of aging men?

3. What do you think contributed to the success of Edward and Bee's marriage? What did you make of Edward's difficulty coping after Bee's death?

4. Edward's family and friends conspire to help him find a new love. But Olga has chosen loneliness over being with the wrong person. Is being part of a couple best for everyone?

5. Why do you think Julie felt more comfortable going to Edward with her dating issues and other problems than to her biological father, Bruce Silver?

6. Do you think Laurel's mental state excuses her for the way she treated Edward at the end of their first love affair, and for her unsettling persistence when she comes back into his life? Does Laurel deserve Edward's keeping her at arm's length?

7. Were you surprised that Edward was finally able to fall in love again, and with whom? Who were you rooting for?

8. When Edward goes to the different members of his family with the news that he's fallen in love, their reactions are not what he expects. Why do you think that is?

9. Is there anyone in your life with whom you would have liked to set Edward up?

10. How would you feel if someone put up a personal ad for you, as Edward's stepchildren did for him?

PHOTO © ROBERT CONLON

HILMA WOLITZER is the author of several novels, including *Summer Reading*, *The Doctor's Daughter*, *Hearts*, *Ending*, and *Tunnel of Love*, as well as a nonfiction book, *The Company of Writers*. She is a recipient of Guggenheim and NEA Fellowships, an Award in Literature from the American Academy of Arts and Letters, and the Barnes & Noble Writer for Writers Award. She has taught writing at the University of Iowa, New York University, and Columbia University. She lives in New York City.

About the Type

The text of this book was set in Janson, a typeface designed in about 1690 by Nicholas Kis, a Hungarian living in Amsterdam, and for many years mistakenly attributed to the Dutch printer Anton Janson. In 1919 the matrices became the property of the Stempel Foundry in Frankfurt. It is an old-style book face of excellent clarity and sharpness. Janson serifs are concave and splayed; the contrast between thick and thin strokes is marked.